COLLATERAL DAMAGE

A TETHERED NOVEL

JESSICA WAYNE

CONTENTS

Collateral Damage
by Jessica Wayne

Edited by Jenny Dillon of Prologue and Prose
Cover Design by Cover Me Darling

To anyone who has ever felt the gripping fingers of loss or the helplessness that follows.
Keep looking forward to the sunrise.

*T*imothy stared down at the gravestone as if he believed it was only a nightmare. Surely she wasn't really gone. Thirty years they'd been married, and he had loved her every single day of it. He would never see her smile again, never hear her bright laugh, or smell her hair that somehow always carried the scent of flowers. How would he navigate his future without her?

A sheep bayed in the distance, but he barely heard anything over the sound of his own heartbreaking. Those who had attended her service had long since moved on, but here he was, stuck in a trance unable to tear his eyes away from the last shred of happiness in his life. From her name etched into cold stone:

CAIT ELIZABETH MCGINLEY
Beloved wife and healer.

How could her life be summed up in one sentence? There was so much more to her, so much more that should have been said about her when she'd been alive. She had been everything to him and had spent her entire life helping to heal the sick and injured.

The pain of losing her and knowing he would never see her again was nearly too much to bear. He wiped a tear from his cheek and knelt in the cool grass to press his hand to the stone. It seemed strange to him that the headstone was cold beneath his touch when she'd been so warm in life. Since the moment he'd met her he'd known she was a force of good in this world. One that would hopefully overshadow the pain he'd felt at losing his two best friends. Aengus and Myria had long since moved on, brother and sister who believed they could only rely on each other. They had shut him out when things had gone wrong, and that was something he couldn't forgive them for.

As it turned out, his Cait had completely eclipsed the pain of that loss with her love, and he'd believed that perhaps he had never truly loved anyone before her. Now that she was gone, he knew he would never love another. How could he?

Anger overwhelmed him when his thoughts drifted back to Myria. She was the very reason he was now stuck in this hell of a life without his wife. He was far too angry to remember just why she'd cast the spell she had. Logically, he understood it had been the only way to save her brother from a lifelong heartache. But here he was, feeling the pain she had spared her brother, and they were none the wiser. Had they ever tried to reach out to him before? Of course not. They were entirely too wrapped up in their own lives to worry about what he was doing.

He and Cait had raised no children, so she was the last person in his world who knew his secret. He had no one left. When she had fallen ill, she had made him promise that one day when the curse was broken, he would live a happy life. That he would marry again and have the children she'd been unable to give him during their time together.

She had told him not to waste the years he had, that they were a gift and a way to do good in the world she had believed he was capable of. But what he always had truly wanted was his one lifetime with her. Now he was completely forgotten and forced to walk this earth alone. And it was all because of a naïve witch who had dabbled in mystics she couldn't have comprehended.

He briefly considered going to her, telling her what she had done to him. But what good would that do? It would change nothing. He doubted even she knew how to undo the spell cast on him. And even if she did, she wouldn't risk hurting her brother by taking away his chance at happiness.

No, there was no hope for him. He would have to continue on with his life, living without fully *living*. No happily ever after's or anyone he would be able to grow old with. He was nothing but a forgotten victim in a world full of empty possibilities.

What good could he do? He felt no goodness left in his heart.

He closed his eyes and willed the lump in his throat to disappear. There was nothing he could do about it now, nothing but wait and hope that one day his curse would end, and he would be allowed to die like everyone else eventually did. Perhaps one day he could see his Cait again.

The wind picked up, and he breathed in the fresh scent of the country he had loved for so long. A country that no longer felt like home without the laughing, smiling, red-haired woman he had loved passionately for the last three decades.

Timothy pulled his cloak tighter around his shoulders and turned away. It was time he began moving forward the best he could.

With each new step he took, his anger for all things magic grew until he made himself a promise. He would never get involved with another person who possessed abilities beyond everyone else. Never again would he offer his help to a witch who had no comprehension of the consequences of her magic.

He refused to ever again be someone else's collateral damage.

*T*imothy McGinley made his way down the busy streets of Boston towards McGinley Antiquities. He had built the company from the ground up over the last sixty years and was more than proud of the well-known reputation they had for being the best artifact authenticators around.

At least in his business, it paid to be well over two hundred years old. He could spot a fake from a mile away since he had more than likely seen the original up close and personal.

He had chosen to walk this morning instead of taking his car, opting instead to stroll amongst the people enjoying their morning in the fresh blanket of snow.

He turned into a coffee shop and ordered his usual cup of black coffee, before slipping back onto the bustling street. It was nearing Christmas time, and Boston was blanketed with snow that shimmered as the sun shined down on it. Had he not seen it every single season for nearly a hundred and fifteen years, he might have been just as enamored by it like everyone else.

Now though, he simply ignored it and moved about his day. He had no reason to celebrate, no reason to even think for a moment this might be the last time he'd experience it.

He couldn't die, and therefore life had lost the edge. He had spent years doing anything he had ever dreamed about. He had fought in both world wars, skydived, climbed Everest, and ran the Boston marathon every year. Why? Because he was bored.

What else was there to do when you were going to live forever?

"Morning, Mr. McGinley!" his secretary called as he stepped into the foyer of his office building.

"Morning Jess, what do you have for me today?"

"We got a new shipment of artifacts from a warehouse in Dublin. They are waiting in the curating room for you as we speak."

"Great. Meetings?"

"A conference call at ten a.m. with the London Museum of Natural History and a face to face at noon with the Boston Museum of Fine Arts."

"What would I do without you Jess?" he asked with a smile and stepped into the elevator. She was pushing forty and ever since her divorce last year, she'd been on a long line of serial dates that made her feel less than adequate compared to the twenty something's wandering around who were doing their best to pull in an older man. He knew that because he made it his business to know everything there was to know about those he surrounded himself with.

He also knew that she was an incredibly sweet woman who wanted nothing more than to be loved and that his head of security and the only one who knew his real birthday, Ashton Hamilton was completely smitten with her and was just too afraid to say anything. Had Timothy's heart been anything but a tool in his body, he might have tried to set them up. But as it stood, he didn't give a damn about the feelings of others. Why the hell should he when no one gave a shit about his?

He had no interest in finding himself trapped in another spell, so he made sure he vetted his employees to the max. He refused to allow any magic around him unless he was the one studying it.

Which, he had been doing, unsuccessfully, for the last sixty-two years. He had tried everything he could think of to break the spell, but no matter what he did, he couldn't muster up even an ounce of magic.

He had only confirmed what he'd always known, you were either born with it or not. There was no way to give yourself abilities if it had never been in your blood to begin with. If there had been, he'd be long dead by now.

Timothy stepped out of the elevator and onto the top floor of the McGinley building. His office spanned the entire fifteenth floor and was by far his favorite place in the entire world.

A dark mahogany desk sat in front of the floor to

ceiling windows that spanned the entire space and overlooked the city he had grown to love. A bar on the left side of the room was stocked with the best whiskey money could buy and artifacts he hadn't been able to part with, so he'd purchased them himself, lined the walls on either side of the room.

The bathroom was the only part of the area that was separated, the door of which was near a large king size bed since he slept here most nights. He had an apartment on the other side of town that served as his private entertaining space.

In all his years he had never fallen in love again, but he definitely enjoyed the company of a woman, even if it were only for a night or two. No matter what he did or who he did it with, nothing ever changed-- he was still lonely, even if he wasn't alone.

He took the messenger bag off and pulled his laptop out. After going through the typical routine of checking his messages and returning e-mails that may have come in since he'd last checked them, he headed downstairs for his favorite part of the entire job: checking the new arrivals.

Each time he held an artifact in his hand, it somehow eased his loneliness. As if, the fact that the object was nearly as old as he was, sometimes even older, it had seen the things he had over the years. Witnessed the horrors that the human race was capable of. It was hard to see the beauty in others when you'd lived through countless wars.

"Morning, Mr. McGinley!"

"Morning, Jake, what do you have for me today?"

Timothy greeted his shipment manager as he stepped onto the fourth floor from the elevator. It was where they kept the majority of their artifacts, unless the item was too large for the elevator, in which case they took it to the basement.

"A new shipment from your home country, boss."

Timothy couldn't help but smile. His favorite shipments were those that came from home. They served as a heartwarming reminder of the place he'd left so long ago and hadn't stepped foot in since.

"Wonderful." He smiled as he pulled on gloves and opened the first crate. Inside, packed delicately, were eleven worn pennies from the first issue to Ireland in the 1280's. They weren't particularly rare and therefore didn't hold an incredible amount of monetary value. However, they would be invaluable to collectors worldwide. He set them back in the crate and cataloged, before moving on to the next one.

The next crate held an assortment of gold jewelry that had been crafted sometime in the early 1800's. He recognized one particular design, as it was strikingly similar to one he'd purchased for Cait as a wedding gift.

The gold cuff was worn down, so the Celtic knots that encircled it were barely recognizable. It didn't surprise him, gold wasn't as hard as steel and didn't hold up nearly as well to the years as the latter.

He cataloged it and set it aside to move on to the next item in the crate.

All in all, it turned out that nearly ninety-five percent of the shipment had been legitimate artifacts, with only a few having been replicas made to appear as if they were the real deal.

He finished logging everything into the books and took his gloves off. He stood for a moment, surrounded by things that were old and full of memories of multiple lifetimes. Just as he was.

"Are we all good?" Jake asked as he walked into the room, chipper as usual. From his research, Timothy had learned that Jake Parish was the only child of two doctors who had their own practice here in Boston. He preferred to play video games rather than going out with friends and other than his online profiles used for gaming—specifically computer games—he didn't use any other type of social media. It had surprised Timothy when he'd interviewed him, to see that Jake was fit. Perhaps it wasn't fair to go off a stereotype, but he hadn't expected the gamer profile to be matched with an athletic build.

Timothy handed him the books, "There are a few items—some glasses and plates—that were only replicas of the real thing. I placed those in the crate near the door. The others have been authenticated and logged and are ready for auction or to be shipped back to their owners."

"Awesome. I'll get them taken care of. Uh, Jess said you are running a few minutes behind for your conference call and asked me to let you know they are waiting on the line."

He looked down at his watch surprised to see that nearly two hours had passed while he'd been down here. "Thank you, Jake, I'll head up to my office."

"Sounds good boss. I'll let you know if anything comes up."

Timothy nodded and headed for the elevator. As the doors closed in front of him, he mentally ran down the list of items on the agenda for his conference call with London. They were begging him to fly out and authenticate a pair of chalices found recently.

Since he wasn't fond of air travel, he didn't care how long it had been around, it still seemed strange for human beings to by flying through the air, he had politely passed on multiple occasions.

If they continued to press the issue though, he might have to at least send someone over there. Jake came to mind. He had recently graduated with a masters in History and had studied overseas dating artifacts they found in Cairo, Egypt. Perhaps he'd be interested in the promotion.

With the idea taking root, Timothy stepped on to the floor of his office and over to his desk to answer the blinking red light.

"Hello gentlemen, I apologize for keeping you waiting. What can I do for you?"

TIMOTHY HUNG UP THE PHONE RELIEVED THEY'D GONE for his idea. He buzzed Jess and asked her to let Jake know he needed to speak with him, then he stood to stare out of the large windows that overlooked the city. *His city*, the only place that had felt like home to him since Cait had died and he'd left Ireland all those years ago.

He'd spent a couple years traveling all over the country and had lived in Illinois, Texas, and even California once it had been deemed a state before he finally settled in Massachusetts and started his business. He carried both mental and physical scars from the battles he'd fought throughout the years. The physical wounds had healed but still turned into the ragged edges of skin that were a roadmap of his injuries. He had thought perhaps the scars would disappear as well, but it seemed he wasn't even allotted that luxury.

He heard the elevator doors open behind him and turned to see a somewhat nervous looking Jake standing just inside his office.

"You wanted to see me?"

"Yes." Timothy offered him a smile. He liked the kid, had since the moment he'd met him and hoped he would take this promotion and use it to build a career above the stockroom. "Have a seat." Timothy gestured to the chair across from his desk and took his own seat while Jake made his way over. "I have an opportunity I think you'll like." When Jake stayed silent, Timothy continued. "The London Museum of Natural History has asked for our help in authenticating and dating two chalices they discovered during a recent dig. I would like to send you."

Jakes face lit up as the words sank in. "You want to send *me*, to London, to authenticate artifacts?"

"Yes."

"Seriously?"

"Yes."

"This is amazing! Thank you so much, Mr. McGinley!" He grinned madly, and fist punched the air before realizing where he was and settling back into his seat. "I mean, of course, this would be an incredible honor."

"I am glad you think so. How long do you need before you can leave?"

"Heck, I can leave tomorrow!"

"Wonderful. I will have Jess get everything in order for you." He couldn't keep himself from smiling at the excitement reflecting on the young man's face. Seeing that love and elation on Jakes' face had made him grateful he'd gone ahead and asked about sending him as a replacement. It surprised him that he felt joy at Jake's excitement. Who knew, perhaps he wasn't such a careless bastard after all.

"I cannot thank you enough, Mr. McGinley, this is an opportunity of a lifetime."

"You are more than welcome. I trust that you will do good work and make a name for McGinley Antiquities while you're over there."

"I sure will Sir."

"Go ahead and take the rest of the day to prepare yourself to leave."

"Will do! Thanks again!" Jake practically ran to the elevator, and Timothy found he was slightly jealous. What he would give to feel that excitement, that absolute enjoyment of the unknown even one more time in his long life.

CHAPTER 2

*P*aislee Adams pulled her hood up over her head and stepped onto the street. She watched closely as people walked nearby and kept her eye out for anything out of the ordinary. Unfortunately, this was now second nature for her.

She pulled her backpack closer to her and pushed her way through the crowd towards the library where she spent the majority of her time researching and trying to find a way to control the part of her she didn't fully understand.

People passed by her, completely unaware that the humming was slowly building in her blood making her feel like at any one point she might explode into a million pieces and destroy everything and everyone around her.

She stepped into the local library but kept her hood up. With her fiery red hair, she stuck out like a sore thumb anywhere she went. People tended to remember the redhead with the giant, ragged scar along her jaw. She was a hard face to forget.

"Can I help you find anything dear?" the elderly woman working the counter asked as Paislee stepped through the entry doors.

"No thank you, I'm just browsing."

"You got it dear. If you need anything just let me know."

"Will do, thanks." She smiled and made her way through the rows and rows of books and to the back of the library towards their magic section. When she'd first stumbled into this library, it had felt like she would finally discover answers to the millions of questions in her mind. Their paranormal and magic section was broader than any of the others. It wasn't long though before she realized most of it was crap written by those with zero-real knowledge about the subjects they claimed to be experts in.

Once she reached the section she was looking for, she placed her bag down on the nearest table and went over to the rack to scan the titles.

She imagined these books were here for amusement purposes rather than actual how-to guides since it seemed the majority of the public didn't actually believe in magic. Shit, she hadn't believed in it even as a child, not until she'd no longer been able to refuse its existence.

She grabbed a book titled *My Magic and I: A detailed look at the magic inside of you* from the shelf and made her way back to her table so she could start her research for the day.

The cover was a deep purple with gold words that stuck up from the thin paper jacket. She opened to the first page and read the inscription, *To my sister with love. I'm forever grateful we were blessed with this power together. Blessed be.*

Paislee rolled her eyes, especially when she started actually flipping through the pages.

This book had clearly been written by a woman who's only power was boring the shit out of people. It was jam-packed full of crackpot love spells that had no actual hope of working.

She looked down at the words of one incantation that was supposed to bring wealth and happiness to any and all that believed.

To me, I call my magic wide
  Show me as I watch the sky
  Bring me love and happiness near
  Show me the path to my monetary ear

What in the actual crap was a *monetary ear?* Paislee shut the book and returned it to its shelf. If she'd had the time, she might have been interested to read what other stupid crap had been put into the book. But she didn't have time, not when her life was on the line.

Instead she grabbed a book titled *Magic: real or hoax* and took her seat at the table again. She *needed* to find something, anything that could help her harness the power inside of her.

Because if he found her and she wasn't ready for him, she doubted she would be able to escape again.

THE DAY HAD UNFORTUNATELY PROVEN TO BE A BUST as far as learning about her heritage. The book's author had some interesting ideas about where magic originated from, but there had been absolutely nothing in there about how to control it if you did possess the gifts.

That was her biggest concern, she was a ticking time bomb. Her magic would grow inside her, and then release itself in whatever way it felt like. Just last month, she'd nearly killed a man who slapped her on the butt as she was leaving a bar.

Sure, he might have deserved an ass kicking for it, but not the jolt of power that shot him back as if he'd been electrocuted.

She supposed the plus was he probably wouldn't be grabbing anyone else's ass for a while. The negative was that she'd liked that bar. The bartender had been cute, and she'd enjoyed the easy conversations they'd had each night over a glass of whiskey. He had looked at her the way men studied women they were attracted to, and Paislee had considered taking him to bed more than once.

The day had darkened into dusk as she stepped onto the street and headed towards the pawnshop she visited every now and then. She was running low on cash, and in the event, she would need to run, it was going to be important to have some on hand.

Giovanni's Pawn was six blocks from her apartment, and while the owner was a disgusting excuse for a man, he never asked her questions, and since her items were stolen, that was more important to her than his manners.

"Hey, look it's the fire crotch!" Giovanni's voice boomed as she stepped into the store. She had to bite back the anger at her nickname, it would do no good to level the shop when she needed the money.

"I have a new item for you." She reached into her backpack and pulled out a plastic container that held an incredibly old painting. She had only briefly looked at it, and it was the first one she had brought in to pawn. Her previous items had been gold coins, pottery, and weapons from the early 1800's.

He took the painting from her and carefully unrolled it than snorted and tossed it back at her. She glared at him, she loved antiques, and he had just tossed it at her like it was garbage.

"What the fuck am I supposed to do with a painting of some dude and his whore?"

"It's an original McCreary painting. Which if you knew your history, you would realize is well worth fifty grand. And that's on the low side."

"You want me to pay 50 thousand fucking dollars for a piece of paper?" He howled in laughter, and Paislee's cheeks turned red. "Oh, look at you! Your cheeks nearly match your hair, fire crotch. I tell you what, you show me what you have down there, and I might pay you your fifty grand."

It was Paislee's turn to let out a laugh. "No, thanks."

"Well, then I suggest you go and get that authenticated before bringing it back to me."

"How the hell am I supposed to do that?"

"I don't give a shit. It's not me who needs the money, if you rethink my offer let me know, it's always on the table. I bet you'd be a hellcat in the sack." He winked at her and Paislee fought the urge to throw him the bird. She was wound tight, and it wouldn't take much before she snapped. It really was too bad she needed his shop standing.

"Any ideas where I can take it?"

He shrugged. "There's a place on the other side of town. It's called McGinley Antiquities. The guy who runs it knows his shit. You get a certificate from there, and I'll buy your painting."

"Lovely. I'll be back." She left before he said something else stupid to piss her off. How the hell was she supposed to get a certificate of authenticity on a stolen item? If his office had been notified of the theft, she could get arrested.

It would help if she knew whether or not the original owner had gotten it through legal channels, but as it was, she wasn't sure that would be the case. She'd be willing to bet the son of a bitch had stolen it himself, or more likely, had paid someone else to steal it. The last damn thing she needed was to get arrested. It would be entirely too easy for him to find her if she was behind bars.

"Fuck!" she yelled once she got outside of the shop and headed towards the other side of town. She didn't have a choice, if there was no money to keep her safe, she was as good as dead anyway.

As she walked, she went through the notes she'd taken over the last week in her head. So far, the closest she'd come to learning anything had been an old book she'd discovered in the library titled *The Mystics of Magic*. When she'd gone back the next day, the librarian had informed her it had been purchased by a man in exchange for a large donation.

The woman had been absolutely beaming, elated that the library was getting new computers and hundreds of new titles for its shelves. Of course, she'd been happy about it, how could she have known that the woman standing before her had needed that book desperately?

It wasn't like she could get a library card since she didn't even have a single form of identification. She lived in a crap hole apartment because the woman that ran it was a junkie whose only concern was when she was going to get her next high.

Unfortunately, Paislee knew all too well what a junkie would do in order to score some drugs.

She shook her head, no sense in dwelling on the past. It was there for a reason and was no use to her now. Now was all about focusing on learning as much as she could before she destroyed the man who had torn apart her entire existence.

Paislee continued walking through parts of town most people wouldn't want to be in alone after dark. She ignored those who asked her for help and pushed through the catcalls from the men sitting on steps of their apartments,

Before long though, those scenes disappeared and were replaced with up kept, gorgeous brownstones and lovers walking together amongst the snow that was now falling lightly.

It stuck to her jacket, and Paislee stopped for just a moment to appreciate the beauty of it. She'd always loved the snow and after going nearly fourteen years without being able to touch it, took every opportunity to feel it. Even now, she stuck her hand out to allow the tiny flakes to dissolve against her warm palm.

She continued her walk into downtown and stopped across the street from McGinley Antiquities. The tall, looming building had been beautifully sculpted with stone, it's elegance portrayed in tall arches above the windows and main entry door.

It was well past closing time, but Paislee had wanted to get eyes on the company before she resigned to her apartment to do research. Knowing the location helped to calm her nerves.

What kind of man, or men, had built this company? Were they honorable and would turn her away at the first hint of trouble? Or were they like Giovanni or the man who'd held her captive and relish at the opportunity to get their thieving hands on such a priceless item?

It was the last of the things she'd stolen upon her

escape, and she'd told herself she had only kept it because it was the most expensive. Truthfully though, there was something in the painting that called to her. Whether it was the haunting eyes of the man standing protectively with the red-haired woman or the way she looked up at him with pure love reflecting in her own. It could have even been that Paislee thought she'd resembled the woman, and wanted to imagine what it would feel like to have someone look at you as if you're the only person in the entire world that mattered.

Paislee wondered if the man depicted in the painting had at one point been a real person and if he and the woman had truly been in love. Because whenever she stared down at that painting that was the emotion she felt.

The artist had captured pure and absolute love.

She saw a man in a black hoodie slip into the alley behind the building, and moments later a shot rang out. It was muffled as if being fired from a silencer and had she not heard that sound countless times in her life, she might have thought it was just another random noise in the city.

But she knew what it was, and while most would have run the other way, Paislee found herself sprinting towards the alley.

CHAPTER 3

*T*imothy stared out of his large windows at the darkening sky. The city was never more beautiful than it was right now as the sun sank lower leaving trails of orange, yellow, and red in its wake.

City lights were just beginning to come on and the combination of them and the sunset as the last rays glinted against the white blanket of snow was pure magic.

He scoffed at the thought, *nothing* good came from magic. Only death and despair. He drank down the rest of the whiskey in his glass and grabbed his jacket off the chair. He never smoked in his office, but damn he could use a cigar now.

Since everyone had gone home for the evening except for Ashton who was in his office watching the security feeds, the building would be silent which was something he dreaded each night.

He had spent a lot of years in the silence, and it was deafening.

Timothy stepped out into the alley behind his building and clipped the end of the cigar he had pulled from his office humidor. He held it up to his nose and breathed in the sweet smell before lighting it.

The darkness enveloped him as he leaned against the door and puffed on his cigar. There was nothing in the world like the taste of a fine cigar as the tobacco seeped into your system.

The calming effect it had on him was one he'd failed to find anywhere else. The chill in the air had the puffs coming out even more defined than usual, and Timothy was enthralled by them as they faded from view. ____

It wasn't until he was half done with his cigar that he saw the shadow lurking in the corner.

"Can I help you?" he asked easily, and the man stepped from the dark. Timothy straightened when he saw the gun in his hand. "No need for that, tell me what you want, and I'll be sure you get it." Timothy wasn't overly worried; the man couldn't actually kill him. But damn, gunshots hurt like hell. He should know since he'd been at the receiving end of one too many times to count.

The man stepped close enough Timothy was able to see the glint of amusement in his eye. Timothy had only ever seen that madness once before, and that man had been responsible for two innocent deaths and the root reason as to why he was trapped.

His back straightened, and he gave the man

before him his full attention. "What is it you want?" he asked again.

"I want to see you bleed," the man said with a smile and pulled the trigger.

It was the pain that hit him first, that sharp tearing of skin and flesh as the bullet forced its way into his body. He fell to the ground, cigar falling next to him, and clutched his abdomen. No matter how many times he'd been shot, stabbed, punched, or even on occasion-burned—over the years, the pain was not something he ever got used to.

The coldness came next and was something Timothy had not been prepared for. His wounds, no matter how severe, had always healed themselves before the numbing fingers of death gripped him as they were now. *How was this possible?* He thought to himself. *What was happening to him?* He tried his best to move but found his body had gone completely numb as he lay there in the pool of his own blood.

And as his attacker knelt next to him, he felt for the first time, as if he wouldn't survive the night.

"I knew he was wrong about you." The man smiled. "Oh well, I suppose it was worth the trouble. There is just something about having the ability to snuff out the light within someone's eyes."

"Hey!" a voice screamed, and the man stood.

Timothy wasn't sure what happened next, but where it had once been dark, a light appeared, and his attacker was thrown away from him. He watched as the light faded, but not before he got a clear picture of the one who had saved him.

A woman, with hair the color of fire, and kind blue eyes, ran to his side and knelt in the blood that poured from him.

"Cait?" he whispered. Was he dead? Was she sent here to usher him into what waited beyond this life?

"You're going to be alright," Cait said as she closed her eyes and pressed her hands to him.

It would always be the pain he remembered first, but the surge of power that came next would be impossible to forget.

PAISLEE FELL TO HER KNEES NEXT TO THE BLEEDING man. "No, no, no you can't die." Had they somehow discovered she was coming here for help? How had they found her? Had Giovanni sold her out?

She had recognized the man holding the gun even in the dark from where she stood at the end of the alley. He was Malcolm's assassin, one that had been gunning for her ever since she escaped. He'd nearly cornered her twice already, and she'd managed to barely evade him.

Fuck this man can't die because of me. She pressed her hands to his wound and willed her magic to heal him, which was something she had never done before. She had absolutely no idea what it would do to the man, especially with the amount of power she'd built up recently. But since he was lying there dying, she figured it couldn't hurt.

She reached inside for the light she had learned

was the core of her magic and pulled at it. She felt the drain as it bled through her fingers and into her captor's latest victim, but she continued anyway. Even as her mind got foggy, and her hands began to shake over his wound.

"Cait?" she heard him whisper, but she ignored him and continued to press everything she had into his body.

What felt like hours later, but had probably been mere seconds, she heard him yell, "Move!" Her eyes snapped open just as she was shoved to the side. Her head impacted with the pavement as a gunshot rang out again and she briefly wondered if the assassin had recovered from her blast of magic and shot her too, it wouldn't surprise her. She had yet to conjure up anything lethal.

"Can you hear me?" The man she healed kneeled next to her, and she nodded. "Fuck," he cursed. She felt herself being lifted and then everything went dark.

"There's a dead man in my alley," Timothy notified Ashton over the phone. He could have easily gone down and spoken face to face with the guard, but he hadn't wanted to leave the woman on his couch alone for long. "Take care of him," he ordered and hung up the phone.

He ran his hands through his hair and fought the urge to curse. What the fuck had just happened? Who was this mystery woman?

She looked just like his Cait. The bright red hair, freckles that covered her nose, even the blue eyes he had seen for only a moment before she passed out, were the spitting image of the woman he had spent the best years of his life with.

The main difference he saw now, was a long scar that ran the length of the right side of her jaw, and a birthmark near her left eye.

So, who the hell was this woman? How had she come to be in that alley? He kept his distance even though he knew that without her he would have died. The fact that he was still breathing meant two things: his curse was broken, and she was a fucking witch. Another magical being crashing into his life and wrecking everything he had worked so hard to accomplish.

He changed his shirt, desperate to get out of the blood-soaked fabric. Ashton would dispose of the body and would hopefully be able to shine some light on who the hell that man was and just why he'd wanted to 'watch him bleed' as the asshole had so eloquently put it.

Timothy looked back at the sleeping form. She had nearly died saving him. This witch had almost completely drained herself while she healed him. Had she meant to? Or was she naïve? Either way, he needed to get her the hell out of his life as soon as possible. He had no time for magic. Especially not when he might finally have the gift of mortality.

"Fuck," he muttered. The last damn thing he

needed was a witch who didn't know shit about her own powers.

Timothy pulled his jacket on over his shirt and headed back out towards the alley.

"You good boss?" Ashton stepped out into the alley with him. Timothy nodded, grateful it was a loyal man who knew his secret on duty rather than one of the others who might have questioned their boss who was unharmed, yet his blood was in a pool on the pavement.

"Yeah, just more shit to deal with." Timothy lit up a cigarette and offered the guard one from his pack.

"Thanks, boss." Ashton took one and lit it. "So, any idea who this guy is?"

Timothy shook his head. "Not a damn clue."

"You good?"

"You know me, I'm difficult to kill." *Except tonight apparently*, he thought to himself. He didn't want to worry his friend just yet though, so he left that part out.

Ashton let out a dark laugh. "I'm glad you are. This guy is packing some pretty serious heat." He knelt next to the body and using a pen, lifted the edge of the man's sweatshirt.

Timothy pulled from the cigarette and felt his nerves relax slightly as the tobacco hit his system. He knelt next to his now dead attacker and looked at what Ashton had uncovered.

Two more pistols in the man's waist, a large knife clipped to his belt, and what looked to be a garrote dangling from a belt loop.

"So, someone sent an assassin after me," Timothy commented as he stood.

Ashton followed. "It would appear so. Now the question is why?"

"Could be a competitor looking to shut my company down."

"Possibly, we need to figure out who he is, so we can find out who sent him."

They looked up as two black SUV's pulled into the alley. "Just in time," Ashton commented and walked towards the men climbing out of the vehicle.

Timothy watched as the men photographed his attacker and then loaded him in a body bag. Another team came in and cleaned up the blood and brass. Ashton would make this disappear and get to the bottom of why the man had been sent to him in the first place.

It was why he'd hired him in the first place. Ashton was ex-FBI and had spent fifteen years in the Army as Special Forces. He was as solid as they came and had contacts high up in both the FBI and the CIA.

It had been a mere coincidence that Ashton had found out his secret. As it turned out, the man was a history buff and had stumbled across a picture of an old platoon from WWII. Ashton had come to Timothy to make a joke about how one of the men resembled him. At first, Timothy had managed to brush it off.

But that night, he had been badly injured when a mugger shot him multiple times, and Ashton had been called in to help clean up the mess. Timothy hadn't had a chance to change clothes yet and was still covered in his own blood.

Ashton had begun asking questions Timothy hadn't been able to answer, so in the end, he'd told the man the truth, and after a few minutes of stunned silence, while he decided whether or not he believed his boss, Ashton simply nodded and went on his way. Ever since Timothy had considered Ashton to be one of his closest friends, well he would be if Timothy had any.

The vehicles pulled out of the alley and Ashton made his way back over to Timothy. "We'll get this taken care of."

"I know you will."

"You sure you're good, boss?"

"I'm good." Timothy headed back upstairs to his office.

She was still asleep when he opened the door, so he took a moment to stare down at her. It was amazing to him how similar she was to his late wife. So much so, that seeing her lying there, stabbed him in the heart the same way it had to watch her dying of old age all those years ago.

This woman's red hair curled lightly around her face, having fallen out of whatever tie she had used to hold it back. He fought the urge to brush it out of her face. *She is not Cait, this woman is a damn witch.* He reminded himself.

She stirred slightly, and Timothy covered her with

a blanket and lifted the backpack she had been carrying from the floor.

He opened it and pulled out a few books on magic, foolish ones that were written by those who only wished they could understand the power some held, a notepad with brief magic notes written on it, a small bag of pens, and a cylinder container.

Abandoning everything but the container, he walked to his desk and pulled out some gloves. Anyone with an ounce of sense could see that whatever the container held was fragile and incredibly old.

He gently tipped the container up and let the rolled canvas fall into his gloved hands. As he unrolled it, his heart thudded in his chest. He knew this painting. Had been there when it had been painted. Now, he thought as he looked down at the smiling faces of he and Cait, how in the hell had this woman gotten her hands on it?

CHAPTER 4

*P*aislee opened her eyes to the light pouring in through a window. It was her first sense that something was off. Her windows were all covered, and she never pulled back the curtains.

Her head felt like it had been split in two as memories of the night raced back to her. A man with a gun. A second man bleeding to death in an alley. A blast of uncontrolled magic and her attempt to heal him.

Her second realization was that this place was *immaculate* compared to the shit hole she hid in. Relics that were triple her age- some more than- covered three of the walls, the only space being where an elevator opened. The fourth wall was covered floor to ceiling in thick glass.

As her eyes traveled, she saw a man standing with his back to her. Her heart began to pound in her chest, had *he* found her? *No*, that's not him. This man was much too tall to be her former captor. From behind she could see that he was heavily muscled. A white business shirt was stretched over broad shoulders and tucked into suit pants that clung to one of the best asses she had ever seen, celebrities included. Her cheeks flushed as if she was worried he could hear her thoughts. She cleared her throat, and he turned around to look at her.

His jaw was strong and covered in light stubble, his dark hair was cut short, and she could tell he had been running his hands through it. If that wasn't enough to make her mouth water, his shirt was half unbuttoned and baring a muscular chest that was lightly covered with hair. She knew she'd never seen him before, but there was something so incredibly familiar about him.

It took her a moment, but she realized the familiarity was because he looked very similar to the man in the painting. That, or she was truly losing her mind.

"Morning," the man's deep voice said softly.

"Morning." She sat up straighter. "Can you please tell me where the hell I am?"

"McGinley Antiquities. I'm Timothy McGinley." *No man this handsome should be allowed to have an Irish accent*, Paislee thought to herself, *it was just wrong.*

So that hadn't been a dream! She really had been in that alley!

"How did I get here?" she asked deciding it might be better to play dumb on the off chance she was crazy.

"You don't remember?" he asked and took a seat in the armchair that was positioned across from the couch she was currently occupying. Now that he was closer, she could see the anger in the way his jaw was set, the way his eyes were unwavering and locked on her. Why the hell would he be mad at her?

"Did I meet you in the alley?"

"Yes."

"Were you by chance bleeding?"

"Yes."

"Maybe even dying?"

"Certainly seemed that way."

Shit, she thought as the realization hit home. She had done magic in front of a stranger. Had, in fact, saved his life; was he going to keep her as a prisoner? Turn her in to be experimented on like some fucking lab rat?

Fueled by anger, she stood. She'd die before she was someone else's trophy witch.

"Well as lovely as this has been, I need to go."

He stood as well. "You won't be going anywhere until you explain to me why you saved my life, and how the hell you gained possession of this." He held up the painting that was the whole reason she was here, and it only stoked the anger.

"Why did you go through my things. That belongs to me, Mr. McGinley, so I would appreciate if you gave it back."

Ignoring her, he rolled it back up, put it into its case, and locked it in a safe next to his desk. "How about you start with why you were in my alley last night? Miss Adams," he added smugly.

She shouldn't have been surprised he knew her name since it seemed he liked to snoop. The word *asshole* certainly came to mind.

"I was sent to you to have something authenticated."

"Who sent you."

"A friend," she retorted, her voice cool.

"What friend?"

"I won't be telling you. Now, if you please-"

"I don't *please*. You might as well get comfortable since you won't be leaving until you've answered my questions." He walked back over to the chair and sat, then he leaned back and crossed an ankle over his knee. "How long have you known you were a witch?"

She let out a nervous laugh. "Are you insane? Witches aren't real." She took her seat back on the couch.

"So, you're a liar then, that's good to know I suppose."

"I am not a liar." Her face turned red, and Timothy grinned, Cait's face would flush when she was angry as well.

"Fine, then answer my question."

"Why do you think I'm a witch?"

"Well, for one, you have a ridiculous amount of magic texts in your bag, all of which aren't reputable by the way. Then there's the fact that I was going to die last night until all of a sudden I'm shooting my attacker and lifting an unconscious stranger in my arms."

She shivered slightly at the thought of this man's strong arms around her. How she wished she could have remembered what it had felt like. Of course, that was before he opened his arrogant mouth. Now she wanted to throat punch him.

"Fine. I saved your life. You're welcome by the way."

"I didn't thank you."

The sudden chill in his voice surprised her, why would someone be angry to still be alive?

"Why was Malcolm's assassin after you anyways?" She hated saying her captor's name, but in this case, couldn't find a way around it. She needed her own questions answered.

His brow quirked. "Malcolm who?"

"Malcolm Gentry."

"I know that name."

"I'm sure you do. He collects antiques." *And people* she added to herself.

"That man last night, he works for him?"

She nodded. "He was here before I was, so it must have been you he was after."

"You have a reason to think he was looking for you?"

Shit, she really needed to shut the hell up before she told him everything. "Malcolm likes antiques," she repeated slowly. "Specifically items that hold power. He's been after me for a while now."

Timothy nodded knowingly. To a man like that,

an actual magical person would be the ultimate prize. "So, you came to me to have that painting authenticated."

"Yes."

"Who sent you?" he repeated his earlier question, and Paislee got the feeling they would continue talking in circles until she answered him.

She ground her teeth together, who the hell did this guy think he was? "I'm not answering any more of your questions." She got to her feet. "Please give me my painting back so I can get going. Unless you feel like authenticating it for me, so I can sell it."

"Why would you want to sell it?" He stood now, and the closeness of their bodies had her reacting in a way she hadn't anticipated. She looked into eyes the color of steel, and she knew without a doubt, Timothy McGinley was a man she needed to avoid. There was a hardness about him, in the way he stared back at her, his eyes unwavering.

"I have no use for it, I do, however, have a use for money if I want to continue living."

"I will buy it."

A slap across her face would have surprised her less. Why the hell did he want it? "Why the hell do you want it?" she repeated out loud and followed him to his desk.

"I like antiques, and this one strikes my interest."

"Why?"

"Does it matter?" He pulled out his checkbook. "I want it, you need money, I have money, seems like a done deal to me."

"How do I know you're giving me a fair deal?"

"Miss Adams," his voice was full of irritation, and he pressed a hand to his forehead. "That painting is an original McCreary and is a hundred and ninety-eight years old."

"Seriously?"

He eyed her. "Yes."

"So how much is it worth?"

Timothy straightened. "It's in good condition, and McCreary was a fairly well-known artist of his time in Ireland. People would travel from all over the country and even further at times, to have their portraits done. However, given that this painting was acquired through less than honorable conditions, I will give you eight thousand for it."

"Are you fucking kidding me. It has to be worth more than that."

"Oh, it is, but since I can't move it because if I'm caught with it, I will go to prison, I'm going to take that into consideration." He folded his arms and watched her with that smug look she was growing to despise.

He was right, of course, but she *needed* the money. She had waited to pawn this particular piece because she felt drawn to it and now if she were going to have to part with it, she would rather do it with enough money that she could leave and never look back.

"Fifty thousand."

Timothy let out a laugh, and Paislee saw the dimple on the left side of his cheek. Why did he have to be so infuriatingly attractive?

"Ten."

"Fifteen."

"Deal."

"This is bullshit."

"I agree," Timothy commented and wrote a check. At least this way she wouldn't have to ever go back to Giovanni. With each visit, she was worried she would burn his shop down because of his 'fire crotch' comments.

"Thanks," she said sarcastically, and put the check in her back pocket. "Hopefully, I won't see you around."

"That seems rude."

She spun to face his eyes wild with anger. "*I'm rude?* Are you fucking kidding me? You've been nothing but an ungrateful bastard since I saved your ass in that alley last night. Maybe I should have just let you bleed to death!"

"While I typically would have welcomed death, I'm grateful to not have met my demise just yet."

"Who the fuck talks like that? 'Demise,' he says. Ugh!" She rolled her eyes and let out a huff of anger.

"Some women like the way I talk."

"Yeah, well, I'm not most women."

"I see that."

"Am I free to go now?"

"If you want this Malcolm to find you, sure." Timothy took a seat at his desk and opened his laptop.

"What the hell is that supposed to mean?"

"It means that he and his men are watching my building. The second you leave, he will follow you."

"How do you know he's-"

"Look." Timothy pinched the bridge of his nose again, something Paislee was noticing he did whenever he was frustrated. "He sent a man to my alley which meant he's been watching me. Seeing as how that man didn't make out alive and I did, I imagine Malcolm will have some questions as to how that happened. You say they're looking for you? The second you exit my building they will be on you quicker than you could run."

"Just why should I trust you. You could have struck up a deal with him for all I know! I don't know you."

"He sent someone to kill me, Miss Adams."

"I swear if you call me Miss Adams again I'm going to punch you."

"You're very violent, aren't you?"

"What can I say? You seem to bring it out in me."

He shrugged. "Fair enough, *Paislee*."

She should have let him continue calling her Miss Adams because her name on his lips was dangerous in itself. "Why did he send someone after you?"

She missed the flash of panic in his eyes. That was something he hadn't spent much time deliberating on afraid that the truth of it was that his secret was out. "I don't know. Perhaps I have something he wants." Timothy eyed her dangerously.

For a moment they stood staring at each other. Both in their own minds reliving pasts, they would rather have forgotten. For Paislee, she was back in that cage. Being forced to perform magic, she had no idea how to use.

Timothy was back in Ireland, staring down at the grave of the woman he loved more than life itself. Or fighting wars trying desperately to end the life he no longer wanted to live.

So how is it they found themselves here? Staring at each other over his desk? He had promised himself he would stay away from anyone who possessed any form of magic, but could he send this woman out to what could very well be her death? Besides, Malcolm was obviously after him as well, so keeping something of value to his enemy could prove a beneficial strategy.

"I would appreciate it if you would stay for a while Paislee. You will be safe here, and perhaps we can determine what it is your Malcolm wants from me."

"He isn't my Malcolm."

Not a refusal to stay, Timothy noted. And while he could see the inner battle she was having with herself, he would be willing to bet he'd won this round. He could sense the fight in her, she had no intention of going down before she got whatever it was out of Malcolm herself.

"Do you have a bathroom in here?"

He pointed to the door next to the bed in the corner, and without a word, she turned leaving him staring after her.

The second she had closed the door behind her, Timothy pulled out his phone and called Ashton.

"Bright," he answered on the first ring.

"Check out Malcolm Gentry. I have reason to believe he is the man who sent the assassin after me."

"On it."

Timothy ended the call and answered the buzzer on his desk that told him someone was asking to come up.

"Hey, boss it's Jake. I wanted to go over a few things with you?"

"Come on up."

He hit the buzzer and took a seat behind the desk.

"Hey, boss," Jake said as he stepped out into Timothy's office. "I'm packed, and my flight leaves in four hours."

"You understand what it is you're expected to do?"

"Check out the chalices, date and authenticate them, and see if they wouldn't be interested in sending a representative over to attend our next auction."

Timothy nodded, and both men turned as Paislee stepped from the bathroom.

"I'm so sorry to have interrupted." Jake blushed.

"You didn't interrupt anything, Miss Adams is an associate of mine."

"Oh, well then, it's nice to meet you, Miss Adams." He held his hand out, "I'm Jake Parish."

"Nice to meet you Jake, I'm Paislee." She took his hand and Timothy couldn't help but detest the fact that they were touching.

"You too, Paislee." Jake smiled and then released

her hand. "Boss man here is sending me to London for a week."

"That sounds intriguing."

"I'm definitely excited." He stared at her and Timothy could feel the attraction coming off of him in waves. Shit, he'd have to be dead to not notice it. "So, um, I usually don't do this, but would you be interested in maybe grabbing dinner or something when I get back?"

Before she could answer, Timothy, interrupted, "Don't you have a flight to catch?"

"Yes, Sir. I'll head out now, nice to meet you Paislee." He smiled widely as he left the office.

"He seems nice," She said easily.

"Yeah."

"What's he going to London for?"

"Company business." He looked back down at his laptop and Paislee could see she'd lost him to whatever it was he did.

CHAPTER 5

"So, when are you planning on letting me go?"

Timothy looked over to where Paislee was sitting cross-legged on his couch, thumbing through one of the useless magic texts she'd brought with her. She looked so normal sitting there, and it pained him. Why the hell did she have to look so much like Cait?

"I told you, you're not a prisoner here."

"But I can't leave because Malcolm is supposedly watching your building?"

"If you want to leave, go ahead." When she remained seated, he said, "That's what I thought."

"What's that supposed to mean?"

"If you believed I was lying, you would have left already. I will take you to your apartment, so you can gather what you need."

"What I need for what?"

"You're staying here."

"Like hell I am. You sneak me out of this place, and I will disappear. It's what I'm good at."

"You're obviously not that good, or he wouldn't have found you."

"He found me because *you* were dying, and I chose to save you. Against my better judgment, I might add."

"Noted. If I take you out of this office, it's to help you gather your things and come back."

"Just what are we supposed to do up here together? Sing kumbaya? There's only one bed, and I'm not sharing it."

"That's assuming a lot Paislee."

"Oh, is it?"

"Yes." He shut his laptop and leaned back in his chair. "For one, you're assuming I would let you take the bed and not make you sleep on the couch. Secondly, that's also assuming I'm staying here too, which I'm not."

"Where the hell are you going?"

"Anyone ever tell you that you cuss like a sailor?"

"No, and I wouldn't give a shit if they did. Where are you staying?"

"My apartment."

"You don't live here?"

He raised his eyebrow. "Hardly."

"Seems strange you would have a bed in a place you don't live."

"I sleep here from time to time if I'm working late."

She tried to not let it bother her that he wouldn't

be nearby. Something about him being here, about her not being alone, was comforting.

"So, I'm going to be here alone."

"This building is secure. There will be a guard outside of the elevator which as you notice, is the only way in and out of here." There was a warning in his tone. It was unnecessary as she had no reason to go anywhere. She knew he was right, Malcolm would be watching this building, and as it stood, Timothy McGinley-arrogance included- was her best shot.

"Why didn't you freak out?"

"Excuse me?"

"When you realized I was a witch, you didn't act weird about it. Or even all that surprised."

"I am not a stranger to magic," he said simply and stood. "Would you like me to take you to your apartment?"

"Yes, please." It pained her to do so, but she tried to sound as polite as possible. She wanted new clothes and her cat.

"Let's go then. If anyone asks, you're an archeologist."

"You got it. Should I call you boss too?" She could have been mistaken, but she thought she saw a glimmer of amusement on his face.

"If it suits you, I certainly won't complain," he responded and pulled a phone out of his pocket. "We need a car in the alley." He hung up, and they walked to the elevator.

"So, have you always been into antiques?" She wondered as the door closed.

"You could say that."

"How long have you been in Boston?"

"A long time."

"Any family?"

"No."

She stayed silent the rest of the way down to the bottom floor of the building. When they stepped out of the elevator, there was a man in a black suit waiting for them.

"Paislee Adams this is Ashton Bright, the head of my security team."

"Nice to meet you." She extended a hand, and the man offered her a kind smile.

"Nice to meet you as well, Miss Adams."

"Please just call me Paislee."

"You got it, Paislee."

"Any updates?" Timothy asked him as they walked down a hallway and towards a door that Paislee assumed let to the same alley where her life had taken a strange detour.

She glanced up at Timothy who walked beside her but was focused on Ashton, *A very strange detour*.

"The assassin was a man by the name of Mitchell Henderson. He was employed as a package delivery man by Gentry Corp. They specialize in refurbishing old properties, specifically those deemed historical sites." Ashton stepped outside first and ushered Paislee and Timothy out after him.

"I'm assuming Malcolm Gentry is the Gentry behind the company?"

"Yes," Ashton confirmed as they climbed into a white SUV that waited in the alley.

After Paislee gave the driver her address, they pulled out of the alley. She stared out of the window tuning out Ashton and Timothy as they went over whatever it was Ashton had discovered. She didn't need to hear it, she already knew who was after him. The question was, why? What did Malcolm have to gain by coming after Timothy McGinley? Who was he? Antique dealer, sure, but there had to be something more.

Could it be that Malcolm was simply interested in something he had? Did the man he sent after Timothy mean to rob him?

"Paislee."

She looked over to see Timothy and Ashton staring at her expectedly. *Damn, had she dozed off?* She wondered. "What?"

"How did Malcolm learn you possessed magic?"

She shrugged. "A lucky guess I suppose?"

"And is it still just a lucky guess? Or has he witnessed it himself?"

He was pretty damn positive since he'd been forcing her to perform magic at his own beck and call since she'd been thirteen, but she didn't tell them that. "He's seen it."

"When?"

"Does it matter?"

"I know it may seem like it doesn't," Ashton's voice was soothing and helped somewhat to calm her fraying nerves. "But everything you can tell us will help to determine why Mr. Gentry has targeted Mr. McGinley as well as helping us stop him from coming after you."

"I don't need help."

"Yeah, you seem to have been doing just fine on your own," Timothy responded sarcastically.

"As a matter of fact, I was doing just fine until saving your ass in the alley."

"So you keep saying."

She stared at him, and he held her glare.

"We're here," the driver announced as he lowered the partition. Timothy looked away, and Paislee let out the breath she hadn't known she'd been holding.

Ashton stepped out first, followed by Timothy and Paislee. She couldn't disagree when Timothy commented, "This is not a safe place Paislee."

"Really? I had no idea."

She pushed into the dimly lit lobby and headed upstairs that creaked as she walked. The yellow walls were paper thin, making it so you could hear the yelling or TV shows from the insides of the apartments.

After stepping onto her floor, Paislee headed for apartment 3C which had been her home for the better part of a year.

"Wait outside," Timothy said to Ashton, and they stepped into her apartment.

Of all the places Timothy had expected Paislee to call home, a drug den hidden in downtown had been last on his list. The complex reeked of mold and dust, and he couldn't for the life of him figure out why she had chosen here.

The inside of her apartment smelled considerably better than the hall, but he knew that to be because of the wax warmer she had on the peeling countertop. She'd tried to make this place a home, he considered as he looked at the colored throw pillows and blankets on the fading mahogany colored couch.

"Hey, baby!" Paislee knelt in front of an orange tabby that had come out of what Timothy assumed was her bedroom. "I missed you."

"You have a cat."

"Yes." Paislee lifted the cat and eyed him. "And he comes with me, or I stay and take my chances."

He held his hands up in mock surrender. "I guess it's a good thing I like cats."

"Good." Paislee smiled and handed Timothy her cat. "This is Garth."

He absently ran his hand down the Tabby's back and carried him over to the carrier in the corner of the room, locked the cat inside, then followed Paislee into her bedroom.

"I'm amazed you haven't been murdered in this place," he commented with disgust.

"Well, when you're broke and trying to hide, anywhere that accepts cash with no identification is an option."

"I suppose that's true." He watched as she packed clothes into a duffel bag, his eyes landed on the only photo in the entire place. He lifted it and studied the smiling faces beneath the glass.

A young Paislee stood next to a slightly older boy with the same red hair as her. Two adults, who he would have recognized as her parents flanked them. There was no argument as to which parent Paislee resembled, her father was the only one out of the two of them with the same red hair and blue eyes. "Your family?" he asked.

Paislee snatched the photo and stuck it into her bag. "Yes."

"Where are they now?"

"You know, for a man who refuses to answer questions, you sure have a lot of your own." Paislee pushed past him and into the living room where she filled a grocery bag with a small container of cat food and two bowls.

She then emptied out the litter box, rinsed it clean, and loaded a bag of litter into the top. After placing it and the food bag into a duffel, she turned to him. "I'm ready." Timothy grabbed the duffel and cat carrier and followed her out of the door.

"A cat?" Ashton commented, amused after they'd gotten in the car.

"Garth is family," Paislee said simply and stuck her finger through the grate of the carrier.

They rode the rest of the way back to Timothy's office in silence, and the driver dropped them back in the same alley as before.

Ashton waved goodbye, and she and Timothy headed back upstairs.

"So why do I have to stay here while you get to be in your apartment?"

"This building is more secure than my private residence."

"Yeah, seems fishy to me. Is your apartment a mess?"

He turned his full attention to her. "Why would you think that?"

"Men tend to not want women in their apartments if they're messy."

He looked offended, and Paislee had to stifle a laugh. "I assure you my apartment is not messy."

She rolled her eyes. "Sure, that's what you all say."

They stepped into his office/Paislee's new place of residence, and Timothy set the carrier down before opening the gate and letting the cat out.

He headed towards his desk and packed his computer into a messenger bag. "I will bring you some more reputable books tomorrow morning. I will have Ashton bring you up some food in a bit as I imagine you're hungry." He eyed the empty plate that had been her lunch. "See you tomorrow."

"Yeah. Pizza please!" she called after him and began unpacking her bags. After setting up the litter box and feeding Garth, she took a seat on the couch.

TIMOTHY STEPPED OUT ONTO THE STREET AND INTO the open door of the car that waited on the curb.

His driver knew the destination, so he leaned back in the seat and closed his eyes.

What did this all mean? Was the curse broken? He

should have done a better job of keeping tabs on the witch who'd cursed him but seeing her face even if just in an image, was more than he could stomach.

Besides, what the hell did it matter anyway? It's not like he'd had control over anything for the past two hundred years. He would continue living the way he was and if he died one day then so be it.

Hell, he'd embrace it. Or so he'd thought he would. But lying in that alley and believing he might actually die had scared the crap out of him. "I'm sorry Cait," he whispered. He should have been grateful for the chance to be with her again, and instead, he had been afraid.

Now, what did Paislee bring into the picture? Not only was she a bloody witch, but a man who had somehow managed to get his hands on an original painting of Timothy and Cait was hunting her. A painting that he had believed destroyed decades ago.

The one shred of evidence of his original life. He should just send Paislee back out into the world. He could pay her handsomely for the painting and let her fend for herself. At least that would keep any attention off him.

"Dammit," he cursed under his breath and ground his teeth together. She looked too damn much like Cait for him to abandon her. Her death would be the result, and he didn't have it in him to let her die at the hands of a man who wanted to control her. Besides, if she didn't die, Malcolm Gentry might be able to manipulate her into using her magic to suit him. If there were anything Timothy had learned over the years, that kind of power in the hands of a mortal man with no respect for it would prove devastating.

"Here, Sir."

Timothy opened his eyes. "Thanks, Geoff."

"See you in the morning."

"Yeah." Timothy climbed out of the car and headed towards the elevator.

"There you are handsome," A woman's voice filled his ears just as Timothy felt hands creep up his arm. He turned to see Giselle standing somewhat behind him. "You know, it's not nice to make a girl wait."

"I wasn't aware we had a meeting."

"Baby, we always have a meeting," she purred.

He studied her. She wore heels that made her nearly as tall as he was, and a long red coat he imagined hid some type of lingerie underneath. Her blonde hair was up off her neck, and her painted red lips were turned up in a grin that he knew meant she was expecting him to take her up to his penthouse.

He was a man that didn't get attached, but physical release from sex helped the years pass quicker than they did for the near century he had been abstinent. And after being near Paislee all day, he could use a release.

"Come on up."

"I knew you couldn't resist," she purred again and followed him onto the elevator.

She used him just as much as he used her, hell she ran one of the most prestigious law firms downtown.

It's how they'd met. He'd been arranging a contract for a month-long acquisition, and she'd been more than ready to satisfy his needs, both in the office and out. So, they'd continued these 'meetings' for the better part of a year.

They stepped off, and Timothy set his briefcase and coat down on the entry table before heading for his bar. He poured himself some whiskey and turned to face Giselle who had made work of the coat and now stood in front of him wearing nothing but a white lace bra and matching underwear.

It should have turned him on, hell it usually did. But now he couldn't get the damn red head out of his mind.

"Come here," he said gruffly, and she crossed the floor smoothly. She pressed her lips to his neck as she worked on his shirt, but he wasn't in the moment.

He closed his eyes and pictured what Giselle was doing, but as her hand crept down towards his pants, he reached down to stop her.

"I can't do this now."

"Excuse me?" Giselle stepped back.

"I can't do this tonight."

"What's wrong with you?" She eyed his groin, "What, can't get it up? They make medication for that." She crossed her arms over her breasts, and Timothy eyed her threateningly.

"You need to leave."

"We have a deal, you get to call me when you want to fuck, and I come here when I want to. You break this deal now, and I'll find someone else."

"Then find someone else, Giselle." Timothy yawned even though nothing about him was relaxed. "I told you I'm not interested."

She stood staring at him as he drank his whiskey. "You will *not* toss me to the side!" She charged at him, and he put his hand up to stop her.

"You're going to want to keep your hands to yourself, Giselle," he warned. "I've asked you to leave, if you choose to put your hands on me I will force you out of my apartment."

She sneered. "You wouldn't dare."

"Trust me, I would."

She stared at him and then grabbed her coat.

"You'll regret this Timothy McGinley. I am not someone to trifle with."

"We'll see about that."

She stormed towards the elevator and pressed the button, before turning around and lifting an antique vase from his entry table.

He stared at her, and she grinned menacingly. "Oops." She tossed the vase to the ground. "You will come crawling back to me Timothy, you're mine."

Timothy watched angrily as the door shut in front of her angry face. That vase had been priceless and over a hundred years old, and she had tossed it to the ground like trash. He left the mess until she had time to get to a car because he had half a mind to go down and drag her ass back up to clean it herself.

It wasn't that Giselle wasn't attractive, sure she was insane, but he'd known that before getting into bed with her. It was part of the reason she'd been an active participant between his sheets for as long as she had. Her craziness kept things interesting.

But that damn redhead at his office kept creeping into his thoughts. Hell, Paislee should have been the last one in his mind. He'd felt guilt the first time he'd sought intimacy in the arms of another woman after Cait. It had taken him three tries before he'd been able to actually go through with it. His broken heart hadn't healed by any means, but it became easier each time.

Over the years, he'd been with countless, willing women who hadn't wanted anything serious. It made it easier when he'd had to step away which he did about every six months. After that, the situation became more difficult, and he needed to protect his secret.

So why the hell did he feel guilty about being with Giselle because of Paislee?

He'd only just met her! Had she bewitched him somehow? Was he at the receiving end of yet another spell? Even as the thought crossed his mind, he shoved it away. She didn't possess enough knowledge of her craft to spell him. That or she was a fantastic actress.

Still, he was angry. He threw his glass towards the wall as the image of her popped back into his mind. It shattered, and whiskey dripped down the pale grey wall.

Damn, now he had to pour another drink.

~

Since Paislee was curious by nature, she refused to call herself nosy, she stood again and headed for his desk. There was nothing but a cup holding some fancy looking pens that probably cost more than her apartment sitting on top. Not a single piece of paper or shred of evidence as to whether or not this man was working with Malcolm. She very much doubted it since he was bleeding on the ground when she'd found him, but what if Malcolm had done it to draw her out?

She closed her eyes and tried to block out the images as they came rushing back to her. So much blood, she could still remember the way it smelled. The copper tang filling the air around her as she fought to control her magic and not show her hand.

Malcolm had been smarter though, he had known she wouldn't be able to allow an innocent to die, even if it had just been a stray dog. She had saved it, and in agreement to do as he asked, he had let the animal be.

A tear slipped down her cheek, and she took a deep breath. He wouldn't get her again, but she needed to make sure Timothy was in no way involved with him. Even if he didn't realize he was. She slipped one of his expensive pens in her pocket and hoped she could find a better weapon to trade it out with as she continued her search.

All of the desk drawers were locked, so she went back to where her backpack sat on the table and pulled out her lock pick set. She had taught herself to use it after she escaped, and kept it stashed in a bag with hygiene products she carried with her every-where in case she was taken again.

After kneeling in front of his desk, she began her work to pick the lock on the center drawer. She was so focused she nearly missed the ding of the elevator and had to abandon her kit under the desk as she sprinted to the couch.

She sat up straighter when a man who was not Timothy McGinley stepped in.

"Hi again, Miss Adams," Ashton said easily as he walked in. "I was informed you might be hungry for some pizza?"

"Yes!" She dashed towards him and he handed her the box with a smile on his face.

"Can I get you anything else?"

She shook her head. "Are you working here all night?"

He nodded. "I'll be right down in my office if you need anything."

"Do you play cards?"

He raised an eyebrow. "What kind of cards?"

"Any kind." She walked to her backpack and pulled out a pack of cards. "I used to play solitaire a lot. It would be nice to play with someone other than myself."

"I'd love to play if you feel like sharing that pizza."

"Oh, definitely." She pushed the large pizza to the center of the coffee table, and they took a seat. "Have a preference?"

"How about war."

She smiled. "That's a good one. My brother and I used to play when I was a kid." She started dealing the cards and then took another bite of pizza as the game began.

"Have you worked for him long?" Ashton raised an eyebrow, and Paislee offered a kind smile. "I am only asking because I want to know that the man I saved is a good one."

"If he wasn't would you have let him die?"

"Yes," she responded without hesitation.

"Then you should know that the man you saved is a good one. I have worked for Mr. McGinley for nearly fifteen years, he is someone worth saving."

"How did you know about magic? You didn't freak when Timothy was talking about it in the car earlier."

He was silent a moment. "I came across it a few years back."

"Care to elaborate?"

"Maybe I will one day."

"So, what did you do before you started working for Timothy?"

"Believe it or not I was an FBI agent."

"I could totally see that."

Ashton laughed. "I loved it for a while, but eventually I decided I wanted to go my own route. That's when I opened The Bright Security Firm."

"What made you want to leave?"

"Timothy wasn't kidding, you like the questions." He smiled.

"I'm inquisitive by nature."

"Some would call that nosy."

She laughed. "I suppose you're right."

They continued playing cards until two in the morning when Ashton excused himself to check security feeds. Paislee climbed into the big bed and stared at the dark ceiling. She absently stroked Garth's soft fur and went through the events that led her to this moment.

Had she not decided to go scope out McGinley Antiquities she never would have heard that gunshot. She never would have ended up in that alley covered in Timothy's blood.

Did she regret saving him? She honestly wasn't sure. She wanted to believe he was a good man, that he was nothing like Malcolm, but it would take more than a few hours for her to make that decision.

She knew one thing, she had to focus more than ever on learning her craft, so she could put an end to Malcolm Gentry and move on with her life. Maybe she would get married, settle down, and start a family. She always wanted to finish school, so maybe she could get her GED and then go to college.

Paislee smiled and closed her eyes as she dreamt of a tomorrow when she wouldn't have to hide from the shadows that plagued her.

CHAPTER 6

"**Y**ou promised me you'd bring her to me."
Malcolm Gentry paced the space in his
office just behind his guest's chair. He'd
rather sit, sure, but the pacing made this particular
man so nervous that Malcolm could practically feel
the fear snapping in the air around them.

"I tried, she's completely off the grid."

"And what about Mitchell."

"Him too."

"The antiquities dealer?"

"Still alive."

"Hmm." Malcolm continued pacing and then
took his seat behind his desk to think. If the man was
still alive, it meant one of two things. Either Mitchell
had been taken out of play before he'd gotten to him,
or McGinley had done something to his best assassin.

"Malcolm," he answered his cell. As the voice on the

other line filled him in on which of those two things most likely happened, he looked pointedly at the now visibly pale failure sitting on the other side of his desk. "Thank you, Allison, you never disappoint." He hung up the phone and smiled. "That was Allison Carver. Seems she found Mitchell."

"She did?"

"Yes, in a Morgue. It appears he died under some mysterious circumstances."

"Wh-what does that me-mean?"

"Well, the coroner believes he was electrocuted and then shot. But the strange thing is that the exterior of his body shows no sign of electrocution. Only a bullet hole in his chest."

The man stayed silent, and Malcolm drank in the fear. It was nearly enough to get him off, enough he needed to find someone to care for his growing arousal. Power made him harder than any naked whore could.

"This means either McGinley has magical powers, which I very much doubt or my Paislee is now in his company."

"I'll get her."

Malcolm shook his head. "Not yet. I want a read from him myself. Set up a lunch."

The man scrambled to his feet "Yes, Sir."

"And send Lindsay up here."

"Yes, Sir." He left, and Malcolm began taking his suit off. He had married Lindsay last year in a private ceremony. She craved power as much as he did, and together they were going to take over the world.

She walked in with a smile on her face. "What can I do for you dear?" She shut the door and clicked the lock. She knew what he wanted without him having to ask. She'd been a whore when he'd found her, but he was going to make her a queen.

CHAPTER 7

"Here." Timothy tossed a stack of books on the couch next to Paislee and set his briefcase down on his desk.

He bent down and picked up a small pouch from the floor. "Yours?" He opened it and raised an eyebrow at the professional lock pick set inside. After zipping it back up, he tossed the pouch to her on the couch, and she set it down next to her without breaking his eye contact.

"Maybe."

"Next time just ask me to leave the drawers unlocked." He took his jacket off to reveal a perfectly pressed shirt below.

Her mouth shouldn't have watered, but it did.

"Have a good night?" She forced herself to look away and lifted one of the texts he had brought her.

"Fine, and you?"

"Definitely. Ashton brought me some amazing

pizza, and I spent the next four hours bored out of my mind. You could at least get a TV or something up here for me."

"You should be studying magic, *not* binge-watching reality TV."

His words chilled her. Not the binge-watching, but the studying magic. She set the book aside and stood. "Why would I need to study my magic?" she asked. "What purpose would that serve you?"

Timothy moved towards her. "I would prefer to not be inadvertently spelled or killed because you cannot control yourself. I assure you, I *detest* magic in all its forms, and once I figure out exactly what it is Malcolm wants from me, I will be sending you packing without a second thought."

"How do I know I can trust you?"

"You don't. All you have is my word."

Paislee focused on the eyes that were staring intently at her. The magic in her blood began to hum as if it were calling to him. *Strange*, she thought to herself.

She relaxed. "Fine. But if you don't let me go, I will use whatever magic necessary to escape."

"As long as you keep it to yourself until then, we have a deal." Timothy sat behind his desk. "So, would you like to tell me why you wanted me to know you tried to break into my desk?"

"I didn't *try*. I went through them early this morning."

"So, you left your tools there why exactly?"

"I wanted you to know I went through them." Her tone of voice told him he should have known that.

"Well then." He leaned back in his chair and folded his arms over his chest. "Find anything interesting?"

She glared at him over the book. "Hardly. You're a pretty boring guy."

"And what exactly was it you were hoing' to find? A handwritten, signed note confessing that I am secretly in Malcolm's employment?"

"Are you?"

"Hardly," he repeated her words back to her, and the ghost of a smile played on his lips.

"I'm glad this is a joke to you. But this is my life and my freedom we're talking about."

His smiled faded. "How did Malcolm learn about you?"

She set the book aside. "I don't see how that's any of your business."

"I do seeing as how I'm protecting you from him."

"I didn't ask for your protection, Mr. McGinley."

"Well you've got it, so how about you inform me as to what the nature of your relationship is with Mr. Gentry?"

She crossed her arms, and the fire in her eyes aroused him, why? He had no damn clue, she was acting like a bratty teenager, and he had no time for it. Not when someone was trying to kill him.

"I don't think that's any of your business," she repeated, this time growling through her teeth.

"I disagree since the second you landed on my doorstep I ended up with a bullet in my chest."

"If you remember correctly, the bullet was already there when I found you."

"Answer my question Paislee. The sooner you do, the sooner I can determine what is going on and put an end to it. Then you will be free to go. Were you sleeping with him? An affair gone wrong?"

She cursed, and Timothy saw sparks on her fingertips. She had no clue how powerful she was, and if she didn't gain control over it, that power was going to build and take the whole damn building down with it.

"Abso-fucking-lutely not," she growled.

The buzzer went off on his desk, and without looking away from her, he answered it, "Yes."

"Mr. McGinley, you have a phone call."

"Send it through." He lifted the receiver. "Timothy McGinley."

"Mr. McGinley, this is Malcolm Gentry. You're a tough man to get ahold of."

Timothy stood, holding the receiver to his ear. He steadied his voice, not wanting to betray any emotion.

"I wasn't aware you were trying to get ahold of me, Mr. Gentry." As he said the name, he looked to Paislee who had gone completely rigid on the couch. Her face paled, and her eyes widened. Her reaction to just the name had his hatred for the man on the other end of the line growing. Just what had he done to the young witch?

"I've been wanting to meet you. I understand

you run an incredibly well-reputed antiquities company."

"Are you looking for something in particular?"

"I'm always looking to grow my personal collection. I was hoping you might be interested in a lunch meeting? I'd love to talk about your inventory with you."

"I think we can set something up. When would you like to meet?"

Paislee shook her head madly, her eyes pleading with him.

"How about next Monday? Twelve Thirty at Rico's Bistro?"

"I will see you then Mr. Gentry." He hung up the phone and crossed the floor to Paislee who was shaking uncontrollably.

"Paislee," he said calmly, but she didn't look at him. "Paislee," he said, his voice becoming sterner.

She didn't meet his eyes. "You can't meet with him, Timothy. You won't stand a chance."

"I will be just fine." He sat in the seat across from her. "How about you tell me the truth . I want to know exactly what happened between you and Malcolm.

She regained her composure, and the fear was replaced with anger. "Fine."

"Fine?" he repeated.

"I'll tell you, but I want a drink first." She walked to the bar, and he stood to follow her.

He had a need to be near her for a moment, and she stilled when she felt him next to her. "Allow me," he said softly and reached around her to lift the bottle of Jameson from the counter.

One look at Timothy had confirmed he was a predator, a lion lying in wait for its prey. Her question now remained, which was she? A predator like him, or his prey?

"Thanks." She took the glass and downed it in one gulp. He refilled and followed her over to the sitting area where she took a seat on the couch, and he sat on the chair, so he faced her.

He leaned back and focused his attention on her.

Paislee fidgeted with her hands as she forced herself to face the past she was determined to block.

"When I was ten my parents died in an accident. My older brother had just turned eighteen, and he was able to legally adopt me. He worked hard, and I never sensed anything was off. He made the transition less difficult for me, but I knew it was more difficult for him. He had left his first year of college to come home and raise me and ended up working at a grocery store." She closed her eyes and took a deep breath.

"Shortly after my eleventh birthday, some men started coming around the house. They dressed nice, and they were always friendly, but Zeke started acting strangely. He wouldn't be home when I got off the bus, he wasn't around to help with my homework, and when he was around it felt as if he wasn't really there." She took another drink from her glass.

"Nearly a year later, the men came back to the house, and I was pulled from my bed."

Timothy's hand clenched on the now empty glass, and he heard the crack from the strength of his grip. He stood to place the glass on his desk, and Paislee lost in her story, didn't notice.

"They brought me downstairs where Zeke was kneeling on the floor, his face bloody." A tear slipped down her cheek, but she continued, "The man I now know as Malcolm came over and touched my face and smiled. He told Zeke 'she will be your payment' and Zeke fought against the man holding him and another punched him. He fell to the ground, and I screamed.

Malcolm told Zeke that if he were to call the police, they would kill me. That he was fired and that I would be better off if he just crawled into a hole and died."

Her cheeks reddened with anger, but she leveled her eyes on Timothy's face. "That was the last time I saw Zeke. I was in Malcolm's possession until eight months ago when I killed two men and escaped."

"Your brother sold you to pay a debt."

She shook her head. "I found out later from one of Malcolm's guards that Zeke had been targeted because of me. He was approached with a job and ended up being injected with heroin. It hooked him, and Malcolm used that to take me. I was angry at Zeke for a long time, but it was never his fault. He only wanted to provide for me."

"How did Malcolm know you had power? Why were you targeted specifically?"

"I'm not sure. Not once did they ever talk about it

when I was around. I was with him for nearly a year before I even realized I had powers."

"How did you find that out?"

Paislee ground her teeth together. "He brought a stray dog in, a yellow lab with big brown eyes and let me play with it for a week. Then, he shot it and told me that if I wanted to, I could heal it. If not, it would die on the floor, and it would have been my fault. I was crying so hard that I could barely see, and I hugged the dog. Before I knew it, the dog was fine, and Malcolm was smiling at me."

Timothy walked to his window and breathed deeply. Malcolm had stolen a young girl because of her magic. Magic she hadn't even known she'd had. He had torn apart a family because of an addiction he had to power. Then he had shot a dog she had grown to love in front of her and forced her to access powers she didn't even know she possessed.

He knew this type well, had dealt with one person or another like that for his entire life. He found himself wishing she hadn't told him right before a lunch where he was going to be face to face with the sick bastard.

It made sense why he was being targeted now if somehow Malcolm had learned of his curse Timothy would be the best kind of acquisition: an actual living antique.

He lifted his phone to his ear. "Ashton I need you in my office." Then he turned to Paislee. "I'm going to fill Ashton in on everything you just told me."

"Okay." She seemed weaker then she had before,

and he imagined reliving the darkest moments of her life was taking its toll on her. It certainly did on him whenever images of his past popped into his head.

Moments later, Ashton stepped into his office. He was the only member of the staff who didn't have to be buzzed up by Timothy himself.

"I got a phone call from Malcolm Gentry who wants to meet for lunch next week."

"Are you sure that's a good idea?"

"I don't see much of a way around it. At least this way I can get a feel for him and perhaps how much he actually knows about me. Not that I need to know much more about him after what Paislee told me."

"She opened up about why he's after her?"

Timothy had never seen Ashton Bright as angry as he was after Timothy finished filling him in on everything Paislee had told him.

"We will get this bastard, Paislee," he growled, and to Timothy's surprise, she walked over and wrapped her arms around his security guard.

"Thank you, Ashton."

Jealousy eating at him, Timothy turned the conversation back to details about the lunch, and Paislee walked back over to the couch.

"I need you to do something for me," Timothy said in a low whisper once she was out of range.

"What is it?"

"Find me everything you can on a Zeke Adams."

Ashton's eyebrow raised. "Husband?"

"Brother. He's an addict so check the streets too. I want to know where this kid is."

"You got it, boss." Ashton turned to leave.

When Ashton left, he took a seat at his desk to do some actual work. Before the items they had on hand went to auction, their bidders would apply to attend, and Timothy personally vetted each applicant. A few times he had stopped frauds who could have turned out to be thieves scoping out the items.

He cared about his antiques as some cared about loved ones and he wanted to make sure each item would be safe even after purchase. At least on his end anyway. There were those select few who boasted about their acquisitions only to have them stolen days later.

He looked up from his computer and saw Paislee was now stretched out on the couch, cat in her lap, with a book. She made a sight in her leggings, and a light sweater and Timothy certainly couldn't help but notice.

"This book is great," she said when she caught him looking at her.

"Yeah, that was written by an actual witch in the eighteenth century."

"You know I actually started reading this book, but when I went back to finish, the woman at the library told me some arrogant rich prick had bought it."

"I very much doubt that. Mrs. Whitten was very grateful for my generosity."

"I'm sure she was. If any rich prick had to buy it, I'm glad it was you."

He eyed her, amusement pulling at the corner of

his mouth. "I bet. Most of your books were written by frauds."

"Hey, I tried. Not all of us have access to old authentic stuff. I got most of my books from the public library."

Timothy rolled his eyes. "Please tell me you're joking."

"Wish I was dude. Besides, that's where this one came from."

"Every now and then a good one pops up on the shelves, and don't ever call me dude again."

"Whatever," she lowered her voice slightly, "*Dude.*"

She was a smartass but damn if she wasn't growing on him.

THE BUZZER WENT OFF ON TIMOTHY'S DESK, AND HE answered quickly, "Yes?"

"Mr. McGinley your lunch order is here."

"Bring it up please Jess."

"Yes, Sir."

A few minutes later Jess stepped off the elevator with two bags of food in her hands.

"Perfect timing, I'm starved!" Paislee offered Jess a smile. "Hi, I'm Paislee."

"Nice to meet you." Jess returned the smile and then set the bags down on Timothy's desk.

"Did you get yourself any food?" Paislee wondered as she searched through the bags.

"Yes, mine is right here." She patted the second

bag and turned to leave."

"Thanks, Jess."

'You're welcome, Mr. McGinley."

"Hang on!" Paislee said and smiled again. "Why don't you join me? Frankly, I could use a little girl time." She had zero clue what girl time actually was, but it had been fifteen years since she'd had any girl-friends to talk to.

"I don't want to be a bother." She looked hesitant, and her eyes darted back to Timothy.

"If your hang up is me, I assure you I don't mind." Timothy smiled, and Jess relaxed.

"Are you sure?"

He nodded and started in on the Philly Cheese Steak Jess had brought him.

"Okay, I would love to. It will be much better than eating downstairs by myself."

"Definitely, and I'm sure your company is much better than that guy."

Jess bit back a laugh and followed Paislee over to the couch.

"So, tell me about yourself," Paislee wondered and took a bite of her burger.

"What's to tell?" Jess laughed nervously. "I don't do much."

"What do you do for fun?"

"I like to read."

"Me too! I'm a huge romance fan."

Jess smiled. "Me too."

"Do you have a favorite author?" Paislee wondered.

"I actually just finished reading Mother Of Shadows by Meg Anne. It's a romantic fantasy, and I was hooked from the first page."

"I'll have to check it out. I love fantasy."

"I own it, I would be more than happy to loan it to you."

Paislee smiled widely. "I would love that!"

They continued talking for a few minutes before the elevator opened and Ashton stepped out. He didn't notice the two women right away, and when he did, Paislee noticed the way his eyes lit up when Jess smiled at him.

"Miss Crew."

"Hi, Mr. Bright, enjoying your day?"

He nodded, the smile never leaving his face. "I am and you?"

"I am, made a new friend." She gestured towards Paislee and Ashton smiled. "I see that."

"Did you need something?" Timothy asked, bringing Ashton's attention back to him."

"I wanted to let you know I'm still looking for that information you asked me for, but that I think I might have found something."

"Great, thanks, Ashton."

He nodded and turned to leave. "Paislee, Miss Crew."

"Bye, Ashton!" Paislee called.

"Have a good afternoon, Mr. Bright." Jess blushed when he smiled at her and Paislee's grin widened.

"You like him!" she exclaimed.

"What?" Jess's eyes widened, but the blush on her cheeks gave it away.

"Why haven't you told him? Is he single? Are you single?"

"I certainly am, and I think he is, but we work together."

"You work in the same building, that's not technically together."

"Trust me, it's better we just stay friends." Jess smiled when Garth padded over, "Hi buddy! I didn't know you had a cat, I love cats!" She reached down to lift the orange tabby into her lap.

So, Ashton and Jess liked each other but neither wanted to admit it, huh? Maybe she could be of some use while she was here.

CHAPTER 8

"So why have you been studying magic if you don't have any yourself?"

Timothy looked up from his desk to see her sitting, legs folded, on the bed. She hadn't changed out of her pajamas yet, and he was annoyed to see the shorts and tank she wore. Annoyed because they aroused him, and he had no business being attracted to her.

"I have my reasons."

"Yeah, I get that, but what are they? Come on, Timothy, you know literally everything about me. Tell me something so I can figure out what the hell is going on with you?"

It was Sunday evening, and the last four days had gone fairly smooth. They had fallen into a sort of routine, and there was a strange comfort in it. He would arrive at eight every morning, she would already be up, showered, and dressed—usually, and he would go about his work while she read up on magic.

For the most part, the days were passed in silence, and how he wished she'd go back to that.

"I have to go downstairs and look at a new shipment that came in yesterday. Care to join me?"

"Seriously?" Her eyes lit up, and he instantly regretted it, because she jumped off the bed, baring her sinfully long legs.

He turned away and acted as though he needed to grab something off his desk. "Yes, but only if you change. I don't need you distracting the guards downstairs."

"You think I'm distracting, Mr. McGinley?" The tone of her voice had warning bells going off in his head, so he summoned all the strength he had and turned around to gaze at her nonchalantly.

"For some people, perhaps, I prefer grown women." He turned back around and heard her disappear into the bathroom with an annoyed, "Uh-huh." After letting out a breath, he waited for her near the elevator with his tablet.

She returned only moments later, wearing jeans, high top sneakers, and a white t-shirt. Somehow, he found her just as mouthwatering as when she'd been in the shorts.

They stepped into the elevator, and he could feel her excitement in the air. This was the first time she'd left his office since they'd gone to her apartment and he felt a pang of guilt at that.

He hated that she felt she was a prisoner here.

Paislee turned and smiled at him, and the close proximity was nearly too much to bear. Thankfully, the doors opened, and they stepped onto the fourth floor.

"Woah!" she exclaimed. Crates, upon crates, stretched the entire floor and as they moved towards the back where the newest ones were, Paislee couldn't keep her eyes from scanning each open ccontainer as they passed.

"Here." Timothy handed her a pair of gloves, and she put them on eagerly, ready to see what it was he did and how items were authenticated. Once she was done, he handed her the tablet and showed her where she needed to input each item description and date of origin.

"This is magnificent." She stared down at the crate he had just opened. Inside were two jeweled bracelets, each with a matching pair of earrings. "Where do they find these things?"

Timothy began to examine one of the bracelets, and she watched in complete and total fascination as he handled it as though it were made of the finest china.

"It varies. These were found in a castle off the coast of Scotland. The current owners were having an estate sale and wanted to make sure these were authenticated before auction, so they could get the most out of it."

"So, people ship their stuff here, you verify it, and then send it back?"

"Sometimes, most likely though I will make them

an offer and then sell them on my own. We hold an auction once a month."

"How can you tell if it's real or not?"

"I start out first by verifying the materials, so in this case, gold plated copper and rubies." He set it down and lifted one of the earrings. "Then I check the design and date the item. I can typically tell based on how an item was crafted. For instance, with the type of clasp on these bracelets, I can determine they were originally crafted in the mid-1800's."

"That's amazing."

Timothy turned to her and saw something in her eyes he'd never seen before, love. Not for him, of course, but for the items that surrounded her. She clearly didn't mind the musty smell or the clutter. "You like antiques?"

"Oh, I love them. When I was a kid, I used to bury things in my sandbox so I could pretend I was uncovering them later. I wanted to be an archeologist who hunted for ancient artifacts." She laughed, and it was the first time he'd heard her make such a happy sound. It did something to him that he wasn't ready to confront.

He continued moving, going through each crate and she kept up with him. Asking questions about the items they uncovered, or about his method of dating them. He hated to say it, but she was quicker than even Jake was, and he wondered if she'd consider a job with him when this was over.

His back straightened at the thought, *she's a witch*.

He reminded himself when this was all over he could never see her again.

PAISLEE HAD NEVER SEEN HIM THE WAY SHE DID NOW. Since day one, Timothy had come off as an arrogant entitled ass hole that probably built his company off the back of his father's checkbook. She had doubted that he actually did much and had even wondered a time or two if he knew anything about antiques or just enjoyed the way they looked on his walls.

But as she watched him carefully handling each object and telling her the date and origin just by looking at them, she found herself intrigued for the first time by the man below the armor she so easily saw now.

What was it that had the head of McGinley Antiquities so hardened on the outside?

He stripped off his gloves, and she handed him the tablet and did the same, then followed him back to the elevator.

"So, do you do that every day?"

"Typically, three times a week."

Oh yay, she thought to herself as the doors closed in front of them, *the short answers are back.*

Once they were back in his office, she followed him over to his desk. She wanted answers, and even if they pissed him off, she was going to pepper him with questions until he told her what she wanted to know.

"So, what's your deal?" She wondered and sat on

the corner of his desk. He looked up at her, and she ignored the way her blood warmed.

"I don't know what you mean."

"Where are you from?"

"Ireland."

"No shit? I thought you were from Queens," she responded dryly. "What part of Ireland."

"A part you have probably never heard of."

"Try me."

"Why the questions, Paislee?"

"You know everything about me, and I know nothing about you."

Timothy pinched the bridge of his nose, he thought he'd bought himself more time by taking her downstairs. Had hoped that she would have been too excited to remember the fifty-question game she seemed to enjoy playing.

"I don't think it's necessary to share my backstory with you."

"But it was necessary to share mine with you? Malcolm is after you too, which means there's a reason. I want to know what that reason is."

"Paislee," he warned.

"No, I want answers, Timothy."

He stood so quickly she nearly fell off his desk. She followed suit and folded her arms as he began to pace.

"You aren't going to drop this are you?"

"No."

"What do you want to know?"

She thought for a moment. "Why are you so interested in my painting?"

"You mean *my* painting." His eyes narrowed. "I bought it from you."

"Okay fine but answer my question."

"It reminds me of someone I lost."

She straightened, that was not the answer she had expected from him. Was she actually getting a glimpse of a man with a heart? One who had at one point, actually cared for someone other than himself?

"Who?"

"Does it matter?"

"Yes, it really does."

He let out a breath. "My wife."

She unfolded her arms, and they fell slack at her sides. "You were married?"

"Yes, a long time ago."

"Oh yeah because you're so old."

"You'd be surprised."

"How surprised? What are you, thirty?"

"Have I answered enough of your questions?"

"Hardly." She studied him. "How old *are* you?" Something wasn't adding up.

The man in the painting had resembled the one before her, there was no question about it, and it was something she'd known from the moment she met him. She had contributed the likeness to her own imagination and bad lighting whenever she'd been looking at it, or even mere coincidence. But now, hearing him say the woman reminded him of his wife combined with the flash of pain across his face, she was starting to think there was perhaps more to the story and she wanted to know all of it.

"I was born August 7th."

"What year?"

He stayed silent, his jaw taut and his body barely leashed.

"What year, Timothy?"

"1787."

Her mouth fell open, and she stared at him searching for the humor that would surely be in his eyes.

Did he honestly expect her to believe he was two hundred and thirty-one years old? *What the hell answer were you expecting Paislee?* She asked herself.

The paintings, the knack he had for being able to date artifacts, the fact that he had been studying magic. All signs pointed to him telling the truth.

"Are you *kidding me?*" She started laughing and before long, was completely unable to stop herself.

"This is funny to you?" The look on his face was annoyance, but his tone was more than that. He was angry.

"No wonder Malcolm sent his guy after you. He is obsessed with old things, and you are literally an antique!" She continued laughing while Timothy stared at her. How in the world was this funny to her?

"Did you just call me an antique?" Hadn't he referred to himself as just that? So why did it bother him so much to have her think of him that way?

"You are an antique."

He crossed the distance between them in an

instant and pressed her back against the wall with his body.

He smiled down at her menacingly, "Do I feel like an antique to you Paislee?" He pressed against her and leaned down, so his breath was on her neck, causing goose bumps to flare on her skin. She fought the urge to press back against him, to pull his mouth down onto hers and give in to the urge she'd felt since the moment she met him.

She did her best to summon strength in her voice and responded, "You do smell a little musty."

He glared at her but moved away, and she relaxed against the wall. Both grateful for and regretting the space between them again.

"At least that explains why you're so damn incorrigible. You've had two hundred years to get set in your ways, and you know what they say about old dogs." She folded her arms unsure who she was more pissed off at the moment. Him for what he'd done, or herself for the way her body had responded.

"I assure you I'm not incorrigible. I just know when I'm right."

"And when you're wrong?"

"I'm still right."

"Ugh." She walked back over to the couch. "So how is it you are so old?"

"Technically, I'm only twenty-eight, give or take a few years based on when my curse was apparently broken."

"Curse?"

"A naïve witch cast a spell which in turn trapped me in time with her and her brother."

"So, this witch, was she like me?"

"If by 'like me' you mean had magical powers, then obviously. I thought that was a given based on the fact that I called her a witch."

"Okay, smart ass. That's not what I mean. There are different kinds of witches correct? Some that possess different types of magic?"

"Yes."

"So, did she have the same type of powers as I do?"

"Yes." He took a seat across from her. "You have the ability to utilize light as a weapon as well as provide healing. Those are two powers that typically go hand in hand together. She also had the ability to move objects and project images."

"Can I do those?"

"I'm not sure, and frankly I don't care."

"What the hell is that supposed to mean?"

"It means that I am not interested in your magic or exploring what it is you are capable of. The last time I was near a witch I ended up frozen in time."

"If you aren't going to help me, then why the hell am I here?"

"Because until I can find out just how exactly to get to Malcolm Gentry, you are the only lead I have."

"I've already told you everything I know."

"And yet, I'm still no closer to finding out just how it is he came to know about me."

"I'm telling you that me learning how to use my magic is the only way."

"The last time magic was the only way I ended up not aging and having to watch everyone around me die."

Paislee visibly winced at the anger he wore on his face. No wonder he was so bitter, what must it have been like to see everything around you changing while you stayed the same? Having to bury everyone you ever loved?

"I'm sorry that happened to you," she said softly and reached forward to touch his arm. "I can't even imagine having to experience that."

The fleeting tenderness on his face surprised her, but his arrogant façade showed up so quickly that she was sure she'd imagined it.

"Yeah, well, it happened, and it's in the past. The fact that I nearly bled to death proves that."

"You think the curse is broken?"

"Any time before I would have healed nearly immediately, this time was different."

"Have you looked into it yet?"

"Why would I do that? It won't change anything. Either I'm going to continue existing, or one day I'll die."

"I would have to know."

"I'm not interested."

He walked to his mini bar and poured a glass of whiskey.

"Can I have one?" she asked.

He silently poured another, and she joined him to look out at the darkening sky.

"It's beautiful up here," she said easily. "It's like being on top of the world."

"I enjoy it."

"How long has it taken you to build this?"

"A hundred years, give or take a few."

"That is insane, the things you must have seen!"

"They aren't as great as you would have imagined."

"Maybe one day you can tell me about it?"

"Not likely." He downed the rest of his whiskey. "See you tomorrow." He grabbed his jacket off the chair and headed towards the elevator.

"Hey, Timothy?"

He stopped but didn't turn around.

"Thank you for helping me."

He nodded and walked to the elevator without another word.

CHAPTER 9

*P*aislee shot out of bed at the sound of a loud buzzer. She checked the clock next to the bed and groaned. It was six thirty am. So, who the hell was buzzing to come up?

"Who is it?" she grumbled into the speaker.

"Is Mr. McGinley around? It's Jake Parish, I have something for him."

"He'll be in about eight," she responded sleepily.

"Can I bring it up? I can just leave it on his desk if that's okay? The time change is not working with me so I am wide awake. I wanted to get this dropped off so I can head straight down to the store room and get to work on the new arrivals."

"That's fine." She buzzed him up and then went back to lay in bed.

A minute later, the elevator doors opened, and the scent of coffee filled her nose. *Oh please, please, please let that be for me.* She got out of bed and yawned just as Jake came into view.

"I am so sorry for waking you up!" He looked appalled and turned around immediately which is when she remembered that she'd gone to sleep in her underwear.

"Oh, crap hang on, sorry." She grabbed a blanket off the bed and wrapped it around herself. "Okay, you can turn around now."

Jake turned around and smiled, showing a dimple near his mouth. "I'm so sorry Paislee."

"You're fine. Even more fine if one of those coffees are for me."

He stared at her for a moment confused and then grinned. "Yes! You can absolutely have one. For some reason I thought it was later than it was, and I was going to leave it on his desk with this." He held up a folder. "But I suppose it will probably be cold by the time he gets in."

"Probably." She smiled and took the coffee and then made her way over to the sitting area. "So, how was London?"

"It was amazing." Stars still in his eyes over his trip, he took a seat across from her. "I had the best time. It's the first time I'd ever been."

"That's awesome, it's on my bucket list."

"Maybe we can go together sometime, now that I'm practically a native and all."

They laughed, and Paislee couldn't help but feel herself relax around Jake. He was kind, funny, and attractive.

"Maybe." She smiled. "So when you aren't running off to London, what do you do?"

"I help categorize the items Mr. McGinley authenticates. I handle all of the shipping and receiving and do the first pass through the crates."

"Sounds important."

"I'd like to think it is, but truthfully Mr. McGinley does all the real work."

Paislee took a sip of her coffee. "What do you do for fun?"

"I play video games."

She nearly snorted out her coffee, that was *not* something she thought this guy would want to do for fun. He looked like an absolute anti-nerd.

"You okay?" he asked with a laugh.

"Yeah, sorry. I guess I never pegged you for a video game nerd."

"What did you peg me as?"

"I don't know, a wrestler, boxer maybe?"

Jake laughed. "I don't *only* play video games. I do go to the gym daily, but it's mainly because I have to."

"Seriously?" She eyed him, he was in incredible shape. She could see as much from the black long sleeve shirt he wore.

"I used to be a big guy in high school. When I went to college, I started eating healthy and working out daily, and now here I am."

"Okay, I get that. What kind?"

"What kind of what?"

"Video games."

"Oh." He let out a nervous laugh. "PC mostly,

although I do enjoy some console games now and then. What about you?"

"Oh, I like to read I guess. I don't have time for much else." She sipped her coffee and hoped he didn't ask any further questions. She was a terrible liar and felt guilty even considering having to lie to her new friend.

"I see that." He picked up one of the magic texts. "Into magic?"

Her cheeks turned red. "A little. It fascinates me."

"So, what are you doing here? With Mr. McGinley?" he asked and set the book back on the table.

"We're friends, I needed to have something authenticated, and he is letting me stay here until I go back home."

"Where's home?"

"South Carolina?" It came out more like a question, but Garth finally decided to make his presence known, and padded over to jump in her lap.

"You have a cat! Wow, you and Mr. McGinley must be great friends."

"Yep, that's us, 'great friends.'"

Jake laughed, "How long have you two known each other?"

"Not long," she admitted. "But it feels like forever."

Jake smiled, and silence fell over the two of them. Paislee's mind wandered to last night, and the dreams she'd had after feeling Timothy's hard body pressed against hers.

"So, I was wondering," Jake started and brought her back to the present.

"Yes?"

"If you wanted to maybe get together for dinner tonight?"

Before she could answer, the elevator opened and an incredibly pissed off Timothy stepped into the room. He looked like he'd just rolled out of bed, his typically styled hair was messy. He wore loose pants that hung low on his hips and a plain black hooded sweatshirt.

"What the hell are you doing up here?" He directed his steel gaze at Jake, who shot out of his seat as if it had been on fire.

"I uh, I brought you the information from the London museum on the chalices." He stuttered and stepped away from Paislee.

"That couldn't wait until eight?"

Paislee was so in shock by the level of anger on Timothy's face that it took her a moment before she stood.

"Who the hell pissed in your cheerios this morning?" She stepped in front of Jake as if her presence would protect him.

"Excuse me?" Timothy's eyes narrowed on her, and his nostrils flared.

She realized at that moment, the blanket had fallen off her, and she stood between both men wearing nothing but her underwear and a tank top. She should have been embarrassed, but she was so pissed off that she didn't care.

"Get the fuck out of my office Parish," he growled, and Jake ran for the elevator.

"Who the hell are you to come in here yelling at him like that? He was only doing his job!" Paislee screamed as the elevator carrying Jake began its descent to safety.

"Why in the fuck are you in your fucking underwear? And why the fuck did you let him up here when I am not here!"

He was so angry that Paislee nearly backed off. Not once in her entire life, had she understood the phrase 'shooting daggers from their eyes' until this moment. But she was just as pissed at the look of horror on Jake's face as he'd fled.

"I am a grown woman, Timothy, I can answer the door fucking naked if I want!"

Timothy was on her so fast, she hadn't had time to react. Before she knew it, his mouth was hot and furious on hers, and she could feel his arousal against the thin fabric of her underwear.

She buried her hands in his hair and gave him back every ounce of anger he fed to her. She bit his lip, and he groaned under it, pressing against where she was already ready for him. His fingers dug into her ass, and she wrapped her legs around his waist, giving herself over to him completely.

Of all the ways she'd thought to start the day, being ravished by a two hundred and thirty-year old millionaire was not one of them.

Just as quickly as he had rushed her, he was gone,

leaving her standing there more aroused then she'd ever been and shivering from the cold.

"Don't you ever let anyone up here when you're alone again," he growled. "Especially not when you might as well be fucking naked."

He stormed out of the office and Paislee could do nothing but stare at him.

AFTER A FREEZING COLD SHOWER, TIMOTHY MADE HIS way back into work. When Ashton had called him after the guard let Jake up to his office, he'd rushed out of his apartment and over to his office.

Ashton had offered to go in, but after witnessing her in shorts, Timothy had known she didn't sleep fully clothed, and as much as he respected the head of his security, Ashton seeing Paislee in her pajamas would have been unacceptable.

But not only was she in her fucking underwear, she was sitting there having coffee with his antiquities manager, who was supposed to have still been in fucking London!

Seeing her standing there in front of Jake, and seeing that assholes eyes look down at Paislee's perfect fucking ass for even an instant, had him seeing red. As far as he was concerned, he was a fucking saint for not killing the man where he'd stood.

The images that crossed his mind once they'd been alone had forced the reaction he'd had to her. And it was mild compared to what he'd wanted which was to bend her over his desk and fuck her senseless until she wouldn't even think of another man for the rest of her life.

"Morning, Sir," Jess greeted him as he stepped into his building.

"Morning, Jess, what's on my schedule for today." He continued his walk to the elevator, and she followed.

"You have a lunch meeting with Mr. Gentry at noon, and a conference call with an archeologist out of Rome at two."

"Great, thank you." He offered her a forced smile as the doors closed between them and he began the rise to his office.

He took a deep breath, there was no telling how pissed off Paislee was going to be after this morning, and since it had been a mistake, *a fucking hot one*, he added to himself, he had no intention of revisiting their kiss.

The elevator dinged, and the doors opened on the fifteenth floor. Paislee was sitting on the couch, legs folded underneath of her, reading a book. She didn't even bother to look up at him, so he set his things down at his desk.

"Morning," he greeted.

"Morning," she responded tightly. *Great, so she was pissed.* This would make for a fun day.

He opened the folder Jake had brought up and looked over his notes. He was going to need to meet with his employee sooner or later, and he supposed getting it over early would be best.

And maybe if Jake was up here again, Paislee would stop seething, because he knew that's what she was doing.

He lifted the receiver, and watching her face closely, called down to his secretary. "Send Mr. Parish to my office."

Paislee didn't move an inch, and he'd wondered if she had even heard him.

Five minutes of silence passed until the elevator sounded. Jake stepped out, looking like a frightened gazelle about to be pounced on by a lion. *Good, you better not fucking touch what's mine again.* He thought to himself.

"Jess said you wished to speak with me?"

"Yes."

"Morning, Jake!" Paislee greeted him happily, and Timothy's jaw tightened.

"Please sit," he instructed, and Jake took a seat across from the desk.

"I'm so sorry about this morning, Mr. McGinley, it won't happen again."

"See that it doesn't," he warned. "Now." He opened the folder. "Tell me about London."

"It went well, the curator was pleased that the chalices were legitimate, and they want to send someone over for the auction next month."

"Good, do we have any items they're particularly interested in?"

Jake shook his head. "No Sir, none that they mentioned to me anyway."

"Okay, thank you. Go to the fourth floor and

begin setting things aside for the auction. I labeled the items I want to incorporate next month, as well as the ones that are ready to be shipped back to the owners."

"Yes, Sir." Jake got to his feet and started to head towards the elevator.

"Jake, hang on!" Paislee called and ran over to him. "To answer your earlier question, I would love to have dinner with you tonight."

Timothy bit back the murderous rage building inside of him as he glared at Paislee's back. Did she really think she could win this game?

"Okay, great. I'll see you later." Jake stumbled towards the elevator and disappeared while Paislee hummed as she walked back to the couch.

"What the hell was that?" Timothy demanded.

She looked up at him innocently. "What was what?"

He nearly flipped his desk over in anger. "Never fucking mind." He responded and waited not so patiently for the elevator to return. He needed to put some distance between them before he went through with his earlier plan involving her and his desk.

Paislee waited until he was gone before she got to her feet and tossed the book she'd been pretending to read on to the couch. How dare he! *How dare he!* Treat her like he owned her!

She wasn't a fool, she knew that kiss this morning had been his way of controlling her. His own personal way of marking her as his. Well fuck that and fuck him. She would *not* be controlled by another man *ever again.*

Besides, she liked Jake. He was cute, and kind, and NOT some condescending, arrogant dick with his own agenda. He wasn't in any way tied to Malcolm, and for once it might be nice to go on a date and not have to worry about anything else.

But then why did she feel so guilty, she wondered. If she knew all of this, coupled with the fact Timothy had treated her like he had every single day since she'd met him, even after their kiss, *why* couldn't she get the asshole out of her head?

"Ugh," she groaned and fell backward onto the couch. If she was honest with herself, she had no inclination to take things past friendship with Jake, but if it bothered Timothy to think she did, she couldn't see the harm in that.

CHAPTER 10

*T*imothy stalked down to Ashton's office. The security guard was the closest thing Timothy had to an actual friend, and what he needed right now was someone to keep him from killing Jake Parish. Because at the moment, that was exactly what he wanted to do. How dense was that kid anyways? Apparently, basic intelligence does not go hand in hand with being book smart.

"Everything alright boss?" Ashton looked up from his computer when the door slammed.

"Just fucking peachy."

"Parish?"

Timothy nodded and took a seat at the desk.

"Want me to have him escorted from the premises?"

"No, I can't do that." Timothy ran his hands through his hair and then leaned back and tried to relax. "Although seeing Paislee's pissed off face would be rather humorous at the moment."

Ashton let out a laugh. "I suppose it would be." His face grew serious. "I was going to come get you, we found the brother."

Timothy straightened. "Where?"

"He was last seen in a house on the other side of town, I have the address."

"When?"

"I called around and a neighbor who apparently lives across the street from 'that house,' which is how she put it, said she saw a man matching his description stumbling into it last night."

"Let's go."

"You got it, boss."

Timothy followed Ashton downstairs and into an SUV waiting at the curb. After making a phone call to the best addict recovery center in Boston, he called Paislee.

"Hello?"

"It's Timothy. I'm running errands, and I will be back after my lunch meeting."

"Fine." The line went dead, he cursed and tossed the phone into the seat beside him.

The drive was shorter than Timothy had thought it would be, and they stepped out onto the street in front of a house that had seen *much* better days. The white paint was cracking and peeling, and the chain link fence that surrounded the piece of property was doing very little to keep anyone out. Weeds and grass were overgrown and had completely taken over the sidewalk. Ashton and Timothy made their way up to the rickety porch. Ashton knocked, but when no one answered, he opened the already unlocked door, and they stepped inside.

The scents of urine and vomit assaulted their senses the second they crossed the threshold. He scrunched his nose and did his best to breath as shallow as possible. *This is just fucking delightful,* he thought to himself as they made their way into what he assumed was supposed to be an entry room but was now lined with people passed out covered in their own excrement.

Groans from the occupants that were scattered all over the floor filled his ears, and he averted his eyes. He had no time for the dying, they weren't why he was here. He had one goal, one man he was here for.

The hallway ended in a living area where torn, and sagging sofas lined the walls.

"Boss." Ashton nodded towards a form on a couch. Even from here Timothy could see the resemblance to the photo he'd seen in Paislee's apartment.

This man was gaunt, pale, and looked one pill away from death, but his bright red hair gave him away.

"Zeke." Timothy stopped in front of the couch, and the man sat up. To Timothy, this man looked very much like a lost teenager, and he bit back the bile that rose in his throat at the stench wafting up off him. He had no pity for a man who would sell his little sister to feed a drug habit. Because even if Paislee didn't necessarily see it that way, he did.

"Yeah, who the fuck are you."

Timothy reached down and ripped the punk up from the couch to slam him into a wall.

"Hey, man!"

Without looking, Timothy pulled the gun from his waist and trained it on the two men who walked in with their firearms out.

"You're going to want to drop those," he warned.

"Put them down." Ashton walked over and kicked the guns away as the men complied. They were too fucking high not to.

"What the hell do you want?" Zeke slurred.

"You're coming with me."

"Fuck no, man."

"You don't have a choice." Timothy drug him out of the house full of the soon to be deceased. Away from the urine and vomit covered floors and walls. Away from the stench of death from those who had died but the others were too high to notice.

When they stepped outside, Timothy and Ashton both took deep breaths, and Timothy tossed Zeke to the car sitting in front of the house.

Ashton opened the door. "Get in," he said gruffly, and Zeke, eyes wide backed away.

"Uh-uh. I ain't going nowhere with you two."

"You don't have a choice," Timothy repeated and lifted him to his feet again to ram him against the car.

"Wh-wh-what do you want from me?"

"I'm taking you to a place where you are going to get clean and stop being a fucking pathetic waste of oxygen."

"You can't make me go nowhere with you." He tried to run, and Timothy slammed him back against the car, so Ashton could pat him down.

"I am a friend of your sister, you remember her? The girl you sold as a fucking twelve-year-old?"

The eyes so like his sisters widened and Timothy saw the sadness reflected even through his dulled senses.

That was what he needed to see to keep him from just shooting the asshole. He actually did care for his sister.

"You know Paislee?"

"Yeah."

"You stole her!" he screamed and to his credit tried to fight back. Timothy pressed his gun against the druggies chest.

"No, I didn't. She is no longer in the care of your old boss. Now that I have your attention you better listen closely. You are going to rehab, you are going to get clean, and if you refuse or I hear that you have been anything but a recovering addict I will put a fucking bullet in your brain, so your sister doesn't ever see you like this again. You *will* do this for her Zeke. You fucking owe her."

Tears fell down Zeke's freckled cheeks, and he nodded. "I will, I will. Please tell her I'm sorry. I'm so sorry. I didn't want him to take her. I tried to save her."

Timothy let him go, and Zeke fell to the ground in tears. He turned away and bit back the fresh anger. Except this time, it wasn't aimed at the addict on the ground but rather at the murderer who had taken advantage of siblings who hadn't known any better.

"Get him out of here," he told Ashton's second, Ty. "Stay with him and let me know if he tries anything."

"You got it, boss." Ty pulled away.

"What are we doing about everyone in there?"

"Call the police and leave an anonymous tip," he said and walked back to his car. Ashton climbed in, and they pulled away from the curb.

Zeke would try to get clean, and Timothy honestly hoped he was able to stay that way. He watched the trees and houses they passed and shook his head.

If he didn't do something about Malcolm, it would just continue to be another family he exploited.

"Fuck," he said aloud. It seemed he wasn't done fighting other people's wars after all. But this wasn't someone else's war anymore, was it? Malcolm had targeted *him* in that alley.

"You worried about this meeting?" Ashton asked him from the front seat.

"No, my guess is Malcolm wants to size me up, see if I'm still breathing for himself."

"What game do you think he's playing at?"

"I honestly have no fucking clue." And that's what bothered him the most.

Rico's Bistro was a well-known gem in downtown Boston. It catered to the wealthy with its elaborate décor, but the food was less than worthy of the price tag that accompanied it.

It had become known as the place for business meetings you weren't sure were going to go particularly well. Typically, it was a place you showed up to and then asked your party if they'd rather take the meeting somewhere else, say a business office, in order to finish with the details.

Timothy had no interest in going anywhere else with Malcolm Gentry.

"I'll be right here," Ashton said and stepped to the side of the front door where he could see the entire restaurant at all times. Timothy followed the hostess who made her way over to a table in the center of the crowded restaurant.

He wasn't sure what to expect as far as Malcolm Gentry was concerned, their research hadn't even uncovered a recent photo of the man they were meeting. So, when the waitress stopped at a table with a middle-aged man, Timothy was fairly shocked.

Malcolm stood and extended his hand, "Mr. McGinley, it's so nice to finally meet you. This is my wife, Lindsay."

"Nice to meet you both," he greeted, and they took their seats. Malcolm's hair was beginning to grey, while the rest was black. His eyes were brown, and his face clean-shaven. He looked like a typical businessman, nothing like the psychotic murderer Timothy knew him as.

His wife though was anything but. She was blonde, but not in a way that came natural and her full lips had not been gifted to her by God but rather injected with more plastic then should be allowed inside any one person. They were painted red, and her blood red fingernails had been trimmed to a sharp point. It was her eyes that set her apart from most businessmen's trophy wives. They reminded him of a shark circling the water for its next meal.

"What can I say is the pleasure of this meeting today?" Timothy wondered as he tried to appear relaxed.

"Can I call you Timothy?" Malcolm asked, and Timothy nodded. "Well, I find I am absolutely fascinated by you and your work. How long have you been in the antique business?"

"A number of years."

Malcolm smiled widely at the lack of an answer. "Well the company you have founded is impressive."

"It was founded by my relatives but thank you."

"Yes, your relatives that's right. My mistake." He smiled again and lifted a menu. "I think I'm going to have the lasagna, what about you my dear?"

"I'm going to have a chicken Caesar."

"That sounds delicious," Malcolm commented. "What about you Timothy?"

"Not hungry."

"Oh, but the food here is great. You have to try something, I insist!"

"Lasagna sounds good," Timothy said easily without lifting his menu.

Once the waiter came and took their order,

Malcolm clasped his hands together and then set them on the table.

"So, tell me about yourself, Timothy. What are some of your hobbies?"

"Is this a date Malcolm? Or is there a point to this meeting?"

Malcolm laughed heartily, and Lindsay smiled. "I'm so sorry, I am just so excited to meet you!"

"And why is that?"

"I've been following your work; your reputation is phenomenal." He leaned in closely, "Between you and I, I have my eye on a rather unique antique. One that is so incredibly rare I'm sure there is only one in all the world."

His words chilled Timothy. Surely the ass hat wasn't talking about him. "If you bring it by my office, I would be more than happy to authenticate it."

"Well, you see, therein lies the problem." He leaned back in his seat. "It's not exactly in my custody at the moment. I wanted to see for myself if it were real or not."

Timothy's blood iced just as Lindsay reached across the table. "That is a lovely watch." Using the tip of her manicured fingernail, she traced the outline of the watch and Timothy felt a bite on the back of his hand as her nail slipped off the watch and into his skin.

"Oh my! I'm so sorry!" She feigned shock when everyone at the table knew she'd done it on purpose.

Timothy didn't move his hand, he saw the glee in Malcolm's eyes as the first drop of blood welled up on the surface of Timothy's hand, and he watched that glee fade to disappointment when the wound continued to bleed rather than heal.

"I'm so sorry about that." Malcolm's now un-amused eyes shifted, so he was looking at Timothy directly. "I keep telling her that those fingernails are going to hurt someone one day."

"It's no big issue." Timothy lifted his hand and pressed a napkin to it. "Accidents happen."

"Yes, it appears they do." He turned to his wife who now looked angry, probably at the fact she had wasted time coming here to meet with a man who was supposed to be immortal. "Dear, can you please have the driver bring the car around, we need to get to our next meeting."

"Not hungry?" Timothy asked him as easily as if they were old friends.

"I'm afraid I forgot about a prior engagement in my rush to meet with you. Perhaps we can do this again?" he asked as they stood.

"You know how to reach me."

Malcolm grinned. "Yes I suppose I do, don't I? Good day, Timothy."

He walked away towards the front, and after tossing money on the table, Timothy did the same.

"You good boss?" Ashton asked as they pulled away from the curb.

"Yes, would be better if my hand would stop bleeding. I think that woman nicked a vein."

"Need to go see someone?"

"No, I've had worse," he commented and stared out the window as the scenery raced by.

He wasn't an idiot, he knew she'd cut him on purpose. So now they knew he wasn't immortal like they'd hoped. But what did that mean now? Would they stop watching his office? Was he free to let Paislee go?

Sure, Malcolm wouldn't leave her alone. But Timothy could get her a one-way ticket out of the country and then perhaps they could both live out their lives separately.

The thought should have thrilled him, he should have been ecstatic over the opportunity to return to some sort of normalcy, and still the thought of her being gone from his life forever, nearly made him sick.

They pulled up in front of his building, and Timothy made his way up to his office. The elevator doors opened, and Paislee glanced up from the book she was reading when she saw the blood covered napkin in his hand, her eyes widened, and she rushed to him.

"What happened? Are you alright?" She reached for him, but he moved out of the way.

"I'm fine. It was nothing but a test. One that I apparently passed."

"They were checking to see if you'd heal."

"Yes."

"Let me guess, Lindsay do that to you?"

"How'd you know?"

Paislee turned and lifted her shirt to reveal scars that matched the one on the side of her face. "She likes her nails long," she commented when she turned back around.

He was nearly vibrating with anger at the sight of the injuries that must have caused Paislee a hell of a lot of pain at one point.

"So, obviously you didn't heal, what do you think his next move is going to be?"

"I'm not sure."

"Want me to heal it for you?"

"No, thank you."

"Why not?"

"Because I like my hand the way it is."

"Bloody?"

"Attached."

"Oh please, I healed you in that alley."

"Something you admitted you weren't sure you could do."

"Timothy let me-"

She reached for him, and he jerked back. "Paislee, I said no." The words came out harsher then he'd meant, and she flinched.

"What the hell is your problem?"

"You," he growled, his breathing ragged. He could still picture her touching Jake's shoulder only hours after they'd kissed.

"You treat me like an employee, keep me at a distance, then you kiss me senseless for nothing other than your own sick pleasure, and now you won't even let me heal you? Am I really so bad?" Her bottom lip quivered, but his pride wouldn't let him give in.

"You're childish."

Paislee stared after him, anger rooting deep down inside of her. "I'm childish."

"That's what I said."

"Then why are you helping me? If I'm so fucking childish that you can't stand me?"

He thought about it for a moment and then looked her in the eye. "Because if I don't, you are going to die. I've done a lot of questionable things in my life Paislee, I have no interest in adding to the list."

"Fuck you, Timothy McGinley." Paislee headed for the elevator. She wiped the tears from her cheeks as she frantically pressed the button.

"It's not coming," he called.

"Excuse me?"

"I told you, you need to stay safe."

"You are no better than he was!" she screamed, and he got to his feet.

"How do you figure that?" His voice held a dangerous edge, but Paislee was too angry to notice.

"You keep me locked in this fucking room forcing me to study magic. The only difference between the two of you is your tactics. He forced me with fear, and you make me feel like you actually gave a shit about me."

Timothy continued towards her until he was inches from her face. He placed a palm on the door and leaned closer until his body was nearly right up against hers. "You would do good to remember I am helping you *witch*. Without me, you would be dead right now whether from Malcolm or a general misuse of your magic."

"You don't even know me."

"That's where you're wrong, as you know I've been around a long time. I've known a lot of people just like you. Naïve, childish, unable to determine exactly what it is they want out of life."

"You're a fucking coward," she muttered.

His jaw tightened, and Paislee had the sneaking suspicion that this man's bad side was not a place she wanted to be. But she refused to be bullied into submission, she had spent too many years behind the bars of a cage.

"You want to go?" he growled. "Then get the hell out of my sight." He typed in a code by the elevator, and the doors opened. "But don't even think about coming back here when he finds you. You walk out that door, and I'm done with you." Timothy turned away, and Paislee stepped into the elevator.

A part of her wanted to stay, she wanted to learn more about the enigma of a man she had saved in that alley, but her wounded pride wouldn't let her.

"I'll be back for my cat." He didn't respond, and she watched his back as the doors closed.

Timothy lifted the phone from his desk and dialed Ashton's number. "Let her out," he said angrily and threw the phone at the wall. She wanted to die? Then who the hell was he to stand in her way? She'd cool off and be back in a few hours, he told

himself. Then she would come crawling back.

He looked around his space that was now covered with her. Before, everything had a certain spot. Every single thing in his office had been organized to a fault.

Now though, her clothes were scattered everywhere. Blankets were tossed on various chairs or areas of the floor where she had simply decided she wanted to relax for a while. The air in his office carried her scent and without her here, although he hated to admit it, his space seemed empty.

She had come into his quietly organized life and disheveled it. Making a mess of things in both his head and his space.

"Fuck," he grumbled and ran his hands through his hair. He was an idiot.

"Fuck!" he yelled again as he grabbed his jacket and headed for the elevator.

He jogged out onto the street and saw her about a half mile away from him on the busy sidewalk.

"Paislee!" he called, but she either couldn't or wouldn't hear him. Fear gripped his heart when he saw the dark SUV pulling up alongside her. "Paislee!" he called louder, and she turned briefly to see him. He pushed into a sprint just as the doors opened and two men hauled her into the vehicle.

"Paislee!" he yelled again and continued running even after the SUV had sped away.

He had been an ass hole, and now Paislee was gone.

CHAPTER 11

The bag was ripped off Paislee's head, and she squinted at the sudden assault of light. She didn't know why they'd put it on her, it wasn't like she didn't know where they were taking her.

The location of her prison was forever ingrained in her memory from the night she'd finally escaped.

Her cheeks were stiff from tears that had dried on them, and she could feel the swelling in her eyes. She'd been crying when they'd grabbed her, and the fear of where they were taking her had caused her to revert back to the frightened child being ripped away from her brother. But no more, she was done crying for these people.

"Paislee, my dear! It's been a long time." Lindsay was the first to greet her, and she rushed forward. The blood from Timothy's hand still on her long fingers.

"Not long enough," Paislee growled.

"Still have a smart mouth I see." Lindsay grinned. "We can work that out of you."

"You know it's a sad thing, to raise a child." Malcolm's voice chilled her to her core. She watched as he moved further into the room and knelt in front of her chair. "You give them a roof over their head, food in their stomachs, books to read, knowledge to consume, and then they leave you."

"Raise me? You think what you did was *raise me?* You kept me locked away as your prisoner! My family, my mom, dad, and brother are the ones who raised me. You were nothing but my nightmare."

The crack across her face was something she'd come to expect from Lindsay. Malcolm had never put his hands on her, but Lindsay had just loved to inflict the pain.

"Watch your tone." Lindsay warned.

"Had I not rescued you from your drug addict brother, you would have either become an addict yourself or been raped by one of his pathetic friends. Or, perhaps both." He stood. "I saved you Paislee, but if you leave me again I will track him down and kill him in front of you." He motioned to the two men who'd brought her in, and they helped her to her feet.

"I will kill you!" she screamed as the two men pulled her out of the room and down the hall to the room she'd spent nearly every day for the last fifteen years.

It hadn't changed at all. The mattress still sat on the floor in the corner, the purple comforter and sheets tossed on top of it. She'd be willing to bet they hadn't been cleaned since she'd left.

The stack of magic books in the corner, and the iron bars on the windows that contained her magic. After she had escaped she'd learned that iron dulled a witch's magic, it was why she'd never been able to blast her way out before, and she'd learned that Malcolm was impervious to her magic when she'd tried to kill him five years ago.

As it turns out, he wore an iron necklace which repelled any magic she threw at him.

He had laughed in her face while the guards around him nearly died from the blast. Paislee walked over to her mattress and reached underneath for the knife she'd stashed inside of it before she'd left.

She wrapped her hands around the hilt and hid it underneath a blanket. Then, she laid back on the pillow and waited. She would *not* go down without a fight this time.

"She's fucking gone, Ashton!" Timothy yelled as he paced his office. "They came, and they fucking took her because I was being an asshole!"

"Timothy calm down."

Timothy eyed him, the only time Ashton ever called him by his first name was when he needed his attention.

"Don't tell me to calm down. They took her. She's gone. Last time, he had her for nearly fifteen years!"

"Last time the only one who knew where she'd been taken was a druggie. This time she has us."

"So, you know where he took her?"

Ashton held up his phone with a picture of a house. "My guy tailed them here. He lost them once but managed to catch up just before they turned into the house."

"Was he made?"

"Not the last time. He said he's not even entirely sure they realized it the first time. Could have just been a coincidence that they got away."

Timothy nodded. "How are we going to go in and get her?"

"That's the tough part. Guy practically has an army guarding that place. He hired BlackPoint security. Other than us, they are the best in the business." He ground his teeth together, "Unfortunately, I know the woman who runs it, and she is as twisted and money hungry as they come. Morality is not her strong suit."

"What's the problem with just storming in? You said yourself your company is better."

"It's not just BlackPoint he has on staff." Ashton zoomed in on another photo and held it up for examination. "Those men walk the perimeter with assault rifles. I have twelve men, and a dozen men cannot take on a compound that size."

"Then what the hell are we supposed to do? We cannot just leave her there Ashton, he will kill her!"

"I'm not saying we leave her, I'm saying we get more men and bigger guns."

"Get what you need."

"You got it." Ashton left Timothy's office, and Timothy turned to stare out at the fading cityscape.

If his death would fix this, he would gladly throw himself off the top of this building. Because at this point, it was what he deserved. The way he had talked to her, the way he'd acted, it was absolutely inexcusable, and now she might die because of it.

Childish? He was the one who had been childish. The buzzer sounded, and without answering, Timothy allowed whoever it was to come up to his office. It was probably Ashton with an update anyways.

The elevator doors opened, and Timothy turned around to see Jake standing in front of him, a bouquet of wildflowers in his hand. He stared at Timothy, wide-eyed and afraid.

"What are you doing here?" Timothy all but growled it and tried to keep his rage in check.

"I, I was meeting Paislee."

"Well as you can see, Paislee isn't here."

"Where is she?"

"Out," he said and walked to the bar to pour himself a drink. "I'll see you tomorrow morning, Mr. Parish."

"Where is she, Mr. McGinley?"

"Out," he repeated and turned to see Jake still clutching the flowers.

"Is she, is she alright?"

Timothy saw the accusation in Jake's eyes, and if

he hadn't currently been beating himself up for her kidnapping, he might have laughed.

"Are you accusing me of something, Mr. Parish?"

"I just, I know you were upset with her."

"I was furious with her, but I assure you I'm past that now. She will be back in a few days, she went to visit some old friends. We both decided we needed a break from our current situation." Garth padded over and rubbed on Timothy's leg. "See I'm even watching her cat."

Jake eyed the cat suspiciously, but then nodded and set the flowers on the stand near the door. "Will you tell her I came by?"

"When I see her again I will."

Jake turned and left the office without another word, and as soon as Timothy was sure he couldn't hear him, he slammed the glass down so hard it shattered, and Garth took off.

Timothy gripped the countertop and hung his head down to fight back the grief tearing him apart.

First Cait, now Paislee. Just what in the hell was he supposed to do? If she died because of him, he had no idea how he was going to survive. He knew he didn't want to ever find out.

"Settling back in?" Malcolm asked as he pulled the door open to her prison. She walked to the bars, the knife tucked securely in her sleeve. She wouldn't waste an opportunity to potentially drive the knife into his neck.

"Home sweet home," she responded dryly.

"Some things have changed since you left."

"Oh yeah? You finally grow a heart?"

He laughed. "You're a funny girl, Paislee, you know, I always liked you. From the moment I met you, I knew you were a little spitfire with power you had no idea you had. Do you remember that?"

"How could I forget? When men drag an eleven-year-old girl out of bed, she tends to remember it."

He clicked his tongue. "Oh my dear it was much further back than that. Your father worked with me at the museum. I was an intern there, and he worked the night security, remember?"

Paislee thought back to the times she'd gone to the museum with her father, but she couldn't place ever seeing Malcolm there before. Was it true? Or was this just another way to control her?

"I see you're still having trouble remembering." He stopped in front of the bars on the door and pulled a necklace from his pocket. "Do you recognize this?" he asked.

She took a step closer and stared at the garnet surrounded by diamonds. It was beautiful, and something about it drew her eye. She stepped closer, and closer again until she was nearly to the bars. It called to her, an enchanting buzz filling her mind, blocking everything else out until she could only see it.

"It's beautiful, isn't it?" Malcolm commented. "You see, I was working late one night when your father brought you in for the night. You hadn't been feeling well, and your mother and brother were away visiting someone, doesn't really matter who. Anyways, you were wandering around with him, and I saw you stop in front of the display case that was holding this particular necklace." He stroked the garnet gently, and Paislee was enchanted by the way the light glint off the stone.

"I asked you if you wanted to see it. I know, I shouldn't have, but when you nodded, I pulled it out. The second it was free from its casing you fell to the floor and started crying." He made a pouting face, but Paislee was too focused to notice. "I pulled the stone back, confused, and put it back in the case. Your father came running over, concerned for his little girl and I told him I had no idea what had happened. But you, you just kept repeating over and over again that the stone was going to hurt you, please get the stone away.

"I thought it was strange, so I researched it, after all, that was what I was good at, and wouldn't you know that this particular stone is known as *mortem auguratricis*. Would you like to know what that means Paislee?" He knelt closer to the bars. "*Mortem* is the Latin word for death, and *auguratricis* is the Latin word for sorceress." Knowing Paislee wasn't paying attention, he moved closer. "This stone is meant to draw in those with magic, but get too close to it, and it will suck you dry leaving you completely powerless to those around and thereby granting the owner of the stone, all the power it possesses. Now that I am so close to my objective, I thought it was time to re-introduce you to it." He grabbed her hand and pulled it through the bars.

The second her arm was past the iron, she felt the drain and screamed. It was so incredibly painful, a complete and total assault on every one of her senses. She yanked and pulled, but the guards had come over to help and were holding her arm securely through the bars.

"No! Please stop! Please stop!" she screamed, but Malcolm simply smiled. She collapsed onto the ground, and he shoved her arm back through the bars.

"Rest up my dear. I'm going to need more when this runs dry." He walked away leaving Paislee unconscious and powerless.

MALCOLM STEPPED INTO HIS OFFICE WITH A SMILE ON his face. Lindsay waited for him next to the roaring fire, and she ran towards him to get a look at the necklace. Power swam inside the garnet, illuminating it from the inside and she giggled.

"That is *gorgeous!*" Lindsay exclaimed. "Try it on baby, how do you make it work?"

He clipped the necklace around his neck and felt as the power began to hum against his body. He closed his eyes and willed the magic from the necklace to seep into his body, and as it did, he felt every single nerve as if they were only now coming to life.

He opened his eyes, and Lindsay jumped back. Curious, he took a look at himself in the mirror and grinned. His eyes, which had once been a simple brown, now blazed like twin flames.

From his studies, he knew that Paislee was probably a light mage, meaning she could conjure light in all its forms and aid in the healing process. But as her power surged through his veins, he felt more and wondered if he hadn't missed something. Was it possible she was more than a normal witch? He closed his eyes and imagined a flame sitting in his palm. When he opened them, he stared down at the fire dancing in his palm, when he sent it flying towards the dartboard hanging on his wall, it disintegrated, and he grinned madly. *He knew she was special!*

"Malcolm, you are amazing." Lindsay stared at him, wide-eyed and he took a step towards her.

"I am power," he said simply and smiled.

"Shall we start phase two?"

"Yes." He removed the garnet and put it in his pocket. Since he still wasn't quite sure how to handle the magic, he didn't want to risk blowing up his house with it. He knew from watching Paislee grow up, it could be fairly volatile. "We are going to need to do something about Timothy McGinley."

"You think he's going to be a problem? We saw today he isn't immortal like we thought."

"Maybe not, but he still poses a threat. Especially if he comes for Paislee."

"What do you want me to do?"

"Let's send him a message."

CHAPTER 12

*T*imothy stood at the window as the sun rose over the sky. *How many times had he done just that?* He wondered. How many sleepless nights had he waited patiently for the light to return to his world?

But even though the sun always returned, he had never felt as though his world would be bright again. Not until Paislee showed up. He wasn't sure when it had happened but having her here had given him something to look forward to each day. How was it that she hadn't been with him long and he already felt lost without her?

Her smile, the rare laugh, the way her fingers sparked when she got mad. It was all of that and more. Had he fallen for her? Or was she just a close friend he'd become accustomed to seeing every day?

He took a drink from his coffee and watched the orange and yellow streak across the skies. It really was a beautiful sight to behold, but he could see nothing except the start of a day without Paislee in it.

He set the mug down on his desk and sat back behind his laptop to go over what they knew about Malcolm Gentry- which as it turned out, was very little. The man managed to stay nearly completely off the radar.

There were no photos of him, no history of any article written about his company aside from a simple website boasting he was the best in the restoration business. As far as the world was concerned, Malcolm Gentry didn't exist.

But he did in fact exist. And Timothy was going to kill him. Perhaps then the world would have something to say about him.

The elevator doors opened, and a grim-faced Ashton stepped inside.

"Anything?" Timothy asked.

"Possibly."

"What is it?"

"If this is true, it could prove deadly to Paislee."

"What is it?" Timothy repeated, irritated.

Ashton set the papers down on Timothy's desk. "There is a record of a Jasper Anderson who worked as a museum curator for a museum here in Boston. They had, very briefly, a garnet necklace in their possession." He opened the folder and Timothy took in the beauty of the necklace.

Based on design, he estimated it would date back to early 1200's. The solid garnet was flawless and surrounded by diamonds of the same quality.

Ashton continued, "This necklace was rumored to be magical, and because of the power it possessed, it was nicknamed *mortem auguratricis.*"

"Death Sorceress?" His face paled, surely a necklace didn't hold that type of power. But then again, he hadn't believed a dagger could trap the souls of its victims, and he'd been wrong on that one.

"It is said to have the ability to drain and hold magic, which can then be used by the wearer."

"Wait, so this necklace can pull magic from a witch, and transfer it to someone non-magical?"

Ashton nodded. "That's not all." He opened the folder to a photograph, and Timothy found himself staring down at a very young Malcolm Gentry. "Jasper Anderson worked alongside a man by the name of Gage Adams." He turned the page again, and a photo of Paislee and her father stood out from the page. "Gage Adams was a security guard, and Paislee would go to work with him at times."

Everything began coming together in Timothy's mind, and he stood to pace. "If somehow, Malcolm had seen the effect the necklace had on her, he would have known she was a witch. There's no way a priceless item like that goes unnoticed by a curator, he had to have known the background of the gem. Which would mean targeting Zeke and Paislee hadn't been a coincidence. She'd been picked when she'd been young. How long did her father work there?"

"The necklace went missing in 2001 and shortly after Adams was fired. Apparently, Mr. Anderson swore he saw the guard take the necklace but since no evidence was discovered, Adams wasn't jailed."

"So, he gets fired in 2001, Paislee would have been what nine at the time? When does Jasper Anderson fall off the grid?"

"2002."

"So, he changes his name and starts building another life. A year later, Paislee's parents die in a car accident, and Zeke returns home from college. Probably not something Gentry had been counting on, but he makes use of Zeke by manipulating him into selling drugs and then eventually using. All of this had to be, so he could get to Paislee. Fuck, I wish we could talk to her brother."

Zeke would be absolutely no help right now seeing that he was probably in the throes of his detox. Hallucinations, shaking, and outbursts of anger would do little to help their current situation. Besides, chances were, nothing her brother would be able to tell them right now would get Paislee back.

"What is our next move?"

"I have a guy watching the house. If Gentry is, in fact, using this necklace, he will be a much worse enemy than we've given him credit for. We need to know exactly what we're walking into before we go. Otherwise we aren't going to be any help to her."

"We can't wait, Ashton, if he kills her-"

Ashton put his hand on Timothy's shoulder, "He needs her, but if we go in there guns blazing and die in the process, there is no one, and I mean *no one* who will be able to help her then."

Timothy knew Ashton was right, but the fact that Paislee was laying somewhere, probably in pain, was nearly too much for him to bear.

"We're coming, Paislee," he whispered. "Hang on."

~

PAISLEE STRUGGLED TO OPEN HER EYES. SHE WAS laying on something hard, and her head felt as though someone had driven a spike through it. The pain itself wasn't unusual for her, after using a ton of magic like when she'd healed Timothy, she'd woken with a headache. But she knew something was off, she just couldn't remember what.

When she pushed herself up and managed to open her eyes, she remembered. She was still lying near the bars, the same bars that Malcolm had used to shield himself while he stole her magic.

There was a significant amount of blood on the floor probably from her nose and ears since both tended to bleed after a blast like the one from last night.

She crawled over to her mattress. She no longer felt her weapon, so she imagined it had fallen out some time during the assault and he had taken it.

Tears stung in her eyes as the realization set in. She was going to be used as a pool of magic which was somehow much more personal than when he had simply been using her to intimidate or carry out a punishment.

Now, he would be stealing her power, stripping away a part of her for his own pleasure. It was sick, twisted, and she was completely powerless to deny him.

Where was Timothy? She wondered. He had seen her get taken and she'd witnessed the fury on his face for an instant when she'd been grabbed. Would he come looking for her?

A fleeting glimmer of hope passed through her at the thought of a rescue effort. Was it possible that he actually cared for her?

Malcolm now knew Timothy wasn't immortal so would he stop going after him? Did this mean that perhaps Timothy wasn't coming? That he would just go back to his life the way, he had before she found him in that alley?

She looked out her barred window as the sun began to rise as the hope she'd been feeling bled out of her. Why would he come for her? He'd called her childish and had told her repeatedly that the second he had taken care of the threat from Malcolm, she would be free to go.

Well, the threat was gone now, so what did that mean for her? Of course, she already knew the answer. She was going to die in this prison, alone, cold, and empty.

~

"Morning, Mr. McGinley," Jake greeted

Timothy just as he was getting off the elevator and onto the fourth floor.

"Morning. What do we have this morning?"

"I just got here, so I haven't had a chance to check out the new stuff, but the roster says a delivery came in that contained a couple crates from China."

Timothy nodded and tried to go about his day as usual. Nothing could seem amiss from the outside, and there was nothing he could do for Paislee until Ashton had more intel to go off of. So, the best he could do was bury himself in work and hope that at any moment Ashton would call him with an update.

"So, have you heard from Paislee?" Jake asked awkwardly as they made their way to the back near the service elevator. The delivery men typically stacked the crates right outside the large elevator since they didn't care to take the extra time to actually put them where they belonged.

"No," he responded curtly. How is it that Jake still didn't get he had no interest in discussing her with him?

"Oh, well, hopefully, she's alright."

"She's fine," Timothy snapped. They reached the crates in the back of the room, and sure enough, they were stacked just outside of the elevator.

Timothy opened the first one and revealed a set of pottery figurines he guessed had been crafted sometime in the early 1300's. They were fairly well preserved for their age, and after Jake finished taking photos and cataloging the era, he placed them back inside and moved the crate to the ground.

As he was standing, he noticed a puddle of dark liquid on the ground just under the crate the figures had been sitting on top of.

His blood iced as he pried open the bottom crate.

"Is that-" Jake started before passing out cold.

Timothy had felt anger a lot of times in his life, felt that fury building up inside of him as his world began to turn red. But never in his entire life, had he felt the cold, unfiltered, murderous rage he felt now as he stared down into the lifeless eyes of Jess Crew.

His body began to shake, somehow, he managed to pull his phone out of his pocket.

"Get to the fourth floor. Now," he said before disconnecting the call and throwing his phone. "FUCK!" he screamed and slammed his fist into the nearest wall. The sheetrock gave out below him, and he did his best to not completely destroy everything around him.

She was covered in blood from a slice at her throat, her eyes frozen open in fear that told him she'd known it was coming.

She hadn't been wearing what he'd seen her in yesterday, but instead was dressed as if she'd been on a date. Was that how the bastard had gotten her? Had he tricked Timothy's lovesick secretary into thinking she'd met someone who might care for her?

He had liked Jess, other than Ashton she had been his favorite person on staff. She was sweet, caring, and had even brought him chicken soup once when she'd thought he'd been sick.

She'd been a kind woman, who had deserved a

happy ending and now she lay lifeless in a shipping crate.

Ashton and his men came rushing in, and Timothy barely noticed until they were practically on top of him.

"Oh, my God," Ashton's voice was shaky, and Timothy could hear the pain reflected in his tone. "Get me security tapes now!" he ordered one of his men. "Get me Holt. He was on duty when these arrived." Ashton turned to Timothy and tried to hide the grief he was feeling.

"Jake pass out?"

Timothy nodded.

"Get him out of here," Ashton ordered one of the men who lifted Jake and carried him away. "We need to call the police."

Timothy nodded and stepped back from the crate as Ashton took a couple photos for his own investigation before phoning the police.

Ashton and Jess had been friends. A friend he had hoped could one day become something more. Her light had been a beacon of happiness for him, and seeing her dead killed a small part of him. He could see on his employers' face, it had done the same to him.

"Malcolm did this," Timothy growled, and Ashton nodded. There was no one else who would have murdered the woman and then stuck her in an antique crate.

"This was meant as a message," Ashton

commented. "Which means he must know we are planning on coming after Paislee."

"But how? How could he possibly know that?"

"I'm not sure," Ashton admitted.

A few minutes that seemed like hours passed before the police showed up. They were ushered in by Ashton's security team and immediately began taking stock of the grizzly scene before them.

"Mr. McGinley," a man in a crisp black suit and a woman in a navy-blue blazer, approached him. "I'm Detective Reilly, and this is Detective Shultz. Can you walk us through what happened this morning?"

"My employee and I came in to go over a new shipment that came in late last night from China. We went through the first crate, the smaller one that was on top of the one I found Jess in, first. When I moved it, I saw the blood and opened the crate."

"The victim was your secretary, correct?"

"Yes, Jessica Crew."

The detective wrote in his notepad. "Anything you can tell us about who might have wanted to hurt her? Or you?"

Timothy shook his head; Malcolm Gentry was his. No way he would be giving up the man to the police. Not when he wanted to be the one to watch the bastard pay for what he'd done. "I don't have anyone who comes to mind."

"Okay, well if you can think about it and let me know if something comes up."

"I will Detective."

"Where is your employee? The one who was with you?"

"Jake Parish. He passed out after seeing her. My security team took him to the break room on the second floor."

"Thank you, Mr. McGinley. We are truly sorry for your loss." Detective Shultz smiled at him warmly and squeezed his arm.

"Thank you." He sounded almost robotic, even to himself.

The coroner came in, and they began removing Jess's lifeless body from the crate. He bit back the lump of grief in his throat. She had been a great woman, and he would miss her. But the best thing he could do for her was get revenge for her senseless death.

Timothy and Ashton made their way up to his office, and Ashton began scanning the room with a device he'd told Timothy could search for any form of transmission that meant someone had been listening to them.

He found none, so they sat in the sitting area staring at the city through the large windows.

The sun was slowly sinking, and Timothy realized it was nearly four in the afternoon. Had it really taken the police that long? He wondered. Between the interviews, the search of the rest of the antique room, and the reviewing of the security tapes, they hadn't turned up anything else.

The delivery men had been the same two men they always were, and they hadn't noticed anything strange when they picked up the crates from the airport. Which meant one thing, somehow between the airport and the office, Jess had been killed and placed in that crate for him to find.

He pinched the bridge of his nose. The two men confessed they'd stopped for coffee on the way in, which must have been where they'd added her body to the crate. But how had they known the shipment was coming in? How had Malcolm known the route they would take?

None of it made any sense. It wasn't like it was public knowledge, and he could simply search for it on the internet. Had he and Jess gone out before? Had he been grooming her for this exact moment?

"Do you think it's possible we have a mole?" Ashton wondered aloud. "Someone that managed to sneak past us in the interview process?"

Timothy pondered it for a moment, he had personally gone through each employee countless times to make sure they were legitimate. Had he missed something? "Send me a list of all the recent hires. Anyone within the last year."

"I'm on it." Ashton got to his feet but paused before leaving. "We'll get him, Timothy."

He nodded, they absolutely would. One way or another.

CHAPTER 13

"*Y*our message was received, Mr. Gentry."

Malcolm turned to face the woman in the doorway. "Tell me, was he distraught?"

"I would say so. One of his employees even passed out."

Malcolm smiled. "Good."

"I would say he is going to be feeling the effects of this one for a while. Your wife does good work."

"Yes, she enjoys it." It was true, there was little Lindsay Gentry enjoyed more than the power that came with taking life. "Keep an eye on things and let me know if it changes."

"You got it." She left the room, and Malcolm pulled the garnet necklace from his safe. He cradled it in his palm gently and smiled.

Soon everything would be in place, and he would be one step closer to achieving his goals.

It was strange, he had worried before that once he

was this close, he would feel less excited, that it would be anticlimactic.

But instead, he was giddy with the wonderment that he would one day have everything he'd dreamed about.

That soon, everything his father had once dreamt of would be within Malcolm's grasp.

"Who has the power now?" he wondered aloud to the empty room.

His door opened, and Lindsay stepped in.

"I'm told your work was exceptional, my love," he greeted her.

"It always is." She grinned.

"Did she put up much of a fight?"

"No, she begged. It was pathetic really. Boring almost." She pouted and took a seat in his lap. "I'm told we have a lead on that item you've been searching for."

"Oh, yeah?"

"But we are going to need to head to London tonight."

Anticipation burned in his mind. "I believe our guest can benefit from one last drain before we depart." He stood, and taking the garnet with him, headed out into the hall. "Have Eduardo file a fake flight plan to Scotland."

"You got it, baby." She pressed a hard kiss to his lips and headed downstairs.

As Malcolm made his way towards Paislee's room, he reflected on their mutual past.

Since the moment he saw the little red-haired girl

following her father around the museum, Malcolm had been intrigued. She was fiery, much in the way his little sister had been before her accident.

It had been that tragedy that had turned him to magic in the first place. He had taken the job at the museum to try and get his hands on the gemstone, but he hadn't found a possible power source just yet, so he'd left the gem there and watched, hoping that it would draw the eye of a witch.

He wouldn't have even considered that witch would be a child. He'd tried on numerous occasions to get the little girl alone so he could capture a fraction of her power to heal his broken sister.

But her father had watched her far too closely after her first reaction to the necklace. Malcolm grimaced at the memory of what followed, his sister died, trapped in her body and unable to speak before he'd managed to get the little brat.

Now though, she was his. His little battery, *his magical creature.*

"Paislee, it's good to see you awake." He nodded to his guards, and they opened the door.

"Please just leave me alone!" she screamed and kicked at them, scratched, and made him hard while she did it.

Not because he wanted her in the typical way a man wanted a woman, but because the power she gave him with her fear was more than he could have ever asked for.

The guards slammed her to the ground just inside her cage, and he pulled the gem out of his pocket.

They extended just her fingers beyond the safety of the iron bars, and she screamed in agony as the gem began absorbing the magic her body had created.

He watched, fascinated, as the color of her hair and skin dimmed as nearly every drop of magic was ripped from her body.

Before he drained her completely, he certainly didn't want to kill his battery, he pocketed the gem.

Unable to move, she lay there while the blood dripped from her nose and ears, and all he could do was smile.

Because she'd refused to help him all those years ago, he was taking full advantage of her now.

"Timothy, we may have a window." Ashton burst into his office.

"What is it?" Timothy shot to his feet.

"My contact who's been watching the house says that Gentry, his wife, and over a dozen guards just left the premises."

"Timothy grabbed his jacket off the back of the chair. "Let's go."

"I don't know how big of a window we're going to have."

"We don't need much," he responded quickly. "Just enough."

They walked down to the alley where four black sedans were waiting.

"Here." Ashton handed Timothy another

weapon, and Timothy stuck it into his waistband where his usual .45 was sitting.

"Call the airstrip and get me a private plane ready."

"You're leaving?"

"Once we get out of there and Malcolm realizes we have her, he's going to be breathing down our necks. We need to make sure we can keep her away from him until we've got something more on him."

"Good point." Ashton made the call, telling the pilot (another one of his security guards) to file a false flight plan sending them to Paris.

"Another thing, I'm going to need you to watch the cat."

"You got it."

They pulled up in an alley near the house and filed out of the sedans. Ashton had assembled fifteen men all carrying assault rifles.

Ashton nodded as another man, clad in black, walked towards them. "You've got three men patrolling the grounds, and I would estimate another dozen inside."

Ashton nodded. "Thank you, Padfield. Keep watch and radio us if you see anyone coming."

"You got it," the man responded before disappearing back into the dark.

Timothy barely listened as Ashton barked orders. He could all but feel Paislee on the other side of those walls, and his body was primed for war if that's what it meant to bring her home to him safely.

"Ready?" Ashton asked, and Timothy nodded.

"Move out." He instructed, and the men began scaling the brick wall around the property. Timothy followed suit, and watched as the three roaming guards were dispatched by two of Ashton's men.

Ashton kicked in the front door, and they blasted through it, not giving anyone enough time to fire on them.

Before he could even think to count, Timothy had taken down three of the twelve men inside. He continued moving towards the stairs, firing when necessary, and when he was in the clear, he bounded up to the second floor and began checking doors.

She'd said there'd been bars on her door, so instead of checking inside each room, he pushed on to the next, counting on his team to clear them for any enemies. He ripped open the last door and found bars.

"Oh, Paislee, please be okay." He knelt to the ground where she was lying, eyes closed, blood dripping from her nose and ears. "What the fuck did he do to you?" He growled.

"Keys." Ashton tossed Timothy a set of keys, and after trying three, he managed to unlock the iron door.

"Paislee," he whispered and lifted her into his arms. Relief for the steady breaths she was taking was little comfort against the anger coursing through his system at the way she looked. Her hair was no longer the vibrant red it had been when he'd last seen her, but nearly a dark grey, as if she'd been drained of all color. Her skin was pale, and her lips chapped.

"We need to go," Ashton warned, and Timothy nodded.

"Let's get out of here," he said and followed the men down the stairs and passing the bodies of those who'd pledged loyalty to the wrong side.

Once inside the vehicles, Timothy cradled Paislee in his lap. Ashton handed him a napkin, and he began to wipe the blood from her. It was still fresh meaning whatever had been done to her had happened only shortly before they had arrived.

It made him wish they'd gotten there sooner.

"Where are you going?" Ashton asked.

"The less you know, the better, I'll call you when we get there."

"Understood." He looked at Paislee, who still hadn't come around. "Do you think it was the garnet? Do you think he drained her?"

Timothy nodded. "It appears that way. I want to know the moment he returns, and if you can tell me where he went, I'd like to know that as well."

Ashton nodded in understanding. "Will you let me know how she is when she wakes up?"

"I will."

The drive to the airstrip was short, and Timothy carrying Paislee gently, climbed into the private plane.

"Where to, Sir?" the pilot asked as soon as the cabin had been sealed.

Timothy took a deep breath. He'd given a lot of thought to where he should take Paislee. She needed now more than ever, to understand how to use her magic. Especially if Malcolm was storing up powers of his own.

There was only one person on the planet he knew he could trust with their current predicament, and he'd sworn never to speak with her again.

"Ireland," he responded and leaned back in the seat.

STILL, IN THE DARK, PAISLEE TRIED TO OPEN HER eyes. She couldn't see anything, but she had the oddest sensation. It was almost as if she was flying, her ears popped with the change in gravity and she cried out, had she died? Was this how you went to heaven?

She mumbled something and heard a man's voice soothe her. "Paislee, I've got you," he said gently, and she curled into the warmth against her body. The scent of him filled her lungs, and one name came to mind, *Timothy*. He'd found her.

CHAPTER 14

*P*aislee opened her eyes to the brain-splitting headache that was a magical overload. Or in her rare case, magical drain. She stared up at a rounded white ceiling, curiously. Where the hell was she?

She sat up and stretched. Okay, *so she was in an airplane*. Or rather, an incredibly expensive private jet.

She looked around the cabin, and when her eyes landed on Timothy, she relaxed. His back was to her, so she stood and after a momentary dizzy spell made her way over to the table.

She put her hand on his shoulder, and he jumped. When he did, her dizziness grabbed hold of her, and she started to fall, stopped only by him pulling her onto his lap and wrapping his arms around her.

She leaned against his shoulder and into the hug, grateful to be back in his protection.

"I'm sorry for the way I acted the day you were taken." His voice was heavy and full of regret.

"I'm sorry I stormed out."

He nodded and helped her to a chair across from him. "Hungry?"

She shook her head and pressed her hand to her throbbing forehead.

"You should be sleeping." He stood and walked over to her.

"I don't suppose I can take a shower, can I?"

"Can you stand?"

"I'm sure I can manage."

He helped her to her feet, and she wrapped her arm around his waist as they walked towards the back of the plane which turned out, to her surprise, to be a master bedroom with a full bath attached.

Her head still throbbing, she made a mental note to comment on it later but didn't want to speak now.

Timothy knelt in front of her and began untying her sneakers. She watched as he gently removed her shoes and socks.

He looked up at her. "Think you can you handle the rest?"

She nodded, afraid to speak and let lose the flood of tears already in her eyes.

He started to walk away, but when Paislee swayed and fell backward onto the bed, decided against it. "Do you want help?" he asked her gently, and she nodded.

"I'm sorry," she whispered.

"You have nothing to apologize for."

Tears stung at her eyes as he helped her to her feet again and held her upright while she unbuttoned her pants and pulled them to just below her hips. Timothy knelt in front of her and pulled them the rest of the way off before gently setting them aside on the floor. He turned around while she finished undressing from the bed, and then handed her a towel to cover herself.

After turning the shower on to warm it up, Timothy returned to see her wrapped in a towel and staring at her feet. "Ready?" he asked, and she nodded. He helped her over to the shower and inside, but as she started to remove the towel, she began to sway again.

"Dammit," she cried, and Timothy steadied her.

"Do you want my help?" he asked her. "I won't look, and I can stay in my boxers."

She nodded, so he sat her down on the toilet and stripped down to his boxers. Once he was done, he helped her back to her feet and into the shower. She tossed the towel to the ground, and he did his best to avert his eyes. He had no intention of moving in on her. She was broken, vulnerable, and in more pain than he could even fathom at the moment.

He couldn't explain it, but he needed the closeness nearly as much as she did, just to feel like she was safe. He held her arm and put soap on a washcloth for her, then he stared at the wall until she handed it back.

When she turned to him, his eyes held hers, and the tears he'd sensed she was trying to hold in came out as she leaned against him.

He wrapped an arm around her and pressed the

other against the wall behind her to keep them both from falling.

"I thought I was going to die in there," her voice broke, and he held her tighter.

"I wouldn't have left you Paislee. No matter what, I would have come after you. I'm just so damn sorry it took me so long."

Her shoulders shook, and he held her under the spray of the water until it turned cold.

Then he wrapped her in a towel and carried her to the bed.

"Please don't leave." She held her hand out for him.

"I won't."

He changed into dry boxers and shorts, then climbed into the bed with her. She scooted close, and he held her against his bare chest while she cried.

WHEN PAISLEE OPENED HER EYES AGAIN, SHE WAS alone. She stretched, thankful her headache had subsided. Timothy was nowhere in the room, and she closed her eyes again, remembering the gentleness of his touch when he'd been caring for her.

She put her feet on the floor and looked around for something more than a towel to wear. Her clothes were gone, so she opened the closet and pulled out a white robe that had been hanging inside.

Finally steady on her feet, Paislee made her way towards the front of the plane. Timothy was sitting at a table, and when he looked up his eyes locked on her. With his gaze on hers, she made her way over to the table and sat across from him.

"How are you feeling?" he asked her.

"I'm okay."

He noted her color was back, the red of her hair had returned, but with it, he could see the bruise that marred the marble skin of her cheek.

"I'm going to kill him," he said it simply, as if it were merely a topic in a typical conversation.

"Good."

"Can you tell me what happened?"

"Can I eat first?"

"Yes, sorry." He stood, "Turkey sandwich okay?"

"That would be great, thanks. Do you have any coffee?"

He nodded towards the pot. "I can get you some in just a second."

"I can get it." She stood and took the mug he offered her. The closeness of his body to hers was electric, and she yearned to feel his arms around her again.

Instead of reaching for him, she finished making her coffee and took a seat at the table again.

He set a plate with a fairly large sandwich in front of her.

"Are you not eating?"

"I've already eaten," he said softly and leaned back in his seat. "Besides, I'm not overly fond of flying. It tends to make me a little nauseous."

A ghost of a smile played at her lips before disappearing. She started to lift her sandwich but stopped. "Timothy?"

"Hmm?" Those steely eyes locked on hers and for a moment she forgot what she'd meant to say. She blushed and looked back down at her food. "Thank you for coming for me. And for helping me earlier."

"You're welcome, Paislee."

His voice was soft, and Paislee offered him a slight smile before taking a bite out of her sandwich. "This is amazing," she commented after she'd swallowed the first bite.

"You don't live for two hundred years and not know how to make decent food." He grinned at her, and for the first time since she'd known him, she felt like he might finally begin opening a bit to her.

"I suppose that's true." She finished eating and then pushed her plate back. "How's Garth?"

"The cat is fine. Ashton is watching him."

"Thanks."

"You don't need to keep thanking me Paislee."

"I just, I would have died if you hadn't come for me. It was different this time, he…" She shut her eyes and felt Timothy's hand reach forward and touch hers. The feel of his hand on hers gave her the strength to continue speaking. "He had this necklace."

"The *mortem auguratricis*."

"You know of it?"

"Ashton found some background on it before we were able to come get you."

She stared at their hands. "He used it to steal my power. It was the most horrible thing I have ever experienced. It was like something was reaching inside of my body, deep down into my veins and ripping pieces of me out." She shut her eyes, and a tear fell onto the table. "He told me that he had met me once when I was a little girl, that I had been drawn to that necklace, and he'd let me see it."

Timothy nodded. "Your father had tried to protect you. He'd known something was off. He had been blamed for the theft of the necklace, but they'd never been able to pin anything on him."

"That explains why he 'quit.' He wouldn't have wanted to tell us he got fired." Paislee pulled her hand away to cover her face. "How could I have been so stupid?"

"Paislee you were a child, you had no idea magic was even real, let alone that you would possess it. You cannot start blaming yourself. If you start down that path, your entire world is going to crumble."

"Oh, because I have so much to live for now?" Her eyes were brimming with tears when she looked up at him.

"Don't you dare give up on life Paislee. If I've made it this far, you can push through this." He stood. "Come with me, we should be landing soon."

She stood and followed him back into the bedroom.

He opened the door to the bathroom where her clothes were all hanging over the shower rod. "I didn't have time to get you new ones, but I did wash these."

"There's a washer on this plane?"

"No. I washed them by hand."

"Seriously?" She tried to picture the man before her, sleeves rolled up, hand washing her underwear, but it was difficult.

"I didn't always have a washer and dryer," he reminded her.

"Mr. McGinley?" A voice sounded over the intercom.

He walked to the speaker mounted on the wall, and pressed a button on the panel next to it, "Yes?"

"We are about to begin our descent."

"Thank you." He headed back to his seat and held his breath as the plane slowly descended into the country he hadn't been to in over two hundred years.

THEY STEPPED OFF THE JET AND ONTO THE TARMAC. Timothy's entire body was rigid, but Paislee didn't notice. She was too captivated by the new land in front of her. They had landed in a private airport somewhere in the beautiful country. Lush green grass surrounded the area that held dozens of private airplanes and one tall tower.

They didn't have any bags, so they quickly climbed into a black town car that was waiting for them. "We will run into Dublin to get some necessities and then we are going to be staying in a small town a few hours outside."

"Why are we going there?"

"I'm taking you to see someone who might be able to help you."

After checking to make sure the barrier was all the way up between them and the driver, she leaned forward and whispered, "A witch?"

He nodded.

"*The* witch?"

He nodded again.

"How long has it been since you've seen her?"

"The last time I saw her, she was breaking my heart on the front porch of her family home. That was two hundred and three years ago."

Paislee leaned back in her seat, it made sense now why Timothy had been so angry at the woman for casting the spell to help her brother. He'd been in love with her, and she'd turned him away forcing him to live out an eternity without her.

His heart had been broken, and she'd mocked him for it.

"I'm sorry."

"For what?"

"For mocking you about your wife."

"Myria was not my wife."

"She wasn't?"

"No, my wife was not a witch. She was a kind woman with a knack for healing the sick using herbs."

The inflection on his words when he'd said she *wasn't* a witch had stung, but Paislee brushed them off. She knew he hadn't meant it that way and that he was already on edge. Picking a fight over something as silly as that would have been pointless.

"Either way, I'm sorry."

"Thank you."

They bought clothes, shoes, toiletries, and luggage to hold it all at a mall in Dublin. Then they climbed into a car that Timothy had rented himself and made their way out of the city. He had checked a map and explained that since he hadn't been here when the roads had been created, he was useless as far as figuring out how to drive to where they needed to go.

She'd never seen him dressed the way he was now. He was completely casual in his jeans, t-shirt, and black jacket. He wore dark boots and sunglasses that made it impossible to see his eyes. She wondered if he'd done it on purpose, so she wouldn't be able to see if he was upset.

She turned her attention out of the window and watched with wonder as the scenery passed her by. A flock of sheep grazed beyond stonewalls, and the grass was greener than she ever could have imagined.

The entire country felt like magic, it was no wonder there were so many myths and legends surrounding it.

"Are you alright?" she asked cautiously.

He nodded and continued driving. "I've missed this place, and I hadn't been prepared for that."

She reached over and squeezed his arm lightly, and he moved his hand over to link his fingers through hers.

The simple act had butterflies fluttering in her stomach, and she suppressed a smile as she turned to continue staring out of the window.

They drove in silence the rest of the way, only breaking it when Paislee had a question about ruins they passed or the small villages that dotted the road between them and wherever it was they were going.

Timothy's hand tightened on hers as he turned down a private gravel road. Trees stood up on either side, blocking the sun and casting gorgeous strands of lights over them as they drove.

They emerged into a clearing next to a large barn, and once she turned her attention off it, Paislee saw the most beautiful house she had ever seen standing before them. It looked like a fairytale cottage, and she tried to picture what it must have been like when Timothy had last seen it. Had it looked the same? Had that ivy climbed its stonewalls the day he left here heartbroken and alone?

He released her hand and gripped the steering wheel, placing his forehead against it. Paislee didn't say anything, she knew there was nothing she could say to ease the pain he was in, so she stayed silent and waited patiently until he opened the door and stepped outside.

CHAPTER 15

*T*imothy stood at the end of the drive, in front of a house he never thought he'd see again. He closed his eyes, and the image of him saying goodbye on that porch step came rushing into his mind.

A mixture of emotions—mainly anger—shocked his system and he ground his teeth together. His past came to the front of his mind, and for a moment he lost himself in it.

IRELAND 1815

Timothy burst into the clearing just in time to see the sorcerer they were hunting drive his dagger into the stomach of his latest victim, the love of his best friends life. Aengus howled in rage and Aengus's sister Myria cried out as they rushed to where she was suspended in a tree.

Aine screamed in pain, but Timothy could hardly hear it over his own blood pounding in his ears.

"Keep them away from her!" Timothy ordered his men as he jumped off his horse and attacked the guards protecting the sorcerer, Caipre.

He fought with anger at the memory of the other death caused by this man all because he had become obsessed with Aine over the years.

Her young sisters face stayed in the front of his mind as he fought those who refused to surrender. As soon as the fight was over, he searched for his best friend who was currently cradling the love of his life in his arms.

Timothy's eyes caught sight of Caipre at the edge of the clearing, seething. He raced towards him and ran through the trees trying to capture the man responsible for all the carnage of the last day.

Timothy's breath came out in ragged puffs as he raced through the trees searching for any sign of the sorcerer. A dizzying wave of magic passed over him and he wondered if Myria had been able to heal Aine. Her magic had grown over the years and he knew healing was something she'd been working towards.

New hope bloomed in his chest at the thought, and he ran back towards the clearing. He saw Aengus kneeling, hands tied behind his back. He was covered in a thick layer of blood from the guards who had surrendered, but were now lying in a lifeless heap on the grassy ground.

Myria was kneeling next to Aine and he felt his own tears. Aine was dead. He could see it all over the faces of those he considered his closest friends.

"Cut him loose!" Timothy ordered one of his men.

"But sir—"

"I said cut the bloody ropes off of him. Can you not see he is grieving? These men deserved to die for what they have done. Do I need to remind you of the little girl who was murdered earlier? I know I don't have to remind you of the woman who was beaten, as she is lying right there!" he screamed, and the guard hesitated just before cutting the binds on Aengus's hands.

Timothy felt a pain unlike anything he'd ever felt as he watched his broken friend pull the body of his true love into his arms and cradle her as one would do a child. He swallowed hard and walked over.

"Aengus." Timothy placed his hand on Aengus's shoulder, he didn't say anything else knowing that no words could soothe his friends broken soul. Within moments, Aengus stood and carried Aine back to his horse.

"Come on, Myria." Timothy lifted her into his arms and cradled her to his chest as she cried. His heart broke for the only girl he had ever loved and the pain she was suffering as well as the grief he knew his best friend was facing now: a life without the one person he loved the most. It was a pain that Timothy couldn't even imagine.

"Wait," she said softly, and turned to look at the ground where Aine had once laid.

"What is it?"

Her eyes searched frantically, "Oh no. Where is it?"

"Where is what?"

"The dagger, the one that Aine was stabbed with."

"I saw no dagger."

"Oh no, this is bad."

"Why? It was simply a dagger."

"No it wasn't. It was the Dagger of Souls."

"*Dagger of Souls?*" Confusion spread across Timothy's face as he looked down at her.

"I learned of it in scrolls Caipre had in his study. It is rumored to trap the soul of the victim. It was why I removed it from her before she——" She choked up at her words.

"We will find it." Timothy stepped away for a moment and went to speak with some of his men. Myria watched as they nodded and he came back to her.

"They are searching for it now."

Myria nodded and let Timothy guide her once again.

TIMOTHY MADE HIS WAY BACK TO THE HOUSE, exhausted and helpless. Aengus had disappeared and after searching for him, Timothy had discovered he was holed up in a small cabin.

He had begged his friend to come home, for his family, for his sister, but he had refused. The house came into view and he saw Myria sitting on the porch. She looked completely and totally broken and Timothy hated he would have to deliver more bad news to an already distraught family.

"Myria." She looked up at him and he saw fleeting hope in her eyes. Hope that he was going to have to extinguish. "He is refusing to come back," he said softly, and took a seat next to her.

Myria nodded.

"I'm so sorry for all you have suffered through, Myria. You are the most amazing woman I have ever known, and I truly hope that one day you find happiness again."

She smiled at him then, and although it didn't reach her

eyes, Timothy believed it was the most beautiful smile he had ever seen.

"Thank you, Timothy."

He cleared his throat. "Perhaps we might spend some time together?"

"I'm sorry, Timothy. I need to focus on bringing my family back together. There must be a way to get Aengus home." She stood, and Timothy followed.

"I understand." He started to take a step down off the porch, but turned back to her. "Actually, I'm sorry. I don't. I know you have lost a lot recently, but you have to know that I will do anything for you. I care for you, Myria, beyond the bounds of friendship, and I need you to know that."

"I know," she said softly, and leaned down to kiss his cheek. "But my happiness is not what matters now. I have to bring Aengus home, and I have to ensure Aine comes back to him." She had told him of the spell she'd cast to offer her brother a second chance, but he didn't understand why she would use it as an excuse. He wanted to though, and had she not already looked so beaten down, he might have pressed for more.

"That sounds like a very lonely future," He said softly, and cupped her cheek with his hand. The feel of the warmth against his palm had a lump forming in his throat. "I cannot wait any longer."

Tears filled her eyes but she nodded. "I understand."

"Goodbye, Myria." He kissed her softly and turned away. He fought the urge to turn around, to rush to her and insist she not drive him away, but he continued. If she didn't wish for him to be in her life then who was he to force it.

They both deserved better.

"Are you sure you're okay?" Paislee asked softly, her voice pulling him from his trance. He hesitated and then nodded, it was now or never, he supposed.

Each step he took towards that house made the panic rise in his chest. *Would they even recognize him?*

The door loomed before them, and he took a deep breath before knocking. He heard voices inside and then a woman with dark hair opened the door, an infant in her arms. The similarities were endless, and he knew he was staring face to face with Aine, a woman he'd watched die over two hundred years ago.

"Hi, what can I-" She stopped mid-sentence, and her jaw fell slack. "Timothy?"

"Aine," he ground out. He had no reason to be angry with her, he reminded himself. It was Caipre who had gone after her, and she hadn't been the one behind the spell, only the object of it.

"Aengus!" she called, and Timothy straightened. The last time he'd seen Aengus, was the night Aine and her sister had been laid to rest.

"What is it?" he asked and stopped in front of the door. Tears filled Timothy's friend's eyes as he took in the scene before him. "Timothy, is that you? But how? I don't understand."

"Aine, Aengus, this is Paislee." Paislee held out her hand, and Aine took it gently.

"Please come in you two."

They stepped into the house and Timothy took it

all in. Aside from the modern upgrades, the house was nearly an exact match for the home he had spent so much time in as a boy. Some of the same paintings and tapestries hung on the walls, and the fireplace was the same stone it had been centuries before.

He heard the sound of giggling and turned to see a young girl chasing after a dog. "Isleen, no running!" Aine called, and Timothy and Paislee followed them into a sitting area.

"Isleen?" Timothy asked, curious about the little girl with Aine's sister's name.

"That's our daughter," Aine said. "And this is our son, Timothy." She gestured to the infant in her arms.

"Timothy."

She blushed. "We named him after you."

"Congratulations, Aine," he said through gritted teeth and tried to be happy for the woman who had to spend so many years in pain. He was moved they had chosen to name their son after him, but the jealousy he felt at the fact that they had children when a family had been all he wanted, rose to the surface. He tried to ignore it though and reminded himself that he had loved these people as family.

"It's Abby now," she corrected him. "At least that's what I go by out in the world."

Aengus still hadn't spoken, he just continued to stare at Timothy in disbelief. "How are you here? I thought you dead?" His voice was barely above a whisper.

"I'd rather not repeat the story. We need to see Myria, and I can tell everyone then." He wished he didn't have to face her, wish they didn't need her help, but without her, they were as good as dead.

"I'll call her," Aine, or rather Abby, said easily and rose from the couch.

"This is a beautiful home," Paislee commented, trying to break the awkward silence that had fallen over the room. She folded her hands in her lap and watched the young girl play with the dog. It reminded her of the dog she'd saved as a young girl, and it brought a pang of sadness to her chest.

"She's on her way." Abby took a seat next to Aengus and smiled at Paislee. "So how did you two meet?"

"It's a long story."

"Why are you here? Why now?" Aengus confronted Timothy. "If you've been around all this time, why are we only just now seeing you?"

"Aengus." Abby put a hand on his arm.

Timothy didn't answer, he just continued to stare at the flames in the fireplace. Ten minutes of awkward silence passed before the door opened and one of the most beautiful women Paislee had ever seen burst in. Her skin illuminated unlike the others in the room, and her magic seemed to call out to the newcomer as if it were sensing a kindred spirit. Those two things could only mean one thing; this was the witch who had cursed Timothy. The one he'd been in love with all those years ago.

"Timothy?" She stopped in front of the couch, and he stood to face her. Paislee saw the barely leashed control all over his face, so she stood with him and placed her hand on his arm. "Is it really you? Of course, it's you." Her eyes filled and Paislee saw love reflected in the depths. But not the same kind of love she imagined had once been in Timothy's.

"I'm sorry Paislee, I can't do this." Timothy pushed past Myria and the red-haired man who had followed her in. He slammed the door shut behind him, leaving Paislee starring at four very confused pairs of eyes.

"Excuse me for just a moment." She eased past them and headed for the door where Timothy had disappeared. She saw him standing at the entrance to what appeared to be a giant flower garden.

"This was all dead," he said softly when she came to stand next to him.

Since the moment she'd met Timothy McGinley, she'd sensed the strength inside his soul. He'd been a stubborn, persistent, sometimes thickheaded ally in the private war she was raging against Malcolm. Seeing him now though, she couldn't help but feel heartache at the pain reflected on his face.

He was broken, damaged, and she had no idea how to put him back together.

"Sometimes things can come back from the dead, you of all people should know that by now." She tried to sound light, but her voice was full of emotion.

He turned to her and the pain reflected in his eyes broke her heart. "I'm not entirely sure how to handle this."

"You aren't alone." She took his hand between

her palms. "I'm here with you, I will help you. Please let me help."

He took a deep breath and turned back towards the house. "I suppose we should go back inside."

She released his hand and watched as he walked back towards the house. She knew that every step he took towards his past was a painful one. And each time he made a move towards moving beyond the pain, the man he'd been before was surfacing.

imothy stepped back into the house and took a deep breath. After confirming Paislee was behind him, he moved back towards the couch. Myria stood, and he forced himself to face her.

He had loved her all those years ago, and after that had convinced himself he hated her. *He had wanted to hate her*, it made things easier. But standing face to face with her, he could still feel shreds of the friendship they'd once shared.

"Somehow the spell kept me here too." He crossed his arms over his chest.

"I don't understand how, and why only come back now? Why have you stayed away all these years?"

"I'm not sure why, I imagine because I was in that clearing with you that day. Or perhaps because I was emotionally involved in the event as well. Either way, I was trapped. And as for why I didn't return, I hated you when I discovered what had been done to me."

Myria's eyes filled, and she covered her mouth. The man who'd come in with her, put his hand on her shoulder but to his credit, didn't say anything.

"I buried my wife. A woman I loved more than anything in the world and the thirty years I had with her hadn't been enough. I wanted to die with her, and you took that right away from me."

"I didn't know, Timothy, you have to believe me," she pleaded.

"I know you didn't. You were still fairly green in your magic. You couldn't have known there would be consequences." He looked over to Aengus who had his arm around Abby. "I'm glad you two found each other again, I truly am, and I am working to forgive you Myria. But I've been carrying a grudge for over two hundred years, and that's going to take some time to let go of."

Myria nodded. "I understand." She took a deep breath. "I know that it probably isn't what you want to hear, but I'm so happy to see you, Timothy. Aengus and I have both missed you." She cleared her throat. "Now, what brings you back here today?"

Paislee raised her hand. "That would be me. I have some magic that I have no idea how to use."

To Timothy's surprise, Myria let out a small laugh. "Well, that I can help you with."

"Tomorrow," Timothy said and turned towards the door. "We need to check into our hotel."

"Hotel?" Abby asked. "Why don't you two just stay here? We have plenty of room."

"No, we can't do that to you guys." Paislee stepped towards Timothy.

"We insist." Aengus stood. "Please," he said to Timothy. "Two hundred years is a long time to go without my best friend."

Timothy hesitated but eventually nodded. If he were truly honest with himself, he had missed his friends more than he cared to admit. They had grown up together, and they were the only ones who truly knew who he had been before the curse had dug its ugly claws into him.

"I'm Sheamus by the way," The red-haired man introduced himself. "Myria's husband."

"Nice to meet you." Timothy shook hands with Sheamus and then turned to Paislee. "Should we go get our bags?"

"We can do that." Aengus, Sheamus, and Timothy headed out to the car leaving Paislee, Abby, and Myria inside.

"So how long have you two known each other?" Abby asked after a moment of silence.

"About two months."

"How did you meet?" Myria questioned.

"He was bleeding to death in an alley, and I saved him."

Both women stared at her in stunned silence, she imagined that was not what they had expected to hear.

Abby spoke first, "That's a hell of a way to meet someone." The men came in with the bags and she stood. "Come on, I'll show you to your rooms."

They followed her up some stairs and down a long hallway to two rooms at the end.

"Myria and Aengus used this as a B&B for a while," she told them as they walked. "Our daughter will bunk with us so you two will have the rooms to yourselves down here."

"Thank you, Abby, I hope we aren't going to be too much trouble."

"You won't be. Timothy is family," she said with a smile and gestured to two rooms.

Aengus and Sheamus set down her bags and then headed back downstairs. Abby smiled. "We'll leave you two to decide who gets which room. Dinner's at seven." Then she turned and disappeared down the hall.

"Shall we?" Paislee asked and pushed open the nearest door. The room was large and held a huge four poster bed covered in pale green bedding, that sat opposite of a dresser with a large mirror. She stepped further into the room and was ecstatic to see an attached bathroom and a door leading to a balcony.

The room was gorgeous. She spun in a quick circle and ran to look out over the balcony. Her view was of a large pasture where she saw horses grazing on the green grass. She'd always known Ireland was beautiful, but from where she stood now, she couldn't imagine a more magical place.

Paislee turned to see Timothy watching her from the door. The strange look on his face had her rushing to him. "Are you alright?"

He nodded. "You don't know the kind of man I

am Paislee, the things I've done would give you nightmares."

She stepped so close she could feel his breath on her face. "And just who are you, Timothy McGinley?"

"I'm bad for you."

"Don't you think I should be the one to decide that?"

"I am not a good man, Paislee."

"From where I'm standing I really don't fucking care."

"Be careful what you're asking for."

"I'm not afraid Timothy, show me who you are."

Timothy's heart pounded in his chest as he looked down at her. Paislee's eyes held nothing but understanding and a promise of a future he absolutely didn't deserve. What would she think when she got a look inside at the demons that raged within him? At the things, he had done over the years. Did he even care? Perhaps that's what scared him the most. If she knew all those things and still wanted him, he knew he would never be able to let her go.

"One day," he said and stepped away from her.

Paislee's chest heaved as she stared at the space he had occupied only moments before. The door shut, and she closed her eyes. Why would fate be so cruel as to put her in front of the only man she's ever cared for, only to make him untouchable? What was he so afraid of her seeing?

～

TIMOTHY SHUT THE DOOR GENTLY BEHIND HIM AND pressed his forehead against the smooth wood. Denying himself, Paislee was getting more difficult the more he got to know her. She was witty, smart, and had a good heart—regardless of what she seemed to think. He had meant it when he told her that he was not good for her. What could he offer her? He was a broken man. A man who wasn't sure how much longer he wanted to continue this life. Now that the curse was broken, he could die. Wasn't that what he always wanted?

He shoved his hands into the pockets of his jeans as he made his way outside. He stood for a moment and breathed in the sweet scent of his homeland. How he had missed the clean, crisp air of Ireland.

Timothy walked to the edge of the flower garden, which had been barren the last time he had seen it. Now it flourished with brightly colored petals, and herbs he imagined had been planted by Myria. She'd always had a knack for gardening.

"Hi."

Timothy turned to see Myria standing behind him. He faced her but didn't respond. She was still beautiful, just as she'd been the last time he had seen her. The years, granted she'd been frozen in time for most of them, had been kind to her. So why didn't he feel the same attraction to her now as he did back then?

"Can we talk?" She folded her hands in front of the light blue dress she wore. He nodded, and together they walked through the gate and into the garden.

"Paislee seems nice."

"She is."

"She is powerful."

"That's why we're here."

"I could sense her magic the second I walked into the room. I honestly would say she's the most powerful witch I've met. Caipre and myself included."

Timothy growled. "I'm assuming he is gone for good."

"Abby killed him two years ago when the curse was broken."

"The curse was broken two years ago?"

Myria nodded. "You didn't know?"

"Until Paislee healed me in that alley I'd assumed I was still immortal."

"It's strange, isn't it?"

"What?"

"Facing mortality again after all this time."

"I suppose it is."

"Timothy, I really am sorry. I don't understand what went wrong, it should have only affected Caipre, Aengus, Aine, and I. Not you."

"Yeah, well it did."

"And you hate me for it."

"I have for a long time, yes."

"Why didn't you ever come back? I mean, I know you said it was because you hated me, but why not return? At least let us know you were okay?"

"After I buried Cait, I spent years trying to die. I starved myself, tried to drink myself to death, fought in wars that weren't mine to fight." He laughed but it was empty. "I even climbed Mt. Everest fifteen years ago and tried to freeze to death."

"But why?"

He stopped and looked at her. "Because even after all of my anger, the pain I felt, I knew that if I came back here I would take one look at you and all would be forgiven. I knew we would all fall back into a routine like we'd had when we were younger and honestly Myria, I wasn't ready for that."

She nodded in understanding. "I hope you know that you two are more than welcome to stay as long as you like."

"Thank you, and you'll help Paislee?"

"Absolutely. I would do anything for you Timothy, you have always been one of my closest friends." Her hands fisted at her sides. "Can I hug you?"

Timothy stared at her momentarily stunned by her request and then nodded. She wrapped her arms around him and squeezed. "I'm so glad you're back," she whispered and then released him. "I need to go get my kids."

"Kids?"

She laughed. "Yes, Sheamus and I have three."

"You all have been busy."

"Never a dull moment." She turned and headed back up the path and Timothy continued to gaze out over the flowers wondering just what he was supposed to do about his feelings for Paislee.

CHAPTER 17

*T*he next day, Paislee sat in the living room with Myria. She couldn't help but feel jealous in the presence of a woman who was so beautiful, especially when the man Paislee was interested in had spent the majority of his life, pre-curse anyways, in love with her.

Timothy sat in a chair in the corner, a book in his lap. His presence alone helped calm the nerves building up inside her. What if when they started peeling back the layers of her magic, they discovered she really was a monster? That was what she was truly afraid of, wasn't she?

When it had just been her, and she was only looking for a way to kill Malcolm it hadn't mattered. But what if all those times Malcolm had told her she was not human, that she was nothing more than a murdering monster, he'd been telling the truth?

Myria smiled kindly, and Paislee wished she could

hate her. But there was something so incredibly honest and kind about her instructor, that made Paislee feel as if they'd been friends for a long time.

"Are you ready?"

"Yes. Let's do this."

"Okay, so tell me what you know about your magic."

"It's frustrating and tends to blow up at random times."

Myria let out a laugh. "Do you practice often?"

"No, because of the whole blowing up at random times thing."

"Magic has a tendency to build up if you don't use it. That's when it will randomly blow up, as you say."

"I shot a man across a bar one time because he grabbed my ass."

Timothy growled so low in his throat that Paislee knew she must have imagined it.

"So, anger is a trigger for you. Tell me, when was the first time you used your magic?"

Paislee's back straightened. Digging into her past had not been part of the deal. "I don't think that's necessary."

"It is if we are to determine the root of your fear."

"Fear?"

"Anyone who spends more than ten minutes with you can tell you are afraid of your power. If you are going to learn how to use it, then you need to address that fear and move on. Your magic is nothing to be afraid of, you should embrace the gift."

"Gift?" Paislee's cheeks reddened. "I'm sorry, I need some air." She got up and ran up the stairs and into her bedroom. Not two minutes into her training and she'd already made an idiot out of herself.

There was a knock on the door a moment before it opened, and Timothy walked in. He shut it gently behind him and turned to stare at her.

"Dredging up my past was *not* part of this whole training thing. I cannot tell her the things I've done."

"You healed an injured dog. How is that anything to be ashamed of."

Paislee shut her eyes tightly. "That was not the first time I used my magic."

"Okay," he crossed his arms. "When was the first time?"

Paislee turned to the window and stared out at the grassy hills before her. Horses grazed on the green, and Abby and Aengus were out pushing their kids on swings. She turned back to him and folded her arms.

"About two months after Malcolm kidnapped me, he started pressuring me to use my magic. Magic that I still had no idea I possessed. He kept telling me that I would be powerful because I was a virgin and that all I had to do was tap into a little of what I had."

"I refused and begged him to let me go. I told him that he had the wrong person and I was not a witch.

He was so angry with me and sent two men into my room. He told me they were going to 'teach me a lesson.'"

Timothy's jaw tightened, but she was lost in her past and paid it no notice.

"I knew they weren't going to rape me because Malcolm had told me repeatedly he was glad he'd gotten me so young, so my magic would be stronger. But they scared me, and when they got close, I held my hands up to defend myself." She shut her eyes, and a tear rolled out. "Their screams were so loud that I don't think I will ever forget it. When I opened my eyes, there was nothing but piles of ash where they used to be." She wiped the tears away again. "I was twelve, and I killed two men. They weren't even the last."

"That is not your fault Paislee. None of that is your fault."

"I'm not done."

Timothy got quiet again and listened.

"After I escaped I took it upon myself to try and lessen my power. I went to bar after bar picking up men. I lost my virginity in the bathroom of a night-club to a man whose name I can't even remember. I spent nearly two weeks screwing random strangers, my silent protest to the hold Malcolm had possessed over me for all those years."

Timothy's throat rumbled thinking of the men who'd put their hands on her. The jealousy was nearly too much for him to handle, but he stayed silent.

"I went back to this man's hotel, he was in town for business, and he seemed nice enough. But when we got there, I knew something wasn't right. His phone kept ringing, and I noticed a ring on the counter. He stepped out to answer, and I realized he was married.

I tried to leave, but he kept pulling me back in, forcing his hands on me and I got so angry that I felt something snap inside of me. When I opened my eyes, he was gone, and the only remnants of him were in a pile of ash on the floor. I am dangerous, I cannot even count the number of lives I've taken Timothy. The years I spent with Malcolm blended together in a horrible array of deaths because of me."

Timothy stepped to her and gently wiped a tear from her eye. "You are not responsible. You were a victim Paislee, a kidnapped child who was forced to do horrible things to survive."

"If I tell her that if I give her that information she is going to refuse to help me. I cannot take the horror that will be on her face afterward."

"You aren't giving Myria a lot of credit . I assure you, she is not going to be any more horrified with you than I am."

She turned her bright eyes up to him. "Are you horrified? At what I've done?"

Timothy leaned down and pressed a kiss to her cheek. It was so gentle, so incredibly sweet, and yet her body roared to life. Even with the memories swirling in her mind, she wanted him.

"Not in the least," he whispered. "You are not the only one who's done terrible things Paislee, but yours were because you were backed into a corner and had no other option. What happens when a predator is cornered?"

Her mind drifted back to that day in his office,

where she'd asked herself whether she was predator or prey.

"They attack," he said. "Don't ever feel like you are anything but a predator. You will never again be his or anyone else's prey."

He stepped away from her and closed the door gently behind him.

As it turned out, Timothy had been correct. Paislee told Myria everything as far as her magic usage was concerned. She was completely and utterly fascinated when the witch began to glow with anger at Paislee's past.

It was refreshing and made Paislee desperate to understand how to control her own power. Perhaps she wasn't a monster after all. Myria was a witch too, and she was kind.

"So, you've told me about your past and how you learned of your magic. Tell me now, what is it you fear?"

Paislee studied her face, had Myria read her thoughts? "What do you mean?"

"Everyone fears something Paislee, especially when you are thrust into a world of magic with no prior knowledge. When I learned I was a witch, I nearly killed my brother with my power. I was afraid I was turning into something horrible." She reached forward and gently touched Paislee's hand. "What are you afraid of?"

Paislee swallowed hard, it wasn't easy for her to bare her soul for others to see, and voicing her deepest fears was not anything she had ever done, at least not out loud.

Timothy had left, off to talk to Aengus she assumed, so it was only she and Myria. If anyone was going to understand, it was her.

"Malcolm used to tell me I was *inhuman*. That it wasn't kidnapping because I wasn't actually a child. He said I was a monster and with each murder I committed, regardless of whether it was self-defense, more of my soul turned down a dark path. He told me that I would never come back from who I was and that it was safer for the world if I were locked up. I suppose I believed him, and I'm afraid that the more I learn about myself, the more of a monster I will become."

"Timothy said you had been looking into magic before, were you afraid then?"

She shook her head. "I didn't have as much to lose. It was only my life on the line."

"Paislee, you have been forced to do some terrible things. I won't pacify you by denying that, but I will tell you that they were done out of self-defense. You are not to blame for trying to stay alive. You are not a monster, being a witch is a gift, not a curse." She straightened. "Now, how about we have some fun?"

Eager to learn, Paislee nodded.

"Okay, magic works off your thoughts. You have to will your power to do something, and there is no room for error." Myria held up her palm and said,

"Light." A ball of light appeared and began to float towards the ceiling before dissolving into a dozen more and eventually fading out.

"That is amazing," Paislee whispered, astounded.

"Now you try."

"With light?"

Myria shook her head. "I want you to try with fire."

"Fire? That seems dangerous."

"Just concentrate Paislee."

Paislee closed her eyes and pictured a flame dancing in her palm. "Fire," she said with conviction. The fire shot up from her hand and into the curtains. They burst into flames, and without moving, Myria conjured up water to put it out.

"I'm sorry, I'm so sorry."

"Please Paislee." She smiled. "That's not the first time those drapes have caught fire, and it probably won't be the last. When I was first getting started, I nearly brought down the house." She looked over at the still smoldering curtains. "Still maybe we should go outside just in case."

AT THE END OF THE DAY, PAISLEE HAD LEARNED HOW to conjure orbs of light, as well as to project memories inside. It had been fascinating to watch a much younger Timothy inside from one of Myria's child-hood memories.

He had been so different then, Paislee could see

the lightness of his heart and wondered just what it was over the years that had darkened him. Had it been the loss of his wife? His mortality? Or things he had witnessed during his two hundred years alone?

Myria gave her a magic text to read that contained actual incantations. Paislee was practically buzzing with excitement over it.

She was walking up the stairs to her room when she nearly ran face first into Timothy as he rounded the corner from the hall.

"Hey! I've got homework," she said with a slight smile.

He nodded. "Can I take you somewhere?"

His curt response had her concerned. "Yeah, let me put this down."

"I'll meet you downstairs."

She set her book down and headed back for the stairs. Anticipation for what Timothy wanted to show her, had her walking so fast she slipped and fell down the last four stairs on her butt.

Face red, she looked up, thankful that no one seemed to see her fall. Timothy stood just outside, hands in his pockets, staring out at the trees.

"Ready!" Paislee announced, and he turned to her.

"Right then. Let's go." He opened the door to their car for her and then walked around to climb into the driver's side.

She could see that he was tense in the way his fingers gripped the steering wheel, and his eyes stayed focused on the road. He didn't say a word the entire time they were in the car, and when he pulled into a cemetery, Paislee's heart stammered. Why were they here?

She climbed out of the car and Timothy walked silently across the grass. They passed new stones of loved ones who were recently departed, but Timothy kept moving until they reached a short wall.

He stopped, just outside of the little iron gate, and took a deep breath. Then he pushed it open and stepped into the part of the cemetery that housed those who had long since passed.

He stopped in front of a stone that had worn down due to the elements and years. Moss grew up the sides, and she knelt to get a closer look at the fading inscription.

Cait Elizabeth McGinley
Born: February 7th, 1799
Died: April 21st, 1849

Paislee covered her mouth with her hands and looked up to see Timothy staring down at the stone as if it might come to life right before his eyes. A tear rolled down his cheek, and Paislee was so stunned she didn't notice the ones falling from her eyes onto the grass.

"This is your wife."

He nodded but still didn't say anything.

Paislee got to her feet and then lightly pressed a hand to the stone.

The scenery around them changed before her eyes, and soon she was standing not in a cemetery, but in a bustling village in what Paislee guessed was the early eighteen hundreds.

She would have been shocked, had her eyes not locked on young Timothy standing only a few feet away from her.

He was watching her, and as he took a step towards her, she stepped back. What was happening?

"Cait?" He was nervous. "May I have a word?"

She nodded, unsure of what exactly was happening. Had she bumped her head when she'd fallen down the stairs?

He grinned at her, and it was completely unencumbered by the pain she'd seen in his eyes since the moment she'd met him in that alley.

"Come." He held his arm out, and she looped hers through it. "I went to see your father today."

"Did you now?" The words came out easily, as if they'd been scripted, and while it was her voice- the words were not hers.

"I went to see him to ask for your hand, Cait." He stopped and turned her. "I wish to marry you, please say yes."

"Yes!" she said loudly, and he swept her into his arms.

"You have no idea how happy you've just made me. I promise I will love you until the day I die, and then I will love you still." He kissed her cheek. "Shall we go see your parents?"

The scenery changed again, and she was standing back in the cemetery, only the gravestone in front of her was fresh.

Timothy stared down at it with a look that could only signify absolute and complete heartbreak.

Tears streamed down his cheeks, and his jaw was hard. Was this the moment? She wondered when he had lost who he was?

She couldn't help it, she reached for him just as a breeze fluttered across the cemetery and lifted a strand of hair from his face. He turned and began walking away from her.

Within moments, she was back in her time, and Timothy stood staring at her.

"Where did you go?"

She shook her head "I don't know, I just touched the stone, and I was there." She looked back down and carefully lifted her hand.

"Did you cast a spell?"

She looked back at him and saw that he was angry, what the hell did he have to be angry about? It's not like she purposely sent herself two centuries into the past!

"No, I don't know what happened. I touched the stone, and then I was somewhere else. Or rather, some-*when* else."

"What did you see?"

"You. I saw you propose to Cait."

"Did you get a good show?"

"Timothy, I didn't do it on purpose-" She stepped towards him, but he moved away.

"I brought you here to share a part of myself with you. A part that I haven't let anyone see, and instead of letting me explain it to you in my own time, you stole it." He turned and headed back towards the car. Paislee ran for him, but when she grabbed his arm, he yanked it away.

"Timothy, I didn't do it on purpose! I swear!"

"You witches never do anything on purpose, do you? Nothing is ever your fault!" He threw the keys at her. "Take yourself back," he growled and walked the other way.

"This is bullshit." She stomped her foot and

headed back towards the stone. He wanted to accuse her of something, *fine*. But she was damn well going to get more out of it than two memories.

She fell to the ground in front of the stone, and pressed both hands to the inscription, "You want to talk Cait?" she murmured and imagined herself stepping into the life of Timothy's wife.

"I do not think I can bear a child, Timothy." She felt the pain and heartbreak as she stared up at Timothy, once again viewing the scene from Cait's point of view. A tear slipped down her cheek and onto her hand, and Timothy knelt before her.

He lifted her hands and kissed them gently. "My love, I will love you whether we have children or not, you are enough for me."

Paislee felt Cait's lip quiver as Timothy wrapped his arms around her. She leaned against him and then suddenly he was gone. She opened her eyes to see him pacing in front of her.

"Timothy, calm yourself. I am sure there is an explanation."

"I know there's an explanation Cait, I was cursed! Myria cursed me just as she did herself and Aengus!"

"Perhaps but getting angry won't solve it."

"What do you expect me to do? Do you understand what this means?"

She laughed lightly. "That one day you'll be married to an old woman."

"That's not funny."

"My dear Timothy." She stood and walked to him. "Everything will be fine."

"I won't get to grow old with you, and I cannot fathom a life without you in it."

"We will figure it out, there has to be a way." She lifted to her toes and kissed his cheek. *"We will find a way."*

The memory faded, and Paislee found herself lying in a bed staring up at Timothy who cried over her.

"You cannot leave, me my love. I'm not ready to be alone."

"You will never be alone." Her voice was old, shaky, and Paislee barely had the strength to lift her hand to Timothy's cheek.

"You will not be here, that means I will be alone."

"You have to promise me your life is not over Timothy. Promise me you will find another and love her as you did me, that you will have the children I was not able to give you."

"Cait-"

Paislee's vision began to fade as a feeling of peace filled her. She opened her eyes, and she was kneeling back in front of the gravestone, only she wasn't alone.

"What the?" She shot to her feet, and Cait smiled at her.

"I see why he loves you," she said gently.

"Excuse me?"

"He may not understand just yet, but one day he will. He's always been stubborn."

"What? How? Why?"

"Easy Paislee, I am glad you came."

"Timothy brought me."

"I had hoped he would. It was the only way I could speak with you."

It amazed Paislee, just how real Cait appeared. She had always believed a ghost would be transparent and look *dead*. But the woman before her appeared very much alive. She wore a green dress, her red hair braided down her back, her eyes were a bright green. It shocked her to see the woman in the painting come to life before her eyes. She could see the similarities between them, but Cait had a beauty that Paislee knew she wouldn't have been able to achieve regardless of makeup. It wasn't that she didn't consider herself pretty, she actually had a very healthy opinion of herself, Cait was just more *graceful.*

"How are we talking?"

She smiled. "I've been waiting to move on, I needed to be sure he would be okay."

"Is that what you wanted to speak to me about?"

Cait sighed,."I love him Paislee, I always have loved him, but I need him to be okay."

"What do you want me to do?"

"Love him."

"Listen, Timothy is a stubborn ass, and I'm fairly certain he wants nothing to do with me."

"Oh Paislee, you couldn't be more wrong. Timothy may be a stubborn ass, as you say, but he is the most wonderful, caring, loving man you will ever know if only you'll give him a chance."

"Did you not see the way he walked away from me just now?"

"He's hurting, he hasn't been back here since the day after I died." Her eyes filled and Paislee wondered if ghosts actually cried. "He's coming."

Paislee looked behind her to see Timothy walking back towards them, and then looked back to Cait who was watching him with longing.

"Love him, Paislee." She faded away, and Paislee turned around just as Timothy reached her.

"Look, I'm sorry."

She grinned. "Thanks for not making me walk, which I would have since I have never actually driven a car."

To her surprise, he smiled back. "Hadn't considered that. I suppose it's a good thing I came back."

CHAPTER 18

"Good, you guys are back," Myria greeted them from inside the door. "I found something on that necklace you told me about." From the look on her face, Timothy could see that whatever it was she'd discovered, was not good. Then again, how could there be anything good about an item that drains witches not only of their magic but their existence as well?

They followed her into the living area where Aengus sat.

"What is it?" Paislee asked as she took a seat on the large couch. Her hands were white from squeezing them out of fear, so Timothy reached over and grabbed one. It was meant to be a simple gesture, a way for him to make her feel better. But as soon as his fingers interlaced with hers, he felt a charge go through his body. Something that whispered *there she is*.

Myria turned the book in her hands around to show them a drawing. "Is this the necklace?"

"Yes," Timothy responded since the very sight of it had Paislee turning pale.

"The *mortem auguratricis* is one of the most sought-after magical items because it grants its wearer limitless magical capabilities. Once the gemstone has connected with a magical creature, the connection remains until said creature loses all magical abilities."

Paislee leaned forward, and Timothy squeezed her hand. "What does that mean?"

"It means that the necklace *knows* Paislee now. It will actively search for her magic, and as soon as she is in range, it's going to start pulling from her. The first time it has to be triggered by an incantation."

"What is considered its range?" Aengus wondered.

Myria shrugged. "I wish I knew. It could be a few feet or a few miles."

"When he had me before," Paislee's voice was shaky, and she took a deep breath to steady it. "I was behind the iron bars, so they pulled my hand on the other side. I wasn't touching it, but I was close enough to have grabbed it if I wanted."

"So that may mean that you have to be very close to it for it to harm you."

"But you don't know for sure." It wasn't a question, and Timothy was not about taking risks. Especially not when it came to Paislee.

"No. The only other thing the text says is that in order for the connection to be broken, the necklace has to be destroyed. But in destroying it, you may destroy the person connected as well."

Timothy released Paislee's hand and began to pace. "So, it's possible that the second we step back in Boston, Malcolm will be able to start draining Paislee, and in order to break this connection and make it so she's safe, we have to destroy the necklace that may very well kill her?"

Myria closed the book. "Sounds like a win-win doesn't it?" she said sarcastically.

"I will come back with you," Aengus spoke again. "I can help you with Malcolm."

Timothy shook his head. "I'm not risking bringing you back with me. If he gets wind of you, he will dig, and if he does that, it won't be long before he finds your family."

"I cannot just leave you to fend for yourself. You helped me when Aine was taken."

"Aengus," Timothy said gently. "Aine was family to me too, and that was different."

"How so?"

"Caipre was an enemy we knew. We understood what he was after. I have no idea what it is Malcolm Gentry wants. I cannot risk you or your family."

"This is bull shit," Aengus said angrily and stormed out.

"He will be fine," Myria added. "What do you know of Malcolm?" she asked Paislee, whose color had returned.

"Other than the fact that he's a psycho? I know

that he's been trying to collect magical items for years now. I just never actually thought any existed."

"So, he's had that necklace for years, why only now use it on you?"

Timothy considered that for a moment, the thought had crossed his mind as well. Malcolm had been in possession of it since the day he'd kidnapped her, so why not use it then? "I believe it was because he was trying to build her power. He needed her to be strong enough to not die the first time he drained her. After all, what good would that do if his power source died?"

"True," Myria considered. "Perhaps he wasn't ready just yet. Maybe there was something else he was looking for as well. I'm curious Timothy, why come after you? It was a big risk for him to send someone after you."

"The man who shot me told me *'he was wrong about you.'* Which led me to believe he suspected I was immortal."

"Okay, but why?"

"Paislee said it was because he loved antiques and I would be a living one." He smirked at her and to his relief, a small smile crossed her lips.

"It has to be more than that. What did *he* have to gain by obtaining someone who was immortal?"

"Can't it just be that he's insane?" Paislee asked.

"It could, but I doubt it," Myria responded. "Is there anything else you can tell me? Anything at all about objects he was interested in?"

Paislee thought back on the years she'd been in his

possession, had he said anything that might give them an idea of what he was after? She shook her head, "I can't remember anything in particular."

"Okay, I'll keep digging," Myria offered.

"I'm going to go talk with Aengus." Timothy got to his feet.

As soon as he was outside, Paislee leaned in and lowered her voice, "Myria something strange happened today."

"What's that?"

"Timothy took me to his wife's grave. I touched the stone, and it was as if I was transported back in time. I was standing in a village, and it was like I was *her*."

"What happened in the vision?"

"He proposed to me, well her. And then moments later I was transported again and was telling him that I couldn't have any children."

"Were those the only two?"

"No, the next memory was him discovering he was immortal and wouldn't age. After that it was me, I mean her, on her deathbed, and then a vision of Timothy standing in the gravesite staring down at her grave."

"Interesting."

"That's not even the craziest part."

Myria lifted her eyes to look at Paislee.

"I met *her*."

"Timothy's late wife?"

Paislee nodded. "When the last vision was over, she was standing in front of me smiling. She told me that she wanted to speak with me. That she needed Timothy to be okay, and that I should-"

"Should what?"

Paislee bit down on the inside of her cheek. "That I should love him."

Myria leaned back in her seat. "That's very interesting. You spoke with a woman who's been dead for nearly two centuries."

"Just tell me I'm insane."

Myria let out a laugh. "You are not insane. Graveyards are powerful. Think about all the powerful emotions that are woven into that ground. The sadness, fear, loneliness, and love."

"So, because the ground is powerful I got visions of a dead woman?"

"No, my best guess is that Cait was a witch."

"What? There's no way. Timothy *despised* witches and all magic. No way he would have married one."

"It's quite possible that he didn't know."

"Myria there has to be another explanation."

"I'll look into it, but that would be my best guess."

"So then how was she with me today? Even if she was a witch, she's a dead one. So how could she reach out to me?"

"I'll need to look into it further. But it's quite possible you share a bloodline somewhere along your family lineage."

Paislee stood. "So not only was Timothy's late wife a witch, but we might be related?"

"It's possible."

"This is insanity."

"I will look into it for you."

"Thanks."

"Not a problem. If I were you, I would be honest with Timothy about what happened today. If I learned anything about him when we were young, it's that he doesn't like being misled or only given half-truths."

"I'll talk to him," Paislee responded as Timothy and Aengus, who now looked in a much better mood, came in.

"Talk to who?" Timothy asked her.

"You."

"Is everything alright?"

"Let's go for a walk." Paislee had no interest in being embarrassed in front of her new friends if Timothy got angry again. Besides, this way she could yell at him too.

Timothy and Paislee walked out towards the flower garden and stopped in front of the gate. "I need you to know that I'm not saying any of this to hurt you, and I need you to listen to the very end."

"Okay." He crossed his arms over his chest.

Paislee began by telling him about the first vision when she touched the stone, as she continued she watched carefully for any sign of anger on Timothy's face. Instead, he was completely and totally emotionless as she talked about what she'd experienced. When she got to the last part, she skipped over the *'he loves you'* and *'you should love him'* parts and just told him that Cait had loved him, but that she needed him to be okay.

Afterward, she stopped and studied him carefully.

"You are telling me that my late wife, sent you visions of our past and then spoke directly to you."

"Yes."

"And you cast no spell?"

"No, I didn't. I wouldn't even know where to begin to conjure up someone else's memories."

"Was there anything else?"

She took a deep breath, this was the part she had feared the most. "Complete honesty?"

He nodded.

"Myria believes Cait may have been a witch, and that somewhere along the way we may share some DNA. That's how she believes Cait was able to contact me."

"Are you fucking kidding me? Cait was not a witch!" His face went red, and Paislee instinctively took a step away.

"She doesn't know for sure, Timothy. And no one is accusing her of anything. It could very well be that it was just the power in the ground or whatever Myria said."

"I need to be alone."

"Okay. I'm sorry Timothy, I just thought you should know."

He nodded, and she headed back towards the house.

❧

A WITCH? THEY WANTED HIM TO BELIEVE HIS CAIT

had been a witch? Were they fucking kidding? There was no way he could have been married to someone for thirty years and *not* known they possessed the same magical powers he despised.

And why would she talk to Paislee and not him? If she was there and was a witch, why the hell couldn't she have spoken to him too?

He climbed into his car and pulled out of the drive. There was no way she was a witch, and he hadn't known about it. Surely, she wouldn't have kept that from him.

He drove to the cemetery and made his way back to Cait's grave. "If you're here Cait I want to talk to you."

Nothing happened, and Timothy balled his hands into fists. "So, you can talk to a stranger, but not to the man who's loved you every day since he met you? Who's loved you even since you've been gone?"

Nothing but a small breeze. "Fuck it then." He turned to head back to his car just as the wind picked up.

"I've missed you," a voice he knew all too well sounded behind him, and Timothy turned slowly. She was so beautiful, just as she'd been every single day of her life. The gown she wore was a soft green that contrasted perfectly with her red hair that was braided down her back. She smiled, and his heart ached to hold her.

"How are you here?"

"We can get to that," she responded, and he

stepped closer. "Paislee is a nice woman." She said with a sad smile. "I'm truly glad you have her."

"We're only friends."

"Don't be ridiculous, Timothy, I know you too well for you to lie to me." She smiled.

"I'm not, nothing has happened between us."

"Why are you holding back?"

"I can never love anyone else Cait, you were it for me."

"Then you are foolish. I am gone Timothy, have been for a long time, and while it saddens me to think of you with someone else, you have to move on too."

"Are you a witch?"

She hesitated but then nodded. "Yes."

"Why didn't you ever tell me? Why keep it a secret?" He was hurt, angry even, but inside he felt as if he'd always known on some level, even if he hadn't wanted to admit it. How else had she been able to help so many people other healers had turned away?

"You had told me of Myria, of the power she possessed and of how you had loved her. At first, I didn't want to be compared to her. I didn't want you to think of her every time I did any sort of magic. After that, it became a secret out of fear that you would leave me if you found out."

"How could you think that?"

"Because after you discovered you were immortal, you made it very clear you hated all things magic."

His eyes widened. "Why didn't you make yourself immortal? So, we could stay together?"

"If I had done that, it would have been unfair to you."

"How would that have been unfair to me? What was unfair to me was having to watch you die!"

"Timothy, I knew no such spell. And had I managed to cast it, you wouldn't have been able to be here today, so you could protect Paislee."

"That's bull shit."

"I had a vision shortly after we married. It was of you, shielding a young witch with your body while a blast of magic hit you. Because of your immortality, you didn't die, but she would have."

"Well, seeing as how I am no longer immortal, I don't see how that is going to happen." He stuffed his hands into his pockets.

"My visions may not happen exactly how they appeared, but they were never wrong."

"Why did you talk to Paislee earlier and not me?"

"You weren't ready to talk to me."

"It was three hours ago, what would have made than any different from now?"

"I knew Paislee would talk to Myria about what happened, in which case she would tell you, and I had hoped you would come back."

"You based a lot on assumptions."

"Or perhaps I just know you very well."

"I miss you, Cait."

"I miss you too, Timothy. But you have to move on, for both of us. I cannot move into the afterlife while I know you are suffering."

"You've been here for two hundred years?"

"It passed much quicker for me, but yes."

They stayed silent for a moment, staring at each other. "Are you and Paislee related? Is that how you were able to contact her?"

"Not related by blood. But by spirit."

"What does that mean?"

"Our magic."

"So, you were able to contact her because of your magic?" She nodded. "Why show her those particular memories?"

She smiled. "Because each one showed the man, you truly are. Beneath this façade, you show the world."

"I'm not the same man anymore ."

"You are still the man I fell in love with, the best man I've ever known."

He shook his head. "You're wrong, I don't deserve her."

Cait reached forward and gently touched his cheek. "I know all you have ever done Timothy, I've seen it all in dreams since the day I died. You are a good man, and you deserve every happiness in the world. Why do you deny yourself love, when it's so plainly in front of you?"

"I don't know what you mean."

She smiled. "Oh Timothy, love her as you loved me. You both deserve it."

She started to fade away, but he put his hand up. "Wait, please."

"It's time for me to go now,. I will always love you." She faded out of sight, and Timothy fell to his knees unsure of how he should feel. The fact that she was gone again pained him, but the weight off his shoulders somehow felt lighter. She was okay, and wanted him to be happy, so what did that mean for him? For the first time in two centuries, he felt a feeling of peace wash over him as he got to his feet and headed back to Paislee.

CHAPTER 19

*D*etective Peter Reilly sat at his desk staring down at the crime scene photos before him. He had researched heavily into Jessica Crew's background and found nothing that would have gotten her killed.

Especially not so violently. She'd been a kind, hard-working woman who everyone adored. *So why was she dead?* What ties did her death have to Timothy McGinley? The man was not a suspect, he had an alibi and to top it off Peter had seen the devastation on his face at the sight of his secretary.

He was good at reading people, and McGinley had cared for the woman. So why was she dead? He asked himself again. After typing some notes on his keyboard, he pulled up the security tape from the coffee house again. The location of her body proved it had to have something to do with the antiquities dealer. Who else would go through the trouble of sealing a body into a crate?

They could see the back of the truck, but no one ever touches it. But it *had* to have happened in that parking lot. After that, the truck was on the move, and the crates weren't touched at the airfield when they arrived.

She had been spotted out to dinner three hours before her time of death.

There was no way their victim could have gotten to China, been killed, and shipped back in the matter of a few hours.

"Wait a minute," he muttered and leaned in closer, there was a shadow on the ground near the back of the truck, and Peter was sure he'd seen a flash of light. Was it possible this video had been tampered with?

"You still here?"

Peter looked up to see his partner standing next to his desk. She looked tired, as if she'd been up all night. He couldn't blame her, this one was eating away at him too.

"I think I might have found something."

"Oh yeah?" She stepped around his desk and leaned in.

Peter forced his eyes forward, he was a happily married man, had been for twenty-one years now, but Madeline Shultz knew zero boundaries as far as where she put her chest.

"Right here." He pointed to the shadow and then

the light that flashed almost immediately after. "Did you see that?"

"Barely." She straightened, and he could see she was thinking. "Were the videos tampered with?"

"That's what I was thinking."

"Tomorrow we need to check with the tech team and have them take a look at them."

He looked at the time, it was well after ten, and he knew nothing else would get done until the morning.

"Yeah, I need to head home. Mildred is going to yell at me if I pull an all-nighter again."

Schultz laughed. "Yeah and I've got a hot date."

"At ten p.m.?"

"Hey, I don't judge you for your monthly board game night."

He shrugged and grabbed his coat. "I suppose that's true."

They walked down to the parking garage together before they went their separate ways. "See you in the morning," he said, and Schultz waved before heading over to where her motorcycle was parked.

Peter was nearly to his car when hands grabbed him. He felt a sharp pain and clutched at his throat, horrified to see his blood on his hands. He crumpled to the ground as a face came into view, but his vision was blurry, and he couldn't make out who it was. His body grew numb and cold as he bled and within moments he was dead.

Timothy sat on the front porch as the sun rose over the trees. The splashes of orange and yellow filled the sky and he smiled.

Yesterday had been harder than he ever could have imagined. Having everything he had thought he knew about Cait being ripped away, only to discover she had been a witch all along had been nearly more than he could take.

And yet, to see her standing there, looking just like she had the day he'd asked her to marry him, had been therapeutic to his soul.

He looked up to see Myria's husband walking towards him. Timothy started to get up but decided he'd stay. After all, he'd been ignoring the man since the day they arrived here.

"Morning." Sheamus stopped in front of Timothy and crossed his arms.

"Morning, Sheamus."

"I wanted to speak with you."

Timothy scooted over so Sheamus could sit next to him on the porch.

"I know that you have some issue with me, but I'm not sure I understand why. Myria tells me I should let it go, that you've been through a lot, but I didn't do a damn thing to you."

Timothy smiled and took a drink of his coffee. "Did Myria ever mention me?"

"She did. She told me you had all grown up together, and that you were with them the night Aine died."

Timothy nodded. "Did she also tell you I was in love with her?"

His eyes widened. "She did not."

"I came to her one day after everything had happened and I told her how I felt. That I cared for her past the bounds of friendship, she told me that her happiness didn't matter and that the only thing she could focus on now, was making sure Aine found her way back to Aengus."

Sheamus stayed silent.

"I was angry at her for that, until I met my Cait."

"I'm sorry, I didn't know any of that."

Timothy slapped Sheamus on the back. "It's all in the past now, and I believe I should be the one to apologize for the way I acted with you. I cannot tell you how happy it makes me to see Myria happy. Both she and Aengus meant so much to me, and I will be forever grateful that they got their happy endings."

"What about you?"

Timothy's face darkened. "Not everyone gets their happy endings . Sometimes a person's soul is too dark for that." He stood and walked inside leaving Sheamus staring out over the grass.

Timothy was just starting up the stairs when his phone rang. He saw it was Ashton and answered quickly, "McGinley."

"We got a problem."

"What's that?"

"One of my guys was trailing the two detectives. He was sitting outside the parking structure when

Detective Schultz left, but when her partner didn't emerge, he went in. Detective Peter Reilly is dead."

"Dead? How?"

"Looks like the same person who killed Jess got him too. He was dead by the time my guy got in there."

"Fuck." Timothy pinched the bridge of his nose. Not only was the detective dead, which was a tragedy in itself, but they were going to be breathing down his neck now since he was directly involved in an investigation regarding a McGinley Antiquities employee. They were going to need to get back.

"Get me my plane. Paislee and I will head back tonight."

"You got it, boss."

Timothy hung up the phone and finished his walk up the stairs. He stopped in front of Paislee's room, and lightly knocked on the wood.

Moments later, she pulled the door open looking sleepy-eyed and absolutely gorgeous.

"What is it?" she asked and rubbed her eyes.

"We need to head back tonight."

"Tonight?"

Timothy nodded. "Some things have come up." Since he hadn't told her about Jess yet, he wasn't sure this would be the best time to explain what those things were.

"Okay." She looked disappointed but disappeared back into her room.

∼

Timothy had just finished hauling his bags down when Myria approached him.

"Leaving?"

"We need to get back to Boston, something has come up."

"Will we see you again?"

He straightened and focused on her. Her eyes were wide, her jaw set. He knew that look well, Myria was upset and didn't want to show it.

He nodded. "I'm sure you will."

She smiled. "Good." Myria lowered her voice to just above a whisper. "Timothy, Paislee is not a typical witch."

"What's that supposed to mean?"

"Most witches have a specific set of magic inside them. Light, for instance, would give them the ability to control light and in some cases, heal."

"Yes, I know that."

"Paislee has both light and dark magic inside her. Which means not only can she heal, she can destroy. The only other person I knew to possess both, was Caipre."

Timothy's body went stiff. "She is nothing like that monster."

"I know she's not." Myria gently touched his arm. "Paislee is a good person Timothy. I never said she wasn't. I only mentioned Caipre so you would know what magic she is capable of. Caipre may have been a monster, but he was an incredibly powerful one." She lifted a stack of books from a table and handed them to him. "She needs to study these. I've given her a baseline how to as far as using her magic, but she needs to learn to control it."

"Thank you, Myria."

She nodded. "It's been so wonderful to see you again Timothy. I hope that one day you find what you're looking for."

Before he could ask what that meant, Paislee came down the stairs with her suitcase. It struck him then, how incredibly beautiful she was. Not just in looks, but in her spirit. The light within her seemed to call out to even the darkest corners of his soul, making it nearly impossible to resist her.

"Thank you for everything Myria." Paislee hugged Myria, then Aengus, Abby, and Sheamus came into the room.

"You are more than welcome Paislee. Call me if you ever need anything."

"Will do."

They said the rest of their goodbyes and then climbed into the car. Timothy was silent for the duration of the drive to the private airport they had flown into only days before.

"Welcome, Mr. McGinley. Miss Adams," the pilot and co-pilot greeted them as they came on board.

"Thanks," she said and walked over to the couch. She was exhausted and ready for a nap.

"We'll be taking off in just a few moments." The captain told them and then disappeared into the cockpit.

"I need to tell you something." Timothy decided

to take her 'honesty is the best policy' approach and fill her in on what was going on.

He just hoped she wouldn't be too pissed off at him.

"What is it?"

"Malcolm killed Jess."

She sat up slowly and stared at him, "Jess?" she repeated, her eyes filling. "She's dead?"

He nodded, and Paislee got to her feet. "When?"

"The day we rescued you."

"Before you got me?" her voice shook.

"Yes."

"I'm so sorry Timothy." She touched his shoulder gently.

"It's not your fault. I know you two had gotten close."

"She is dead because you got involved with me."

"I don't think that's it. I think he was coming for me anyway. I'm just sorry Jess got caught in the crosshairs."

"Me too. She was so sweet, I was just getting to know her."

"He will pay for what he's done." Paislee's fingers began to spark, and Timothy took her hands to calm her and then he smiled, although there was no humor in it.

"I know he will. Oh, poor Ashton, how is he?"

"Holding up, I think he's holding it together until he can get his revenge. It seems we're all out for blood."

"So, you knew then? That he had a thing for her?"

"I made it my mission to know about my employees, and I've known Ashton and Jess for quite a long time." *Knew Jess,* he reminded himself. He still wasn't used to the idea of his life without her in it. She had become a staple in McGinley Antiquities.

CHAPTER 20

*M*alcolm walked towards his house with a spring in his step. London had proved to be a completely beneficial trip. He hadn't been able to get his hands on the exact item he'd been looking for, but he had been able to obtain some texts that should help to point him in the right direction. Plus, he had added another item to his collection, and he was sure it would prove to be quite useful in the coming weeks.

Either way, the country was beautiful, and he and Lindsay had enjoyed themselves for the week.

They pushed open the front door and immediately assaulted with the stench of death. His guards rushed around him and into the house and began clearing rooms leaving them in the foyer to assess the scene around them.

"What the hell happened? Did *she* get out?" Lindsay accused.

"These men were shot, Paislee would not have been able to take them all down with bullets alone. She must have had help."

"McGinley."

"Yes." Malcolm felt the blinding rage digging its fingers into him. That man had been getting in his way entirely too often as of late.

"The witch is gone," one of the guards announced as he made his way down the stairs.

"Would you mind explaining to me how my house was attacked when *your* men were on duty?" Malcolm turned to the now wide-eyed guard.

"Sir, I assure you they would have done all they could to keep your location secure."

"It seems to me that if they had done all they could, this wouldn't have happened."

"Sir-"

Malcolm held his hand up and allowed the power from the necklace to build in his body. He then released a blast of magic that turned the man before him into dust.

Lindsay laughed darkly.

Malcolm smiled.

CHAPTER 21

They exited the plane and were immediately greeted by Ashton. Paislee ran to him and gave him a loud kiss on the cheek. "Thank you for saving me."

Ashton grinned. "Anytime."

"Anything new?" Timothy asked as he shook Ashton's hand.

The guard shook his head. "My contact said the Gentry's arrived back at the house today, but as far as the detective I haven't heard anything."

"Detective?" Paislee asked as they climbed into the SUV that had been waiting for them on the airstrip.

"The detective who had been looking into Jess's murder was killed in a parking garage," Timothy answered.

"Oh no." She ground her teeth together, bodies were piling up, and they all started with her.

"It's not your fault," Timothy reminded her and then turned back to Ashton.

She let them drone on as they drove, and it wasn't until they were pulling into a parking garage she didn't recognize, that she spoke up.

"Where are we?"

"My apartment."

"Why are we here?"

"Because they found a way to get into my office and I really don't want to risk you being there alone."

"Oh." *What would his space be like?* She wondered. Would it be just like his office? Filled with old antiques and completely organized?

"Garth is here too."

She smiled and climbed out of the car after him.

They rode the elevator up with Ashton and then stepped onto a small entryway. There were only two doors, and Ashton headed for one.

"This is the back entrance," Timothy explained. "Ashton has an office just over there."

"Ashton," she called just before he shut the door He leaned back out, and she could see the pain he was trying to hide in his eyes.

She walked over to him. "I'm so sorry about Jess. She cared for you deeply."

He sighed. "I shouldn't have waited as long as I did. If I had told her how I felt perhaps things would have turned out differently. I could have protected her."

"It's not your fault, you were both afraid of jeopardizing your work relationship."

He smiled emptily. "Well, I suppose it's jeopardized anyways, isn't it?"

She wrapped her arms around him. "She loved you Ashton and hopefully knowing that will bring you some peace."

"Thank you, Paislee."

She nodded and walked back over to where Timothy waited for her.

"That was nice of you," he said quietly.

"It was the truth, she loved him."

He typed in a code, and they stepped into the large open space. The living area and kitchen were completely open and about triple the size of his office. It wasn't decorated with antiques, but rather what looked to be incredibly expensive artwork. A grey couch sat in front of an impressive fireplace, and a large television hung on the wall next to it.

It was a place she could absolutely relax in.

She heard a meow and dropped to the ground to greet Garth, who was padding over to her. "Hey, buddy! I missed you!" She lifted him and carried him to the couch, before dropping down on the soft cushions and petting him. "Timothy, this is gorgeous."

"Thank you." He walked over to a set of monitors hanging on the wall near where they'd come in, and she him check through the footage from when they'd been gone. "If you like, I will show you to your room."

"Yes, please. I'm exhausted." And she hadn't had the chance to cry about Jess, which was something she had no intention of doing in front of the steel backed man before her. "So how many bedrooms is this place?" she asked as they walked up a few stairs and down a hallway.

"Two."

"Which one do I get? I'm exhausted."

"The couch is incredibly comfortable."

She eyed him, grateful for his attempt to lighten the mood. "Then I guess you will sleep well." She followed him over to a door and gaped when he pushed it open revealing a large bedroom. "This is massive!"

A huge sleigh bed with an emerald green comforter sat against one wall, and directly across from that was a large armoire that after further inspection, Paislee saw it boasted a TV as well. Large doors opened to a balcony that looked over the harbor. She pulled them open and took a deep breath as the breeze lifted the hair from her neck. The salty air filled her lungs as she breathed deeply. Man, it felt good to be home. Boston would always be her home no matter what happened to her within its limits.

"This is the guest room, is it to your liking?"

She turned to see him leaning in the doorway, his mouth turned up in a lopsided grin. It made her heart stumble in her chest to see him standing there that way. What had changed between them? She wondered. Had it been the kiss? The tenderness he'd shown her the night he'd rescued her? Whatever it was, Paislee couldn't help but wonder if he felt it too.

"Absolutely." She grinned back.

"I figured." He smiled. "I'll be down the hall in my office if you need me."

"Thank you."

With a single nod, he disappeared out of the door leaving Paislee standing alone. She turned back towards the bed, aching to feel the softness of the sheets on her skin. She was exhausted and figured closing her eyes for only a few moments wouldn't be a bad idea.

Once she was buried under the covers, she closed her eyes and drifted into the sweet abyss that accompanied sleep.

TIMOTHY RUBBED HIS EYES AND STARED AT THE computer screen that held the images of the items for their upcoming auction. It seemed wrong, planning something so scheduled for their monthly event without Jess to help him with the details. But the best thing they could do now was keep business as usual.

Malcolm would pay for what he'd done to her, Timothy would make sure of it, and the longer it took, the angrier he got. Ashton had taken care of finding homes for Jess's animals and had carefully packaged her things. She'd had no family, but per her request, she would be cremated, and Timothy would make sure her ashes were spread over Lake Tahoe like she'd written in her will.

Just as soon as the damn investigation was over, they could lay her to rest. But who knew when that would be. With Detective Reilly's murder, things would be taking another turn he was sure of it.

The phone rang, and Timothy lifted it to his ear.

"I'm here, got what you asked for."

"Come on up."

Minutes later, the elevator dinged, and Ashton stepped out. He handed Timothy a small black box, and Timothy opened it to reveal an iron cuff. His hope was that it would protect Paislee should Malcolm get close enough to use the amulet on her.

"Thanks, Ashton."

"No problem."

"Anything new?" Timothy set the box down and walked to his mini bar where he poured two fingers of whiskey into two glasses, then handed one of them to his friend.

"Not yet. We haven't been contacted by the other detective yet, but I imagine it's coming." He took a drink.

Timothy nodded and walked to the window that faced the harbor. "We have to find a way to get to Malcolm. Part of me thinks we should just storm his house and take them all out."

"Unlikely that would be a successful mission."

"Especially not with the amulet. Our best bet is to wait it out until we have more information, but dammit if I'm impatient."

Ashton let out a laugh that had Timothy turning towards him. "You are over two hundred years old, now is not the time to lose that patience you've acquired throughout those years."

"I suppose you're right." Timothy smiled and downed the rest of his drink. "Send Jake over tomorrow, I don't want to leave Paislee alone, but I need him to set up the rest of the items for the auction."

"Will do." Ashton walked towards the elevator. "We'll get him, boss."

"I know we will." The doors closed, and Timothy turned to see Paislee standing in the doorway to the bedroom. Her red hair was loose around her face, but the curls were wild just as the eyes that were looking at him now.

His mouth watered as he took her in, she wore nothing but a tank top and shorts, and although he had done his best to not see her naked body when he'd helped her wash, he had still felt it pressed against him.

Blood pounding in his veins, Timothy forced himself to look away. "I'm calling out for dinner, I was thinking Chinese if you're interested."

"That sounds great."

He nodded without looking back at her. "Get a good sleep in?"

"Yes, the bed is really comfortable."

"Good." He headed back down the hall towards his office, needing to put as much distance between himself and the fiery redhead that was currently burrowing herself past his defenses.

Paislee watched him walk away, irritated at herself for believing, if even for a moment- that he was going to cross the distance between them. Then, she was angry at herself for not just doing it anyway.

She heard the door to his office shut, and it angered her further. The mixed signals he was giving off was giving her a headache especially when she knew exactly what she wanted- *him*.

Without putting too much thought into it, Paislee walked down the hall to his office, and after taking a deep breath pushed the door open. He turned away from the window he had been looking out of, and they stood staring at each other, the air pregnant with tension.

Her blood pounded in her ears, making it impossible to hear him when he said her name as she began moving towards him on legs that felt as if they might give out any second.

She stopped just on the other side of his desk, so they were so close she could all but feel his heart as it thundered in his chest.

"I'm not a good man, Paislee," he reminded her.

"I don't care."

"You will." He warned just before slamming his mouth down onto hers. Teeth nipped at her bottom lip begging to be allowed inside. She opened her mouth and buried her hands in his hair. She didn't hear the items on his desk being thrown to the floor, all she could hear was her own heart pounding and her body begging for release.

His hands trailed down to her ass, and he lifted her onto his desk and pressed between her legs that wrapped around his waist. Fingers gripped the front of his shirt, and she ripped, sending buttons flying in all directions.

Paislee splayed her fingers on his hard chest, feeling the muscles below. Her heart skipped when she could feel them trembling underneath her palm, Timothy was a beast who had been kept chained, and she was finally setting him free.

He lifted the tank over her head and growled deep in his chest at the site of her bare breasts. A rough hand cupped her, and her head fell back on a moan when he pulled a taut nipple into his mouth.

She gripped his hair and arched back into him, wrapping her legs harder around him so she could feel his hardness against her.

When he released her, she slid off the desk and trailed her lips and tongue down his chest and stomach until she reached his waist. Holding his gaze, she lowered to her knees and began to work on his belt.

His pants fell, and he sprang free, and Paislee leaned forward to press a kiss to the very tip of him. He groaned as she took him into her mouth his hands buried in her hair for a moment before pulling her back to her feet. He took her mouth again as he lifted her back onto his desk and removed the shorts she wore.

She leaned back onto his desk and wrapped her legs around him, so he moved closer. He watched her face as he buried himself deep into where she ached for him and had been aching since the moment she'd met him, she realized.

"Timothy," she moaned as he drove her closer to the edge she'd never quite reached before. She reached for his head and caught a glimpse of her hand. Her skin was illuminated. It would have frightened her if Timothy hadn't lifted her, so their foreheads were touching. When she was with him, the world could come apart at the seams, and she wouldn't worry. He was her rock, her shield, and if need be her sword.

Just before they reached their release, he kissed her again, and Paislee couldn't see anything but him.

"Paislee," he groaned, and the room erupted with light just as he collapsed on top of her.

Their breathing was ragged, their bodies coated in sweat as they tried to regain control. Paislee had had sex before. She'd even enjoyed it a few times. But she had never experienced the mind-blowing, body shattering, raw and primal fuck that she'd just had with Timothy.

He had completely shattered her, and she would be picking up the pieces for a long time to come.

"Shit, I'm hurting you." He stood, leaving her lying on her back on top of his desk. He looked down at her and growled low in his throat. "That's a sight I could get used to." He trailed his fingertips down between her breasts and to her navel, stopping just below it. "Are you hungry?" He pulled her to her feet, and she leaned against his chest, still having difficulty catching her breath.

"I could eat."

"I'll make us something." He pulled her out into the hall and towards the kitchen.

"You can cook?"

He snorted. "I've been alive a long time, I picked up a few skills."

Paislee grinned at the humor in his voice, it was nice to see him smile. She watched him, both of them completely nude, as he prepared pancakes, bacon, and eggs.

He moved smoothly in the kitchen, and the muscles in his body were relaxed. She wasn't, however, she was already ready for another taste of him.

Her eyes narrowed on the scars that covered his body. The largest was a ragged scar that ran from just below his right shoulder, down to his stomach. He must have seen her eyeing it because he responded. "I've been in a lot of wars."

"War?"

He nodded, his eyes darkening. "I craved death for a long time, sought it out whenever I could."

"So, you fought in wars."

"Yes, I fought in both world wars, after the latter, I came to Boston and started my company."

She hopped off the counter and ran her fingers down the largest scar. "Did it hurt?"

"Yes."

Her fingers brushed a healed gunshot wound in his abdomen. "This was the night I met you, wasn't it?"

He nodded. "That one hurt like hell too."

The jagged edges of the wound on his stomach felt rough under her fingertips. She wished she hadn't been so shocked by his admission, she had wished for death more times than she could count. How horrible it must have been to be forced to live on while those you loved died around you. She had wondered that same question before, but it hadn't truly sunk in until she witnessed the scars that marred his body.

"I'm sorry."

"For what?"

"For everything." Her eyes filled as she continued to run her fingers over the canvas of pain that had been painted all over his body. "I can't even begin to imagine what you've been through."

"Paislee," his words were soft, and he tipped her face up to look at him. "For the first time in the last two hundred years I am glad to be alive. I may have been breathing, but it was you who brought me back to life." He brushed his lips against hers, and pancakes forgotten, they lost themselves in each other.

CHAPTER 22

"So, this is supposed to protect me from Malcolm?" Paislee turned the cuff over in her palm. The metal was cool against her skin and sent a chill through her. She assumed that was due to the magic blocking capabilities rather than the temperature itself.

Timothy nodded. "It will keep you from being able to use your magic, so it's up to you whether you choose to use it or not."

"You're sure it will keep him from being able to use the amulet on me?"

He nodded again. "You said he had to pull your arm out from behind the bars in order to use it on you before."

"Yes, but this is just a cuff, wouldn't it only protect part of me?"

"In theory, yes, but it's the best we've got. We can't

line my apartment with iron or keep you in a lined box."

She slipped the cuff onto her arm and shivered. "I can feel it."

Timothy walked around his desk and rubbed his hands on her arms. "I only want to keep you safe."

"I know." She smiled up, and he brushed his lips against her forehead.

The buzzer went off on his desk, and he answered it, "What is it?"

"It's Jake, Sir. I'm downstairs with those folders you asked for."

"Come on up." Timothy buzzed him up and kissed Paislee gently. "You had better go, it appears he has a thing for you, and I'm a jealous bastard. I might kill him if he looks at you as if you're naked since I've seen you that way."

Paislee smiled. "You got it. We wouldn't want any blood on the carpet." She turned to leave and purposely swayed her hips as she walked. A smile of satisfaction spread across her face when she heard him groan.

Timothy took a seat at his desk when Jake walked in. He studied his employee, the bags under his eyes showed additional stress, and it made Timothy wonder just what was going on in the young man's life. Though he supposed seeing the murdered remains of a coworker would cause anyone to appear drained.

"How are you doing?"

Jake seemed shocked by the question, and he

looked up from the stack of files he was staring at in his hand. "I'm fine, why?"

"This is your first day back since Jess's murder. I want to be sure you are operating at a hundred percent. If you need more time-"

"I'm fine."

Timothy didn't miss the subtle hints of irritation. He hadn't meant to be so crass, but when it came down to it, he needed to be sure everything was moving smoothly.

"If that changes, be sure to let me know."

Jake nodded and pushed the files across the desk. "Any particular reason you needed these?" he wondered.

"I am interested in finding an artifact that is said to have a lot of value. If we are able to acquire it, it could prove incredibly beneficial for the company."

Accepting his answer, Jake moved on. "Well, I combed through and found all known artifacts dating back to 800 BC. There are twenty-two that are said to possess great power, although only four have any actual credibility as to granting something similar to immortality."

Timothy opened the top folder and lifted the photograph of a bronze shield.

"That's the Shield of Age. Ridiculous name but it's said to collect the youth of those who mean to do the user harm. Basically, if you are in battle and are using that shield, it will suck the life out of whoever strikes against it."

"That's brutal."

"Absolutely. It's disappeared, but previous owners discredit the rumor."

"Probably started by a general hoping to gain the upper hand by inciting fear in his enemies."

Jake nodded in agreement and moved on. "The next item is a chalice that was rumored to at one point heal any who drank from it. It is believed to have been lost during the great storm of 1703 when the ship carrying it sank to the bottom of the ocean."

"No recovery effort?"

"People have tried, but no one has ever found it."

Timothy nodded and studied the next image. It was a painting of a gem-encrusted gold chalice, Celtic markings surrounding the base. It was beautiful, and a shame that it was rumored to be buried at the bottom of the sea.

"Next on the list is a pair of earrings that are believed to make the wearer alter whatever physical attribute they wish. So, if someone wanted to look twenty years younger, all they had to do was wish it."

Timothy doubted Malcolm would ever wear a pair of earrings, but it was still worth looking into.

"Where are they now?" he wondered.

Jake pointed to a note in the file. "In a museum in France."

So, they were safe for now. Of course, there was always the possibility that the ones in the museum were fakes. "The last item?" he asked as he put the photo away and lifted the last manila folder.

"An emerald crusted cuff. It's believed to keep the

wearer the same age for as long as they choose and shields them from any harm."

Timothy's jaw set as he stared down at the cuff. Why anyone would choose immortality was beyond him, but if he had to guess, that had to be what Malcolm was after. If only he could inform him, it wasn't worth it. Timothy doubted the bastard would care.

"Where is it now?"

Jake shrugged. "Last known owner died two years ago, and it's been missing ever since."

Timothy nodded curtly. "So either they weren't wearing it, or it doesn't work. Thank you, Jake. Keep going back and see what you can find me. This is great."

"If you could tell me what the item is, that would make the search easier."

Timothy shot him a glare. "Keep looking for anything."

Jake sighed. "You got it, boss." He started to leave but turned back around. "How's Paislee? Is she back yet?"

Timothy ground his teeth together. "She's fine, got back just this morning. She's napping right now," he added sharply. "Please get back to the office and let me know if you find anything."

"Sure thing. Can you tell her I asked about her?"

"Do I look like a messenger?"

"No, Sir, I just-"

"I will tell her you said hello. Please leave."

"Thank you." Jake turned and left quickly, and

Timothy pinched the bridge of his nose. His phone rang, and he answered without checking the ID.

"McGinley."

"Hey boss, Zeke is starting to come around and is asking to speak with you."

"Has he been staying clean?"

"According to the staff he's been doing well."

"Good." He was glad to hear it, maybe soon he could tell Paislee and let her decide whether she wanted to see her brother again or not. But he wanted to see for himself that Zeke was doing well before he got her hopes up.

"Thanks, Ashton. Let them know I'll come by Wednesday."

"You got it."

Timothy ended the call and looked up to see Paislee standing in the doorway.

"I saw Jake leave, so I thought it was safe to come out." She stepped into the office, and Timothy's body tensed. How did she still have this effect on him?

"He said to tell you hi."

"That was nice of him."

"Nice isn't the word I would use for it."

Paislee grinned. "You jealous?"

"I told you not ten minutes ago I was."

"Why?" She moved closer to his desk.

"Because, you are mine," he said it simply, and his words slammed into Paislee's chest. She never thought she would enjoy being claimed by anyone. Not since Malcolm had repeatedly told her, she belonged to him over the years.

But when Timothy said it, it made her heart yearn for more.

She stepped around and sat on the edge of his desk. "You have nothing to worry about."

A smile spread across his face, illuminating it. "I certainly hope not."

They stared at each other for a moment before Paislee broke the silence, "So where are you going on Wednesday?"

"I need to talk to someone."

"Who?"

"Aren't you full of questions this morning."

"Can't help it, I'm bored."

His eyes darkened. "Perhaps I can help with that?"

"Perhaps you can."

His mouth was nearly on hers when his phone rang. "Rain check?"

"Absolutely."

"McGinley," he answered.

PAISLEE SET THE BOOK SHE HAD BEEN READING ASIDE and picked up Garth from the floor. Stroking the orange tabby, she strolled to the large picture window and looked over the city. How long would she have to stay hidden away? How long would it take before she could watch Malcolm leave this world- permanently?

She'd be lying if she didn't admit she was becoming incredibly restless. Before Timothy, she'd felt like she had been working towards *something*. She had made daily trips to the library, and anywhere else she thought she'd find something to help her move forward with her plan.

Now though it seemed as if she were simply sitting around waiting for Malcolm to make his next move, and who knew how long that would take.

Never one to stay in the same place for long, Paislee knew it was only a matter of time before she needed to move forward. Even if it meant leaving what she'd found behind.

CHAPTER 23

*H*e saw her step to the window and bit back a growl. How he wanted to wipe that smug look she wore on her face off. She believed she was untouchable. Well that was a lie, wasn't it? He could touch her if he wanted. Watch how she bled when he cut her.

His hand clenched the binoculars. Hell, he had a rifle. If he wanted to, he could take the shot now. That glass barricade was nothing compared to the round he could fire her way.

He'd been so close and somehow that bastard McGinley was keeping her just out of reach. Soon he would have her within his grasp though, soon enough she would no longer have the protection of the antiquities dealer.

When she stepped away from the window, he started to lower his binoculars until he caught sight of the woman watching the apartment building angrily from the street. *Well, isn't this interesting?* Perhaps he could make his move sooner rather than later.

CHAPTER 24

"eel like going away with me?"

Paislee lifted her head from where she lay on Timothy's shoulder. "What do you mean away?"

"I need to go check something out in France."

"An artifact?"

He nodded. "I think that perhaps Malcolm is trying to locate something that offers him immortality."

She sat up. "Seriously? Why do you think that?"

He put a hand behind his head. "I had Ashton look into his movements over the past few months. Nearly every trip he has been on has been to locations where it was rumored certain artifacts might be located."

"Artifacts that grant immortality."

"Yes."

"Because there are actually items out there that can do that?"

He eyed her, partially amused. "Paislee, you are in bed with a man who is over two hundred years old, and you have magic of your own. How can you not believe there are items out there that are capable of keeping someone alive?"

She considered and then shrugged. "We are people though, we are both here because of magic of some kind or another. An item is not alive, it just is there. It's made by man, not created by God."

He raised an eyebrow. "So you believe in God?"

"You don't?"

"I didn't say that. I was just surprised to hear you say it."

"Look, just because I've been through a lot and think it's really shitty that it happened to me, doesn't mean I don't believe we weren't created by something more powerful than us."

He put up his free hand in mock surrender. "Easy, I wasn't attacking you. As far as the artifacts, some were said to have been spelled by witches, others cursed. It's all a matter of perspective."

"I suppose. But why would he want immortality?"

"Because those who have never suffered through it don't understand the nightmare it brings."

"So, you think one of these items is in France?"

"Possibly, there are a pair of earrings located in a museum that can offer the wearer the ability to alter their appearance. I have my reservations as to whether they are legitimate or not, but it's still worth checking out."

"When do you want to go?"

"Tomorrow. We can bring the cat."

"Seriously?" She couldn't hide the smile from her face.

"Seriously. Ashton is coming with us, and I don't want to leave Garth in the hands of anyone else"

She leaned down and pressed her lips to his. "Have I told you that you're amazing?"

"Not lately, but I know." He grinned, and she laid back down.

THEY ARRIVED AT THE AIRPORT AT SEVEN THIRTY IN the morning and Paislee couldn't have been more exhausted. Nightmares had kept her up nearly all night, and the lack of sleep had made her cranky.

Garth meowed from his carrier, and she absent-mindedly stuck her finger through the slats to pet him. She was excited to visit France for the first time, but something was nagging at her.

Why hadn't they just rounded up a group of people and stormed Malcolm's house? Just go in and kill him before he had a chance to get his hands on anything that would potentially make him harder to kill?

Now if they waited, there was always a chance he was already one step ahead of them. Who knows how they would stop him if he gained any more power. The amulet made him difficult enough.

"Are you alright?" Timothy asked as he guided her onto the jet.

"Yeah, just tired."

"Once we're air born you are more than welcome to go back and sleep."

"I probably will, thanks." Her voice was anything but cheerful, but if Timothy noticed, he kept it to himself.

She took her seat across from Timothy and Ashton patiently waiting for the jet to take off. A scowl plastered on her face, she listened to them talk strategy while the aircraft was filled with fuel and prepped for departure.

She closed her eyes as the scenes from her nightmares plagued her. Last night she dreamt of death. Not of her own, but the deaths of all those she'd come to care for since that night in the alley.

She had seen Timothy die, no longer immortal due to his curse. Some invisible force had struck down Ashton, and Jake was slaughtered before her very eyes. It was the end of the dream that had stuck with her though because after all the bodies lay in pools of their own blood, after they had each taken their very last breaths, it was her who had stood victorious in the center of the horror. And she had been smiling.

"Paislee."

She opened her eyes to see Timothy and Ashton both staring intently at her. "What?"

"We're in the air if you'd like to go lie down."

"Already? We just got on the plane."

Ashton shook his head. "It's been about forty-five minutes since we sat down."

Paislee shook her head to clear it. "Thanks," she muttered and headed back towards the bedroom area.

Garth followed her, apparently, Timothy had released the feline from his carrier as well. Had she been asleep? Or simply wrapped up in herself?

"What is going on with you?"

Paislee turned to see Timothy standing in the doorway, his arms crossed. "I told you, I'm tired."

"You're lying," he responded calmly, but the irritation in his voice told her he was feeling anything but.

"I really just want to lie down."

"I heard you cry out last night in your sleep. If you don't wish to talk about your nightmare that's fine. But don't take it out on me."

She glared at him. "Don't act like you know what I'm thinking. And I wasn't taking it out on you."

His eyebrow raised. "Really? So, you didn't just snap at Ashton and me."

"Had I 'snapped' this plane would be in a flaming heap on the ground. I assure you I am in control."

His tone took on a deadly edge. "You will do well to remember that you are on this jet with three people other than myself. Whatever you're pissed off at me for can be dealt with when we land." He turned and left the room leaving her seething.

～

SEVEN HOURS AND TWENTY-TWO MINUTES LATER THEY were walking off the plane and getting into a black town car. Their luggage and her cat had stayed behind to be driven over to the hotel for the night.

Why they were getting a hotel and actually staying, she had no idea. Not that she wasn't excited to see Paris, but every day they refused to make a move was another day that Malcolm gained power.

Her hands clenched into fists as she watched the town pass them by. The iron cuff she wore kept her magic in check, but she could feel it building. She only needed to get close enough to Malcolm to let it consume them both.

"We're here," Ashton announced as they pulled up in front of a large museum. Paislee climbed out after he and Timothy, and stared up at the impressive building. Large stone steps led up to the entrance, and even as volatile as she was feeling, she had to appreciate the beauty of it.

"Shall we?" Timothy asked and offered her his arm. She took it, grudgingly so, and let him lead her through the doors and into the plush lobby. Ashton walked over to check them in, and within moments they were greeted by a slender woman who looked to be in her early forties.

"Mr. McGinley, so lovely to meet you, Sir. I am Katarina Devaux." She offered him her hand, and it did nothing for Paislee's mood to see him press a kiss to her knuckles.

"Pleasure to meet you, Mrs. Devaux."

"Oh," she blushed, "It's Miss Devaux, I'm not married."

"What a shame." He grinned, and Paislee rolled her eyes. Asshole had laid his accent on thick too.

"You flatter me, Sir. I am the director of this museum, and I have to say, I am incredibly happy to have you here with us. To what do we owe this immense pleasure?"

"I merely want to take a look around. As you know, I love antiques and being amongst them in such an exquisite museum thrills me."

She blushed again, and Paislee stuck her hand out. "Hi, I'm Paislee."

Katarina eyed her hand and reluctantly took it. "A pleasure I'm sure." She released it quickly and turned back to Timothy. "Come, I will show you around."

"I'm sure you have much more important things to do lass. My associates and I would hate to take up your time. Perhaps after we have a look around I can come tell you about a very interesting artifact I found recently."

Katarina's face lit up, and she nodded. "That would be most wonderful, Mr. McGinley, I do hope you enjoy yourselves."

They began walking, and Ashton hung back to give them some space.

"Disgusting," Paislee muttered as soon as Katarina was out of earshot. "Perhaps you would like to stay in her room tonight?" She did her best to re-create Katarina's accent but failed miserably.

Timothy eyed her, amusement pulling the corners

of his lips. "Why Paislee it sounds to me like you're jealous."

"Of course not. What reason would I have to be jealous? There was never any talk about us being exclusive was there?"

Timothy stopped and faced her. "Make no mistake, Paislee, I do not share. I simply exploited her attraction to me in order to get what we needed, which was alone time with the artifact."

"Yes, I'm sure you took no pleasure in that."

"In watching your irritation? Absolutely." He grinned, but there was little humor in it. "But I would never act on it. I am sleeping with you and only you, understand?"

"Perfectly. But if you do that to me again, you won't be sleeping with me either."

"Fair enough." He began walking again, and they made their way through the museum.

Every once and awhile Timothy would stop to tell her the history of a certain artifact, and a few times pointed out items he had donated to the museum. She felt stupid and childish for her reaction earlier.

Timothy had been right, she'd been taking her nightmare out on him rather than simply voicing her fears. Right now, it was imperative they stay focused, and fighting with each other could prove to be an unaffordable distraction.

"I'm sorry," she offered as they walked down an empty hall. "I shouldn't have acted that way."

Timothy shrugged. "I've gotten used to your mood swings."

She turned to him angrily. "Mood- sw-" And then saw the humor on his face. "You're an ass."

"I've been called much worse."

"I'm sure you have."

He stopped suddenly. "There they are."

The earrings were stunning in their glass case. The room was focused entirely around them, and Paislee and Timothy moved forward to get a better look. Garnet stones dangled from large diamonds on the sides of the mannequin's head. The stones glinted in the light and to Paislee, she had never seen anything more beautiful.

"Are they real?" she wondered as Timothy bent for a closer look.

"Possibly. It's hard to say without getting my hands on them."

"How are you planning on doing that?" she wondered as he pulled a device from his pocket.

"This will disable any alarm on the case, including the pressurized sensor and won't trigger any secondary alarms."

She gaped at him. "I didn't know anything like that existed."

"It doesn't, at least not to anyone but me."

"*You* made that?"

"As you know I had quite a bit of spare time, I got bored."

She watched in complete fascination as he held the small black box up to the edge of the glass before slipping it back into his pocket. He then pulled fabric gloves on and lifted the glass to set it aside.

The stones glinted with new light almost as if they were coming to life at the idea of being used. It was hard to describe, but the stones looked and felt *alive* to her.

Timothy carefully lifted one of the earrings to study it. "The stones are real, but the craftsmanship is strange and not likely to have come from the era the earrings themselves are said to have been made." He lifted it closer to his face. "These are not the earrings from the legend."

Paislee barely heard him, she felt as if she could hear the stones screaming in her mind. She focused closer and reached out to touch one just as Timothy gripped her arm.

"Paislee," he said sternly, and she tore her focus from the stones.

"What?"

"Don't touch. These are not the actual earrings, but you don't have the best luck with garnets."

"Right." She shook her head trying to clear it.

Timothy had just replaced the glass and stashed the gloves into his pocket when Katarina walked in.

"So, have you enjoyed yourselves?" she asked, and Timothy nodded.

"Thank you for the hospitality, but I'm afraid we must be going."

Her mouth turned down in a pout. "But I was really looking forward to seeing that item you spoke about."

The way she said 'item' irritated Paislee so much that she just couldn't help herself. "I assure you, Katarina, he had no intention of showing you his dick." Ignoring the horror on the woman's face, Paislee lowered her voice. "That's for my eyes only." She winked and could almost hear Timothy's internal laughter.

"Well, I suppose we had better be going now," Ashton, who had apparently joined the party, commented.

"You most absolutely should." Katarina straightened the hem of her jacket, "I have never been so embarrassed in my life."

"I'm sure that's just not true," Paislee coddled and turned to leave.

"Was that truly necessary?" Timothy asked her, his voice low enough so only they could hear.

"It absolutely was necessary, and it made me feel better."

"It was crude."

Paislee shrugged, "I told you I had a potty mouth."

"A potty mouth? How old are you?"

"Much younger than you," Paislee added with a grin.

She could see the humor on Timothy's face, and it only made her feel even better about what she'd said to the director.

CHAPTER 25

*H*e watched them walk into the museum and had nearly given in to his urge to rush them right there and taken her as his. They would have been surprised, and he was so smart it would have been easy. She was so damn powerful it made his skin itch. But his employer had insisted there was a plan in place, a reason for the wait.

And if he moved on her now, he would surely get his own throat cut. That arrogant bastard McGinley had strolled in there as if he didn't have a care in the world. Personally, he couldn't wait to watch that man bleed to death. Two hundred years was long enough to plague the earth with his pathetic existence.

He had no want for immortality, no drive for more power. What he wanted was money, and the death of Timothy McGinley would give him that and allow him to live like the king he was.

As for Paislee Adams, his employer had plans for her, and once she was drained of her power, she was promised to him.

Then he would make her pay for what she'd done to him.

CHAPTER 26

*P*aislee lounged on the couch and listened while Timothy let Jake know the search wasn't over. She was surprisingly relaxed given her reaction to the earrings. Timothy, however, had told her they would be researching any and all references to garnets and their strange effect on her.

"Jake will continue searching for anything that might point us to where the real earrings are." Timothy took a seat on the couch near her feet.

"Mmhmm," she said with her eyes closed.

"Tired?"

"Exhausted." She opened her eyes slightly when she felt a hand on her leg.

"Not too tired I hope." Timothy's eyes were dark, and there was something incredibly heavy in them.

"I suppose I could muster up some energy," she responded breathlessly as he kneeled between her legs.

"That's good because I have a few activities we could take part in." He leaned over her and kissed the hollow of her throat.

"A few activities, huh?"

"One in particular."

"What did you have in mind?" she whispered as he moved down her body and lifted the hem of her shirt to bare her stomach. He pressed a kiss to her abdomen, and her heart stammered in her chest.

The short beard on his face scraped against her skin, leaving a trail of fire in its wake. Did he know what he did to her? How he set her soul on fire and made her feel as if she were perfect? He was the cure to every bad memory she carried within her. Every scar, both mental and physical were erased when he touched her like he was doing now.

"I thought that perhaps," he moved her shirt up and over her breasts before placing a kiss just above the cup of her bra, "We could start slow." He removed her shirt the rest of the way and Paislee's body readied in anticipation.

Timothy moved back down and undid the button of her jeans. The pop noise it made caused her to jump slightly. His fingers played with the line of her underwear, and Paislee groaned, arching up against him, ready for what would come next.

"Timothy" she moaned as his hand slipped beneath the fabric and cupped her heat. His fingers made quick work of her, driving her up over the crest but stopping just before she fell.

"Not yet," his voice came out like a growl as he

moved off of her to remove the rest of her clothes. When she lay naked in front of him, he removed his own.

Paislee's mouth watered as she drank in the sight of him, completely naked, in front of her. When he covered her body with his and buried himself in her, she moved with him as if it were the last time they would ever get together.

For all she knew, it could be.

MYRIA SHOT OUT OF BED, AND SHEAMUS SAT UP sleepily. *There had been so much blood*, she pinched the bridge of her nose on the memory of the nightmare.

"What is it, love?" Sheamus asked her.

"He's going to die," she nearly whispered it, afraid to say the words out loud.

"Who's going to die?"

"Timothy."

"What do you mean?" All hints of sleep had disappeared from his voice, replaced by genuine concern.

"She is going to kill him."

"Myria, stop with the half sentences. Tell me what's happening."

"I saw it Sheamus. I saw Paislee slaughter, every-one. Timothy tried to stop her, but she killed him."

Sheamus climbed out of bed and knelt in front of her. "'Twas only a nightmare, my love."

She shook her head. "'Twas a premonition."

He studied her face. A face he knew better than his own. "You're sure then?"

She nodded.

"Then you must warn him."

"He won't listen to me, Sheamus. Even before, Timothy was stubborn, now he's dug his heels into helping the lass."

"Okay, then how do we help him? Why did she kill him?"

"I don't think she meant too. Twas a blast of power."

"Okay, what can we do?"

ANOTHER SEVEN-AND-A-HALF-HOUR PLANE RIDE LATER, and Paislee's feet were happily planted on solid ground. Before Timothy had rescued her from Malcolm and taken her to Ireland, she'd never actually been on a plane.

While flying was interesting, to say the least, it was absolutely not her favorite thing to do.

She set Garth's carrier on the floor of the apartment and opened the gate so he could come out.

"Happy to be back?"

She looked to where Timothy watched her from the doorway and smiled.

"Absolutely."

"Good." He grinned back. "I need to run somewhere tomorrow. I shouldn't be gone but a few hours."

"Okay."

"There is security in the room downstairs, so you will be safe."

"I'm honestly not worried about it Timothy, I'll be fine."

"I know, it's just hard." His jaw set in a hard line as Paislee walked over to place her hand against his cheek.

"I will be fine," she repeated. "Besides, I'll have my alone time to start studying some of those books Myria sent me back with."

"So, you haven't started then?" His tone was mocking, and he raised an eyebrow.

"I was going to, just haven't gotten around to it yet. You are a distraction."

"So, it's my fault?"

"Absolutely." She smiled and turned towards the kitchen. "Are you hungry?"

"Famished."

"I can put something together if you'd like?"

"Oh Paislee, it's not food I'm after."

She looked over her shoulder at him and shot him a wicked grin. "Then come and get it."

"DO YOU UNDERSTAND WHAT YOU ARE TO DO?" Malcolm asked his wife one last time.

She nodded. "I am to get the cuff off of her arm and use this on her." She clutched the garnet necklace in her hand.

"Good and then?"

Her grin was full of hatred "I will kill her. I won't let you down, my love."

"I know you won't." Lindsay transformed before his eyes, and he looked smugly at the woman currently bound and gagged in the corner.

Her fear filled eyes widened, and Lindsay laughed. "Look familiar, bitch?" she asked and slapped the woman across the face. "This is going to be fun." She clapped, and Malcolm kissed her deeply.

TIMOTHY SAT IN THE BRIGHT WAITING ROOM OF THE Addiction Recovery Center just outside of Boston. The room was a cheerful sunshine yellow with paintings depicting parks with brightly colored birds on the walls.

If anything, the decor made him want to pop a pill of something that would make him forget he ever sat in a room like it.

But there must have been something to it because they had the best recovery rating in this part of the country.

"Mr. McGinley come right this way please." A woman wearing all white stepped from the back, and he and Ashton followed her down a hall and into a large room that was empty except for one person.

Zeke Adams had only been in this place a short time and already looked significantly better than the last time Timothy had seen him.

"Hi, Mr. McGinley, thanks for coming to see me." Zeke offered him his hand and Timothy took it easily.

"Of course, what can I do for you?"

"I wanted to talk about-" he sighed, and his eyes shifted down to look at his hands. "My sister."

"How are you coming along in your recovery?"

"Fine. I haven't used since you brought me here." His tone was defensive as his eyes shot back to Timothy's face.

"That's good."

"It was hard at first, a lot of pain came back to the surface, but I'm dealing with it."

"I can imagine."

"I want to talk about Paislee."

"What about her?"

"Where is she?"

"That's none of your concern right now."

"She's my sister."

"A sister you didn't even know was alive until I told you in that drug house. A sister mind you, that was taken, and you didn't even bother looking for her." Was he being rough? Definitely but Zeke Adams needed to understand just what he had sacrificed that night Malcolm and his men had taken Paislee away.

"He said he would kill her."

"I understand that, but you didn't even try Zeke." Timothy leaned forward. "I don't know if I can trust you enough yet to tell you where she is. I will tell you that she is safe, cared for and that I will protect her with my life, if necessary, but that is all."

Zeke nodded, fresh tears rolling down his lightly

freckled cheeks. "She was my world, you know. I worked my ass off to provide for her, all I wanted was a good, solid life for my baby sister."

"I believe you, but that's not the way it turned out. The easy road is hardly ever the best option."

"I know that now." Zeke wiped a tear from his cheek. "Can you give her this? Please, you can even read it first if you're that worried about it. I just want her to know that I am doing this for her and that I'm so damn sorry."

Timothy looked down at the note in his hand. "When the time is right." He took the folded paper and stuck it into his pocket.

"Thank you." Zeke offered him the ghost of a smile. "And thank you for doing this for me."

"I'm doing this for Paislee," Timothy responded quickly. "Now I need you to tell me everything you remember about Malcolm Gentry."

PAISLEE'S ATTENTION WAS PULLED FROM THE BOOK SHE was reading when a knock sounded at the door.

Thinking it was one of the guards, she didn't bother checking the peephole and simply pulled the large door open.

"Hi, can I help you?" she asked, surprised to see a woman on the other side.

"Yes, I think you can."

She never saw the punch. It landed on the corner

of her jaw, and Paislee's head whipped back, sending her body with it. She landed on the floor, dazed and the woman rushed her, kicking the door shut behind her.

Paislee put her hands up to block the attack, but the woman had successfully caught her off guard. "What the hell do you want?" she screamed at her attacker.

"Your blood, bitch." She pummeled her fist back down into Paislee's jaw, and her eyes settled on the silver cuff around her bicep. "This is what I need."

"Don't take it off," Paislee warned, dazed.

"Oh, I'm going to take it off, and then I'm going to kill you." She ripped the cuff off and stared down into Paislee's face. "Do you know who I am?" She sneered.

Paislee shook her head.

"I am Giselle, Timothy is *mine*, do you hear me? Every single part of him is *mine*. *How dare you* try and take what is mine!" she screamed and pulled something out of her pocket.

Paislee caught the glint of red and her eyes widened. "No!" she screamed just as the stone was within view. She screamed in agony as the stone began to pull the magic from her veins.

"How does that feel, bitch? He told me it would hurt you, but I had no idea how enjoyable it would be for me to watch."

Paislee couldn't hear a thing she said, her mind so overtaxed due to the pain the garnet was inflicting on her. The only thing she could focus on was that it would soon be over and then she wouldn't have to feel anything anymore.

"Paislee!" a man yelled her name, but Paislee could barely hear it. Tears slipped down her cheeks as she held on to what little life she had left. Was it Timothy?

"Get away from her!" someone, not Timothy, yelled as Giselle was ripped off her. "Paislee, can you hear me?"

Jake's face came into view, and Paislee caught sight of his worried expression. She did her best to nod and opened her mouth to speak, to warn Jake that he needed to get the stone from Giselle.

"What happened?" A deep growl sounded in the room, and Paislee tried to stop the tears from streaming down her face. Timothy knelt beside her and glared at Jake.

"It was that woman, she had Paislee on the ground when I got in here. I don't know what happened."

"What woman?" Paislee heard Ashton ask.

"She was right-" He turned, but Giselle was gone. "I don't understand, she was right there. I came in and pulled her off Paislee."

"Paislee," Timothy said softly. "Can you hear me?"

Paislee nodded.

"I'm going to lift you, okay?" he said softly.

"We need to call an ambulance. Don't move her," Jake insisted, but Timothy ignored him.

"Ashton, figure out what the hell he was doing here before I kill him myself."

"What? Kill me? I didn't do anything!" he insisted as Ashton pulled him down onto the couch.

Timothy carried her into the bedroom and laid her gently back. "I'm going to put the cuff back on, okay? Just in case whoever was responsible is still nearby."

Paislee nodded and felt the coolness from the steel against her skin. She could see Timothy clearly now, his face hardened in anger.

"It was Giselle," she whispered.

Paislee had been prepared for anger, but the unfiltered rage that crossed Timothy's face had surprised her. "Fuck," he growled. "I'm so damn sorry, Paislee." He leaned forward and pressed his head against hers. "Dammit, I'm sorry."

She lifted her arms up and wrapped them around him as her body began to shake. Death was not something she was afraid of. In fact, she was prepared for it. But as she held on to him, she realized just how much she enjoyed living.

∽

"Did you get her?" Timothy asked into his phone.

"We can't find her. It's as if she disappeared." Ashton's voice was full of frustration and he cursed under his breath.

"Keep an eye out. I know Giselle, she won't go far."

"Were watching. How's Paislee?"

"Still asleep, I don't know what the hell happened. How did she get up here?"

"She killed Jim."

"How?" How in the world had Giselle killed a fully trained ex-GI?

"His throat had been cut."

"Something about this isn't fitting. Giselle is insane, sure, but I don't see how she could take down a fully trained man and make it out with no injuries."

"She took down a witch," Ashton reminded him. "Paislee is no easy target."

"Yeah, I suppose so." He rubbed his forehead. "I guess we won't know anything for sure until Paislee wakes up."

"Did you get anything out of the brother about Malcolm?" Ashton asked him.

"Unfortunately, no, he didn't remember much, the drugs had seen to that, and what he did remember were things we already knew."

"Shame."

"It is, but we hadn't counted on him remembering much anyway."

"True."

"We need to know what Malcolm has before we can make an executed attack on his estate. We could go marching in there and be shot down before we let out our first breath."

"I fear that if we wait much longer, we're going to

end up with Malcolm on our doorstep. I'm going to get into touch with my contacts with the bureau, see if there's some way we can get some intel. I was hoping not to do it, it could raise flags if I'm not careful but at this point, I think it's our only play." The phone line disconnected, and he set it down on the table.

Timothy knew Ashton was right, every single day they sat on it was another day Malcolm had to prepare. There was a war coming to them, and they needed to be sure they were ready for it.

CHAPTER 27

*J*ayde Walker stepped out into the dark with a smile on her face. She had finally gotten her term paper finished and was certain she was going to get an A on it.

Her professor was tough, but Jayde had poured days into making sure the paper was up to expectation. She was one step closer to graduation and then she could start her work as a resident in at Seattle General. Her future was just within reach. She wouldn't be known as the 'freak' anymore, or 'the weird girl' because of the strange things that happened around her.

She would be known as Dr. Walker, M.D. She grinned into the dark as she pictured herself helping others while wearing the coveted white coat.

"Excuse me," a man's voice sounded behind her, and she turned to see a handsome blonde man with a bright, kind smile.

"Yes?"

He blushed and stepped towards her. "I saw you in the library."

"Yes, I was in there."

"I, uh." He rubbed the back of his neck and Jayde could see he was nervous. It was cute and added to his kind demeanor. "I was wondering if you wanted to grab a drink?"

She smiled. "I would love too, but it will have to be another night. I just finished my term paper, and I want to get back to my dorm to give it one more look over."

"I totally understand, I just, I really want to take you out. What about dinner? Or coffee? If you're going to be up, I bet you'd like some coffee."

She thought about it as she studied him. He had kind eyes, and he wasn't being overly pushy with her. Besides, she could use a cup of coffee to help her get through the rest of the night.

She smiled. "Okay, I'd love to grab a cup of coffee."

"Awesome." He grinned, and Jayde was glad she'd agreed. "Shall we?" he asked and held out his arm.

She slung her arm over his and allowed him to walk her through the dark. They turned a corner, and for the first time since meeting him, she began to feel nervous.

"What are we doing? The college coffeehouse is that way."

He pulled her into an alley and slammed her against the wall. "I promise this part won't hurt a bit."

The kindness that had been in his eyes was gone, replaced by madness Jayde couldn't understand how he'd hid. She tried to access the power in her veins, but in an instant, he had covered her face with a cloth and her world fell away.

CHAPTER 28

*P*aislee opened her eyes and winced as the light from the window enhanced the pounding in her head. *What the hell happened?* She asked herself as she tried to sit up. It felt like her body had been hit by a semi that then had the courtesy to back over her afterward.

She rubbed the heels of her hands against her eyes as the memories came flooding back to her. The woman had attacked her over Timothy. Who the hell was Giselle anyways?

The stone. How had she known? Did Timothy let it slip? Was he still seeing her? How did she get it? One word came to mind: *Malcolm.* It was more likely the sadistic bastard had exploited Giselle, used her feelings for Timothy against her.

Her old captor certainly had a way of using people against each other. She'd seen him do it.

The door opened slightly, and Timothy stepped

in. She saw him visibly relax as soon as he saw her sitting up.

"How are you?"

"My head feels as if it's on fire and my body aches but I'm alive."

Timothy took a seat on the bed next to her and wrapped his arms around her. The gesture was so sweet, so *normal* that it took her by surprise.

"I'm so sorry, Paislee."

"What are you sorry for?"

"Giselle and I, we used to see each other." He released her and sat back.

"I gathered as much. Doesn't mean you are responsible for her psychotic ass."

"What happened?"

"I'm an idiot, that's what happened."

"What do you mean?" he wondered.

"There was a knock at the door, and I opened it without checking to see who it was first. I got comfortable and didn't see the punch until it was too late. I may be good with my magic, but I'm not very physical. I never got the chance to learn, so when she punched me, it knocked me back and stunned me long enough for her to land a few more good ones on me."

"You were able to get your cuff off, is that why we can't find her?"

Paislee stared at him a moment. "I didn't take my cuff off. She did, and then pulled a garnet out of her bag."

Timothy's hands fisted into balls. "She did *what?*"

"She used the stone just like Malcolm had and started to draw out my magic. I don't remember much after that, just the pain."

Timothy stood and walked to the window. "How in the hell did she find out about you?"

"Probably Malcolm."

"Malcolm."

"Makes sense doesn't it? How else would she have gotten it?"

"What doesn't make sense is why garnets are suddenly your kryptonite. I thought it was only the necklace. You're sure that's not what she had?"

"Positive. Malcolm would never let her to take it on the off chance she lost it or was killed. He's way too paranoid."

Paislee turned at the sound of a light knock and saw Ashton standing just outside of the door.

"Hey, Ashton." She offered him a smile. "Come on in and join the party."

"I'm happy to see you're alright Paislee."

"Me too."

Ashton turned to Timothy. "Parish claims he didn't see anything and has no idea where she went."

"Jake?"

"He claims that he stopped Giselle."

"I need to thank him then."

"No. Not until he is cleared."

"Cleared? You don't think he had anything to do with it do you?"

"I think it's suspicious that he was here in the first

place, on the very day you are attacked and one of Ashton's men is killed."

"Killed? Who?"

"Jim, who was working downstairs."

"Oh no, I'm so sorry, Ashton. He seemed so nice."

"He was a good man, and it appears he didn't try and fight off his attacker. Since he is happily married, I cannot imagine it was Giselle he invited in."

"Do you really think Jake has anything to do with it?" she wondered.

Timothy didn't hesitate. "I think it's possible."

"Then let's go talk to him."

"Paislee, you need to rest," Timothy insisted.

"I need to stop sitting on my ass doing nothing. Before you, I was careful, on edge, and watched everything around me. Now, I've been attacked because I got complacent. I won't let that happen again."

"Paislee-" he started, but she put her hand in the air.

"I'm no delicate flower, Timothy, so stop treating me like I am."

After a moment he nodded. "Fine, but we do this my way."

PAISLEE, TIMOTHY, AND ASHTON MADE THEIR WAY downstairs to the security office. It was hard to wrap her mind around the kind-faced Jake having anything to do with Malcolm, but unfortunately, she was smart enough to recognize the signs and knew it was worth looking into.

They stepped into the security office, and Ashton cursed. It took Paislee a moment to notice the feet sticking out from under the desk.

"Is he dead?" Timothy asked through gritted teeth.

"No, just unconscious."

"Fuck," Paislee muttered.

"Fuck is exactly right. Turns out we've had a traitor in our midst this entire time."

Ashton got on his radio and told them to lock down the building, but if Paislee had to guess Jake was long gone by now. Which meant their only lead had disappeared.

"We have to make a move soon Timothy. You might be okay waiting around to see what happens, but I'm not." She turned and walked out of the office.

"You failed." Malcolm eyed the woman standing before him.

"That asshole interrupted me." She shot her finger to Jake who leaned against the wall.

"This asshole interrupted you because McGinley was headed upstairs. We can't risk him getting his hands on that stone."

"She was nearly drained. I could have killed her!" Lindsay insisted.

"I told you," Malcolm warned. "You are not

allowed to kill her until her magic is completely drained. That itself will kill her."

Frustrated at her own failure, she rolled her eyes. "What does it matter anymore? You have that other one." She pointed to the woman in the cage situated in the corner of his office.

"Paislee is special to me, her magic is pure and the strongest I've ever tasted. If we're going to have ultimate power, we need it all." He turned to Jake and gestured to the other woman still bound in the corner. "Kill her."

Still gagged, she tried to move.

Jake pulled out his gun and fired a single shot. Giselle fell to the ground, and the woman in the cage flinched.

"Get rid of the body and find a way to get me Paislee. By any means necessary. We need to be able to move forward, I have people waiting for my orders, and the longer they have to wait, the more their fingers itch for the trigger."

"I will bring her to you," Jake assured him.

"Alive."

"More or less."

"Be sure it's more."

"Please." The woman in the cage reached for Jake as he started to walk by. "Please let me go."

Jake stepped closer to the bars and grinned. "Haven't you figured it out yet Jayde? You belong here."

"Why me?"

"Because you have something I want," Malcolm

spoke up and dismissed Jake. "You should feel proud Jayde, you are going to be the one who helps me to shape a new world."

Her eyes widened. "A new world?"

"Oh yes, we are going to destroy this one and rebuild it." He reached into his shirt and pulled out the garnet.

"No, please, not again. Please!" she screamed, and he yanked her arm through the bars. She crumpled as he felt the power being pulled from her body.

She was no Paislee, but her power was strong nonetheless, and before long he would have all he needed.

"Shit." Timothy hung up the phone and began to pace.

"What is it?" Paislee looked up from the magic book she was studying.

"This is so much bigger than we could have imagined."

"What do you mean?" She set the book aside.

"Ashton called some buddies he has with the FBI. It seems Malcolm is on their watch list. Apparently, the reason we couldn't find any information on him before was that they have been sealed for security reasons. They think they may have a leak somewhere up the chain and didn't want to tip him off."

"Why would the FBI be watching him?"

"Not just the FBI. He has been tied to some

recent terrorist organizations. Homeland Security is watching him as well."

Her jaw dropped. "What? Which ones?"

"Does it matter?"

"Absolutely. I helped him force people to do his bidding, what if I helped in some way-"

"You didn't."

"How do you know? How could you possibly know?"

"Paislee," his voice was calm, but there was an edge to it that told Paislee she wouldn't win an argument right now. No matter how guilty she felt.

"Which attacks, Timothy?"

"As far as anyone knows, none, yet. But there has been word that one is coming."

"They don't know anything else about it?"

He shook his head.

"Is that why he wants my magic? So, no one can question him? So, no one will stand a chance against him?"

"He won't get you or your magic."

"We can't wait around Timothy, we have to make a move sooner rather than later. Do they know when the attack might take place? Or where?"

He shook his head. "If anyone knows they aren't saying anything. But my guess would be it will take place in an incredibly populated area that would cause enough bloodshed to get him whatever power it is he wants."

"This is horrible." She put her head in her hands. Never in a million years would she have considered this possibility. Murder, manipulation, torture, those things she knew Malcolm was capable of. But killing thousands of innocent people just to gain the upper hand against who knew what? She wouldn't have thought him capable of such horror.

Timothy rubbed his hand on her back. "We will get him, Paislee."

"I hope so."

CHAPTER 29

"*M*cGinley," Timothy said when he answered his phone three hours later.

"It's Myria."

He smiled slightly at the sound of his old friends' voice. "What can I do for you?"

"You're going to die," she choked out. "Helping Paislee will kill you."

He straightened in his chair. "What the hell are you talking about?"

"I had a vision, Timothy. You tried to save her, but you died instead. You cannot die, we just got you back."

He could hear the tears in her voice and tried to steady his own. "I'm not going to die Myria, it was just a dream."

"It wasn't just a dream. Do you not think I can differentiate from a dream and a vision?"

"That's not what I said-"

"That's exactly what you said," she interrupted.

"I am not going to give up on her because of a dream Myria. You should know I don't scare that easy."

"You are going to die, Timothy. Is her war worth your life?"

"Her war *is* my war Myria."

She was silent a moment. "You love her."

"This is none of your business."

"You're wrong. Aengus and I are your friends, whether you live, or die is our business."

"What do you expect me to do Myria? I won't turn my back on her."

"Because you love her."

"Because she will die and whatever Malcolm is planning will come to fruition if I do."

"Do you still have the cuff I sent you for her?"

He pinched the bridge of his nose, a headache setting in. "Yes."

"Wear it," she said, and the line went dead.

Timothy slammed down his cell and cursed. Just who in the hell did she think she was? She had turned her back on him two hundred years ago. One trip out to see her wouldn't erase that.

Did he wish things had turned out differently between them? He used to. He'd believed that he was in love with her all those years ago and he'd be lying if a small part of him didn't still hate her for turning him away.

But things *had* turned out differently, and that was

the fact of it. No amount of time would change it, and if he had the chance, he wouldn't even change it.

She had Sheamus and their kids, and he had Paislee. Whatever came next could be handled as long as those two constants remained.

"Is everything alright?" Paislee stood framed in his doorway. The light behind her cast an orange glow and made her appear as if she were the one providing it rather than the fading sun outside.

He nodded. "Myria was just checking on our progress."

"Myria."

He didn't miss the tone of her voice, and it brought a small smile to his lips. "You jealous then?"

"No, of course not."

Timothy leaned back in his seat and folded his arms across his chest. "How are you?" he asked, changing the subject.

"Tired and a little sore, but fine. Any word on Giselle?"

"Unfortunately, not but that's not surprising."

"Oh?"

"If she's working with Malcolm we may never see her again."

"Does that bother you?"

His eyes narrowed on her face. "Not in the way you're thinking it might."

"I just thought that-"

"Whatever you're thinking right now needs to be forgotten." He got to his feet. "I want you Paislee. It was over with her before I even knew how I felt about you."

"Look, Timothy, what if we're only distracting each other? What if this is a mistake?"

"Who says we don't deserve to be distracted every once and awhile. You may have been fighting this war most of your life, but until I met you, I was fighting for a reason to stay alive. You've given me that reason. Don't give up on me now." He walked over and looked down into her eyes. "Give me time, and I swear to you we will nail that son of a bitch."

"Okay," she said softly, and he pressed his lips to hers.

"I want you to teach me to fight."

Timothy looked up from his computer. "What?"

"I want to learn to fight. I never had the time and always assumed since I had magic, it wouldn't be necessary."

"It's not necessary."

"Don't you want me to be able to protect myself?"

"I don't want you running off into a fight because you think you are a professional boxer."

"I won't ever think that I just want to be able to defend myself. My magic is temperamental at best and the chances of me mastering it in time to stop Malcolm is a pipe dream. I need to be able to have other means of fighting back."

"Paislee-"

"Please? If you won't teach me, I will find someone else who will."

The thought of her rolling around, sweaty, with someone else was too much for him, so he nodded. "Very well, we can start tomorrow."

She kissed him loudly. "Thanks, Timothy."

Ashton passed her as she was leaving Timothy's office. "She looks happy." He commented and shut the door behind him.

"Apparently I'm going to teach her to fight."

"Good idea."

"You think?"

"After Giselle, definitely."

"Any word on her or Jake?"

Ashton shook his head. "We found the real Jake Parish though."

"I was afraid of that. Where?"

"In the deep freezer of his parents' basement."

"They knew about it?"

He shook his head. "Apparently, they didn't see their son much. There was a private entry in and out of the basement where he was living, and they rarely interfered."

"He was missing for at least seven months. How did they not notice?"

"The mother said he had received a letter asking him to travel and be the test bunny for some big gamer company. They had been receiving letters from him every two weeks but according to those letters, couldn't call because it would breach the security of the companies."

"They never questioned?"

Ashton shrugged. "Between you and I, I think they were happy to have him out of the house."

"So, if the real Jake Parish has been dead seven months, who the hell has been working for me?"

"Isn't that the million-dollar question."

ASHTON TOOK A SEAT ON HIS COUCH, A GLASS OF vodka in his hand. He closed his eyes as images of Jess played through his mind. He hadn't realized until she was gone how deeply he cared for her.

She had been the bright light in his day, and someone he had envisioned himself ending up with, but all that had been torn away. Had Jake killed her? His hand tightened on the glass, the bastard had come to work every day smiling, pretending as though he was the poor bastard they'd found in the freezer.

He took a shaky drink and tried his best to fight back the tears. He was not an emotional man but seeing Jess wide-eyed and lifeless had broken him.

There was a knock on his door and he stood to check the peep hole. His hand clenched on the pistol at his back when he saw who it was, but he pulled open the door anyways.

"Allison."

"Ashton, it's good to see you." Allison Carver smiled brightly at him and stepped into his apartment.

"Wish I could say the same, what are you doing here?"

Allison had been his partner at the bureau and the very reason he had left in the first place. She'd been caught trading secrets with a criminal and even though he turned her in she had gotten off on a technicality.

He'd had it with the corrupt assholes at the top of his chain of command, and so he'd left to start his own company.

Not long after she had done the same and named it BlackPoint Security.

"I wanted to see an old friend."

"Sure, that's it." He folded his arms.

"The years have been kind to you, Ashton." She eyed him with all the heat a lioness has in her gaze just before she pounces.

"Did you come here to give me small talk or do you actually have business?"

"I came to offer you a job."

"No thanks, now goodbye."

"I know you're working for McGinley. You're on the wrong side Ashton."

"I think you've got that backward, Malcolm is a psycho, and he's got you doing his dirty work."

She shrugged. "He pays well. Much better than McGinley it seems." She sneered as she looked around his small apartment.

"At least I can sleep with a clear conscience."

"Alone to it seems." She pouted. "It really is too

bad that secretary ran into a blade isn't it? I hear you
had a thing for her."

His body stiffened. "You responsible for that?"

She laughed. "I don't get paid enough to kill in
cold blood."

"No, of course not, you just protect the ones who
do. So, who killed her then?"

She shrugged again. "What does it matter?
She's dead."

"Leave. Now." His body was shaking, and the
longer she stood in his presence, the more likely he
was going to snap. He was not a murderer though,
and killing Allison would do nothing to stop Malcolm.

"I'm not done yet."

"What. Do. You. Want."

"I want to warn you. I have a bit of a soft spot for
you, even after what you did to me."

"Warn me about what?"

"Malcolm has some things planned, things that
are going to change the world."

"Tell me why I shouldn't put a bullet in you? That
would put a hitch in his plans wouldn't it?"

"Hardly." She laughed. "It's not just BlackPoint he
has on his payroll anymore." She smiled. "That's what
I have for you, sure you don't want a job? I would
triple whatever you're making now."

"No thanks."

"That really is too bad Ashton, I've missed you."
She stepped forward and pressed a hard kiss to his lips
before he could move.

"See you later."

"I ever see you again I will put you down."

"Oh honey, we both know you don't have the stones for that. Otherwise I wouldn't be standing here today."

She shut the door behind her and Ashton picked the bottle of Grey Goose up off his counter. He turned it up and drank deeply, desperate to feel the burn from the liquor. Desperate to feel anything but the dagger in his heart. He prided himself on being an honest man, one that followed the rules otherwise he would have killed her right there, or at the very least taken her into Timothy for questioning.

But doing anything against his carefully laid out guidelines went against who he was. The rules were changing though, and if he didn't catch up, Ashton knew he was going to be the next one in a body bag.

He pulled out his phone and dialed Timothy, who answered on the third ring.

"What is it?"

"Allison Carver was just here."

"Allison Carver of BlackPoint Security?"

"That's the one."

"What did she want?"

"To offer me a job. and warn me that Malcolm is planning something big."

"Where is she now?"

"Gone."

"Anything she say credible?"

"Definitely. She wouldn't have come here without a reason. Other than the job offers, which I know to have just been a way to get under my skin, everything she said will check out. I'll look into it tomorrow, but I'd be willing to bet we're running out of time."

"Alright, thanks, Ashton. Watch yourself, I don't want you to be next on Malcolm's elimination list."

"I will." He disconnected the call and took another drink.

"WHY HAVEN'T I SEEN THIS BEFORE?" PAISLEE ASKED stunned as she stood in the doorway to the home gym in Timothy's apartment.

"I never had much of a reason to show you."

"This is amazing." Professional equipment lined the walls and a giant bag hung in the center of the room over some mats. She watched him walk over to it, and after pushing a lever, he shoved the bag, and it slid over against the wall on a track.

"Seriously? This is awesome!" She had never been one to exercise, she'd been young when Malcolm had taken her and hadn't had the opportunity to enjoy that particular pastime while in his custody. Then after she had escaped, her sole focus had been on learning as much as she could about her magic.

After her run-in with Giselle though, Paislee was beginning to understand just how important it was to learn to protect yourself hand to hand.

You never knew when you would need it.

"Okay, we're going to start with some basics." Timothy pulled his shirt off, and Paislee did her best to not let her mouth water as he stripped down to nothing but a pair of shorts that hung low on his waist.

She suddenly felt very overdressed in her baggy t-shirt and yoga pants.

He cleared his throat and Paislee blushed. "You said basics, I'm listening," she defended.

"I can see that." He smirked and stepped onto the mats.

She followed suit and let him walk her through how she was supposed to stand and the rules of throwing a punch.

"You want to be sure the contact is coming from your knuckles and not the flat parts of your fingers." He ran his index finger over her knuckles and then stood next to her. "When you execute, you want to put your body weight behind it, but make sure you stay balanced otherwise you're going to end up on the ground."

Paislee mimicked what he'd shown her, trying her best to not feel embarrassed by her lack of knowledge. It was hard enough to focus on him standing there half naked. She didn't need her own embarrassment adding to it.

They worked on her form for an hour, and then Timothy moved the heavy bag back into the center of the room, so she could practice on it. Another two hours later, Paislee was sore and drenched in sweat.

"You alright?" Timothy asked as she practically crawled out of the gym.

"I'm good."

He handed her a Gatorade, and she drank deeply.

"You are going to want to take these." He handed her two gel pills. "And drink this." and a shaker bottle.

"What are these?"

"These." He pointed to the pills. "Are fish oil and will help with your recovery time, and this is a protein shake. It will help rebuild muscles, so they are stronger."

She took the pills with her Gatorade, and then took a drink of the shake. "This is awful."

He grinned. "We can get you a different flavor, but peanut butter is all I have here."

"Blah," she complained but drank it anyway. "I'm going to go shower now if I can make it there."

His eyes darkened. "Want help?"

"Normally, I would say yes, but since my body feels like jelly at the moment, I will have to take a rain check."

"I could hold you up."

"Rain check."

"Alright, if you insist." He grinned and headed back towards his office.

~

TIMOTHY OPENED THE DOOR TO SEE AN ANGRY Detective Shultz on the other side.

"To what do I owe this surprise visit, detective?"

"Do you know this woman." Shultz held up a photo of Giselle and Timothy nodded, not changing his expression.

"I do, what is this about?"

"She was found dead last night. A single gunshot wound to her head."

"That's terrible."

"I agree. She was an incredibly successful woman who had a lot of years ahead of her. It's such a shame when you get mixed up with the wrong people." She glared at him to get her point across. "Mind if I come in?"

"Not at all." Timothy stepped aside to let her in.

"I hear that you and Miss Ray had quite the relationship."

"What are you implying?" Timothy wondered as he closed the door gently behind her.

"Simply getting my facts straight, Mr. McGinley."

"Giselle and I had both a working and physical relationship for a time, although both ended over a month ago."

"Why is that?"

"I no longer needed her professional services, and we didn't have quite the connection we thought."

"So, you both ended it."

"Yes," he lied.

"Amicably."

"Yes."

"Have you seen her since?"

How much to tell her? "Am I going to need a lawyer, detective?"

"Are you guilty?"

"No, but these questions are making me think you believe I am."

"If you aren't guilty then you have nothing to

worry about. Did Miss Ray come and see you at any point since your relationship ended?"

"Yes, she came to see me two days ago."

"Why?"

"To talk, as I said our relationship ended amicably and we remained friends."

She studied him, searching for a lie. "Do you know of anyone who would have hurt her?"

"Not that I'm aware of. We were physical yes, but never shared anything about our personal lives."

Her jaw tightened, and she nodded. "If you think of anything let me know. Don't leave town, there seems to be a trail of bodies following you and I plan to figure out why."

"I have no travel plans."

"Good."

"Have a great day detective," he said with a smile and shut the door behind her before immediately pulling out his phone. "Ashton, Detective Shultz was just here. She said they found Giselle's body, look into it." He disconnected the call and looked up to see Paislee standing with her arms crossed.

"She's dead?"

He nodded.

"And the detective seems to think you did it?"

"Or that I know who did."

"Malcolm."

"Can't exactly prove that. We don't even know where he is since he abandoned his last property after we rescued you."

"We could find him."

"How?"

"Me. You use me to draw him out."

"Absolutely not." He headed for his bar and poured a drink.

"Timothy, look at it rationally, it's me he wants. As far as he knows, you aren't immortal. He saw that much with his own eyes after his skank wife sliced you with her nasty fingernails."

"Paislee, we are not using you as bait."

"Come on, we have to get him. If you have a better plan, I'm open to it. This is bigger than me, bigger than us. He is going to hurt a lot of people if we don't find him."

"And what if we fail? What if he managed to get his hands on you and your magic? Are you okay risking that? Risking being the reason he is able to hurt all those people?"

"That's a low blow."

"I'm sorry, but we have to look at all possible scenarios, and that bastard has been ten steps ahead of us since day one. He planted someone in my company seven months ago. Before I even knew you existed, which tells me he's been watching me constantly. I'm having to comb through every little bit of work Jake did while he was here to see if anything was altered or taken. If he's been that far ahead, what makes you think he isn't planning for that exact scenario?"

"We don't know."

"Exactly, and until we do we are not risking your life." His phone rang, and he answered without taking his eyes off Paislee, "McGinley."

"It's Ashton, they did find a body. She was killed execution style with a single GSW to the head."

"Where?"

"They found her body in an alley behind her office."

"So, nothing to tie it to me?"

"As far as I can tell, no. But the bodies are lining up Timothy, we need to make sure they don't point to you. Schultz is out for blood."

"I could tell that much."

"Let's not give her any."

"Thanks." He ended the call as Paislee was walking away.

"I told you I'm not sitting around much longer," she warned over her shoulder and disappeared into her room.

imothy pinched the bridge of his nose and looked at the clock on his desk. *Four a.m.* He groaned, he'd been combing through these files for nearly twelve hours and still had nothing to show for it.

On the surface, it appeared that Jake, or whatever his name was, had done an expert job. Everything was professionally documented, thoroughly explained and from the shipment records to what he had put in the files, nothing seemed to be missing.

But that was on the surface, there had to be something buried that didn't belong. There was no way Jake had worked for him for seven months and not done anything to further Malcolm's goals. There was just no way.

He stood and stretched before stepping in front of the large window. The city below was dark with only a scattering of lights. What was it like, he wondered, to live a normal life? To wake up at the same time every day, go to work, put in an effort, come home to a spouse, to children? To eat dinner and then curl up on the couch with a good book or to watch a show?

He had never known a normal life. At least, not since before he found out about his curse. The vision of Cait from the graveyard popped into his head. He had believed she would be his normal life, his chance at happiness, and now he wondered if he would ever get the opprotunity.

He wasn't stupid, he knew Paislee wouldn't wait much longer, and he also knew that when she went after Malcolm, he would go with her because Myria had been right. He was in love with her, she was his second chance, and he would protect her with his life, if necessary.

If fighting her war meant dying in the trenches, he would gladly sacrifice his life to free her from the horror.

"You okay?" He looked up to see her framed in the doorway by the glow of the light in the hall. It struck him then, just how incredibly beautiful she was. Her features were shadowed, but the lines of worry for him made pieces of his heart, he thought long gone, fall back into place.

"Yes, just going through the inventory and sales records."

"Anything?"

"Not yet, but there has to be something."

"Maybe there's not, it's possible he only planted Jake here to test out your immortality."

He had considered that, but it didn't fit. "Then why wait so long before sending someone to try and kill me? Jake had plenty of opportunities to get rid of me, or at least to try. I never had any hint at the thought he was anything but an outstanding employee."

"Is that what's bothering you?"

"What do you mean?"

"You've been off since you found out about Jake. Timothy, there is no way you could have known." She walked in and crossed her arms over her chest.

"I allowed him into my office, shit he was in there with you when I wasn't here. Paislee if anything had happened because I missed something-"

She touched his arm gently. "Nothing happened. Could he have smuggled something out?" she asked as she straightened.

Timothy shook his head. "It would have been impossible. All my employees go through security when they leave. They are scanned, their bags checked, everything. I don't see how he could have snuck anything out."

"Maybe paid a guard?"

"Those are Ashton's men, I'll let you bring that theory up to him."

"We need to check every angle."

He changed the subject. "How is the magic coming along?"

She held her palm up, and a ball of flame appeared. He stared at it, dumbfounded.

"I'm getting the hang of it."

"You definitely are."

"It's amazing what a little proper motivation will do."

"And what's motivating you now?"

"The idea that Malcolm is planning an attack and I haven't done anything to stop it is motivation enough."

"We will stop him, Paislee."

She nodded. "We can't fail."

"We won't."

PAISLEE AND TIMOTHY LOOKED UP FROM THEIR breakfast at the sound of a knock on the door. Timothy got up to answer it, and Paislee watched after him just in case. Ashton was off on some secret mission Timothy wouldn't share with her just what that was, and as far as she knew they weren't expecting anyone.

Timothy looked in the door, and Paislee watched his body relax, so she followed suit. He pulled open the door to a familiar face.

"Aengus, what are you doing here?" Timothy asked and embraced his friend.

"Myria said you might need some help."

"We'll talk in my office."

"What is it?" Paislee asked. "It's nice to see you Aengus," she offered with a smile. "What does Myria think he needs help with?"

"Not now, Paislee," Timothy warned and abandoned his breakfast as he ushered Aengus into his office. "What are you doing here Aengus?" he asked once the door was closed behind them.

"Myria told me of her vision."

"What about it? It was just a dream."

"I get that you haven't been around us much, but her dreams are rarely just dreams."

"What does it matter? I already told her, I wouldn't leave Paislee."

"Nor should you. I'm not here for you to abandon your mission, I'm here to help."

"Help? Do you not realize what this is? You have a family Aengus."

"And you are part of that family. When Caipre took Aine, you were right there by my side and with me to the very end. Let me do that for you. Let me fight beside you like we used to."

"We aren't the same people we used to be."

"We aren't that different either," Aengus rebutted.

Timothy stared at his old friend. Aengus's jaw was set, which usually meant there was no room for argument except there had to be this time. His friend couldn't risk his life, his family, on him. "You cannot help me Aengus."

"Like hell, I can't. I'm not leaving, you kick me out of here, and I'll go find this Malcolm character myself."

"Dammit, Aengus."

Aengus grinned, and Timothy couldn't stop himself from returning it. Damn, it felt good to have his friend back.

"That's what I thought, so tell me where I can put my stuff."

"Guest room, down the hall, turn right."

"Perfect, I've had a long trip, so I'll be retiring to my room and calling Abby. Once you're ready to fill me in, let me know." He turned and left the room.

Paislee was right at the door. "What dream?"

"Shit, Paislee were you listening to everything then?"

She crossed her arms. "What dream and why does Myria think we need help?"

He had dreaded telling her, but he had promised he would never lie either. "Myria had a dream that I died."

Paislee's face lost just enough color for him to notice and her body stiffened. "You died."

"It was a dream, Paislee, nothing more."

"How do you know? Have Myria's dreams come true before?"

"That was different."

"Why would you keep this from me?"

He narrowed his eyes. "You know why."

She did know why, and she knew exactly how he expected her to respond, so she did her best to do the opposite. "Well, you should have told me, but it was just a dream." His eyes widened in shock, *that's right. Not what you expected is it?* She smiled. "Are you going to come finish breakfast?"

~

"WE GOT A PROBLEM."

Malcolm sighed on the other line. "What type of problem?"

"A man showed up at McGinley's apartment this morning, I don't recognize him, and can't seem to pull any information as to who he is."

"That's not necessarily a problem, from what you told me McGinley met with clients at his apartment from time to time."

"This guy flew in from Dublin."

"Still not seeing a problem." Malcolm's voice took on a dangerous tone that he knew would warn the man on the other line. He didn't have time to waste on random men who just so happened to pop up from time to time. He had bigger things to focus on. He looked down at the map on his desk. "Find what you can about him, and let me know if it's important. Otherwise, I'm not interested." He hung up the phone and studied the map closer.

The plan needed to be executed flawlessly. He needed to maximize damage while ensuring he got his desired outcome. His eyes narrowed on a spot on the map that would meet both his criteria.

He smiled, *boom*.

"SO, THIS MALCOLM IS A BASTARD, ISN'T HE?" Aengus commented after Timothy finished filling him in over whiskey that night.

"More than." Paislee took a drink of her own. "We need to stop sitting around and do something."

"We need a plan. We go in there guns blazing, and we're likely to get cut down."

"My magic-"

"Is only useful if he doesn't bring the necklace out. If he does, you're powerless."

"Maybe not entirely, what about the cuff?" Aengus asked.

Timothy shook his head. "It blocks her from being able to use her magic."

"But at least the necklace wouldn't be able to touch her."

"True, but it still doesn't solve our problem," Timothy responded.

"What do we need to move forward?" Aengus asked.

"We need to know where his new compound is, and how to get in."

"How are we going to do that?" Paislee asked.

Timothy rubbed his hands down his face. "Ashton is working on it. He's hoping to have a location in the next few days."

"We may not have a few days. If he attacks-"

"Paislee, we don't have a choice. If we go after him and die, who is going to save all those people?"

"I know you're right, but that doesn't mean I have to like it," she nearly growled it, and it surprised even her to hear the animosity in her voice.

Aengus stood and pushed his chair back. "I'm going to go and call Abby."

Timothy and Paislee kept their eyes locked on each other. Even now as angry as she was, electricity snapped between them and all she wanted to do was run and jump into his arms so they could forget everything going on in the world.

"Are we okay?" Timothy asked carefully, and Paislee nodded.

"I'm going to go to bed though, I'm tired." She got up to walk past him, and he gripped her arm.

"Please trust me, love."

"I do trust you,. I just hope you aren't making up excuses because you're afraid of what might happen to me. If you're willing to gamble with your life, why should mine be any different." She pulled her arm away and walked towards the room.

CHAPTER 31

"Well I'll be damned," Timothy muttered and studied the file in his hand.

"What is it?" Paislee and Aengus both asked at the same time. They had been going through inventory files for nearly two days, and Paislee thought if she had to continue, she might burst into flame.

"There's a very faint line right here." He pointed to the bottom of the form, where it looked like an item had been removed.

"Could be a smudge," Aengus pointed out. "We've seen a few of those."

"Not this, see how the list is shorter?" Paislee compared her list to the one in Timothy's hand. "There was something covered up at the bottom of this page."

"But what?"

"Are you sure he hadn't gotten anything out?" Paislee clarified.

"Nearly a hundred percent, but I want to be sure." His phone rang. "McGinley. When?" His body straightened, and his blood began to pound. Coincidence? Perhaps, but he doubted it. "On my way."

"What is it?" Aengus asked.

"Someone broke into my building, it looks like something from crate one-forty-two was taken."

"One-forty-two?" Aengus began looking at the forms in his hand until Timothy tossed his sheet down on the table and pointed to the crate number.

"Well, that's one hell of a coincidence," Paislee commented.

"I need to get down there."

"I'll go with you." Aengus stood, and Paislee followed suit.

"Paislee-"

She put her hand up. "I get it. It might be a trap, stay put, don't feed them after midnight."

"What does that have to do with anything?" Aengus wondered.

"Have you never watched a movie?"

He stared at her blankly, and she shook her head. "Never mind. I'll be here. Unless, of course, you have any other ex-girlfriends who want to drive a dagger into my heart?"

"None come to mind," he responded sarcastically.

"Good, I'll get a shower and hang out here until you guys get back. I can keep looking to see if anything else pops up."

"Thanks." Timothy kissed her on the cheek, and he and Aengus left the apartment. She watched them go and then walked in to wash the grime of the day away.

Paislee was drying her hair by the window when she noticed a man on the street watching the building. With how high they were, she couldn't see his face, but he was the same build as Jake.

He wore a dark jacket and cap over his head, but his eyes were focused intently on the apartment building. She rushed into the bedroom and finished dressing, before dashing downstairs and onto the street. She had managed to sneak out quickly, but she knew the guard was probably already calling Timothy, which meant she only had minutes to figure out who that man was and where he was going.

Her hair up in a ball cap, she stepped out into the cold and searched the street for the man. She saw a dark jacket walking away and chose to follow. She kept her distance, and her head down as she walked trying to not draw attention to herself.

The streets were crowded today, which could make for a quick getaway if necessary. After all, if there was anything she knew how to do at this point, it was run.

The man turned down a corner, and she kept walking, only sparing a quick glance into the alley. There was only one exit, so she could circle around the building and wait for him to step back out.

Just as she was stepping around the corner, her

shoulder bumped into someone hard, but before she could say excuse me, she looked into the familiar blue eyes of the man she believed had been Jake Parish.

"Isn't this a treat?" He grinned, and Paislee turned to run, but his grip on her arm was strong. "Let's have a chat, shall we?" He pulled her down into the same alley he had disappeared into only moments before and slammed her against the wall on the other side of a dumpster.

"I could scream you know," she growled.

"You could, but anyone who came in here would have to be put down if you did. Can't have any witnesses."

"You wouldn't dare. Too many bodies would equal a hell of a lot of questions."

"Perhaps, but do you really want to risk it?"

"What do you want?"

"I told you, to talk."

"I don't have anything to say to you. You're a murderer."

He shrugged. "I do my job."

"Your job is to kill innocent people."

"Was Giselle innocent?" He asked her.

"So, you were the one who pulled the trigger on her then?"

"I told you, I only do my job. Although, I would be lying if I didn't say I took some pleasure out of putting her down."

"Why doesn't that surprise me?"

"It should, it certainly surprised me. Typically, I have no emotions when it comes to performing my duties, but after seeing her on top of you, it did something to me." His devilishly handsome face contorted slightly into a frown.

"Why is that?"

He shrugged, and it was gone. "Who knows. Maybe I grew mildly attached to you."

"You're so full of shit."

"Am I?" He laughed. "It probably is because I want to be the one to kill you," he growled and leaned closer to her. For the first time, she saw the glint of a blade in his hand.

"Why is that?"

"You and I aren't so different Paislee. We both do our jobs right?"

"My job isn't to kill people."

"Oh, it's not? Because I have a very vivid memory of you murdering my brother."

She paled. "What are you talking about?"

"When I was about twelve, my brother and I went with our father to Malcolm Gentry's house. You were on proud display in his living room, and my brother became rather interested in you. He was older, closer to your age, so I suppose about sixteen at the time."

She stiffened, she knew exactly who he was talking about now. The blade pressed against her jugular.

"He wanted to get a closer look, and you coerced him into opening the cage. Do you remember that Paislee? Do you remember using him to free yourself?"

"I didn't kill him," she choked out as his hand closed around her throat.

"You might as well have. You nearly escaped, and Malcolm killed him for opening the door. Don't you remember? He killed him right in front of my father and I. Do you know how it feels to watch your brother bleed to death on the floor?"

"I'm sorry, but it's not me you should be after!"

"Oh, Paislee." He pressed his lips to her throat just above the blade. "I have every intention of killing Malcolm as well."

Her neck began to sting, and she could feel drops of blood on her skin. She knew she only had moments, so she did what Timothy had taught her, and attacked.

～

"Shit, this is a mess," Timothy commented as he stepped around the mess of crates in his storage room.

"It is," Aengus agreed. "Any ideas as to who it was?"

"One. But now I'm thinking it may have been someone else."

"Why do you say that?"

"Jake knew exactly where that crate was, he wouldn't have needed to make such a mess looking for it."

"Perhaps he did it on purpose."

Timothy thought about that for a moment and then shook his head. "No this was done by someone in a hurry, someone with no love for antiques." He looked disgusted at the nearly three-century-old vase that had shattered on the ground.

Ashton nodded. "Someone cut the feeds, so we've got nothing. I'm going to pull from the ATM on the street to see if it caught anything, but as of now we're blind."

"We need to know what was in that crate," Timothy insisted. "Can you look into it?"

Ashton nodded. "I'll put a call into the company that shipped it."

Timothy handed him the roster with the contact information, and Ashton turned to leave the room.

"I'm sorry your business has been harmed like this," Aengus offered.

"I'm just disgusted at the amount of damage to the antiques. These are priceless artifacts from history, and some asshole came in here and destroyed them."

"We'll get whoever did this"

"I know we will." Timothy stood, and Aengus clasped a hand on his shoulder.

All in all, Timothy was glad his friend was there. He still worried about Aengus risking his life, but it was nice having someone he knew he could trust completely.

He trusted Paislee, sure. But there were some things he couldn't tell her just yet. He couldn't risk her running off after Malcolm by herself on a whim. Aengus was level-headed though, and for once Timothy wasn't the oldest thing in the room.

Ashton rushed back into the room. "We've got a problem."

"What is it?"

"Paislee snuck out of the apartment. Andrew tried to stop her, but she ran out quicker than he could get to her."

"Fuck," Timothy growled, and headed towards the door. "Any idea where she is going?"

"Andrew said the reason she managed to get out, was that he was studying a man who appeared to be staring at the building. He had focused in on him with the camera, and was running facial recognition software when she left."

"Whoever this man is, she must have recognized him."

"My guy couldn't get a hit, but he believes it was Jake."

"Son of a bitch." Timothy quickened his pace, Aengus, and Ashton right beside him.

JAKE GROANED AS PAISLEE KNEED HIM IN THE SIDE. HE had been blocking his groin otherwise that's where she would have aimed.

Once he had pulled the knife away, she brought her hands up to break the grip he had on her throat. He slammed his fist into the side of her face, and she saw stars.

"I will bleed you bitch." He gripped the back of her hair, but dammit she wasn't going down that easy. Knowing it would hurt like hell, she twisted in his grip and bent over to wrap her arms around his waist. She used all the strength she had and rammed him backward.

When he fell to the ground, she released the magic she had instinctively been holding back.

"Feel like an asshole now?" She grinned as the magic sparked on her fingers.

Jake grinned at her, his teeth bloody from biting his lip as he fell. "I'm not the one who should be feeling like an asshole."

Paislee's skin began to glow as she knelt in front of him, the fear in his eyes would have made her smile, but she knew all too well the anger he was feeling. "I was not responsible for your brother. His death is something that weighs on me every single day."

Jake's mouth turned up in disgust. "You are a liar. You and I both know you don't give a shit about anyone but yourself." He charged her again, and her magic shot him back the second he touched her.

His head cracked against the wall behind him, and he slumped forward. Paislee knelt in front of him and was checking his pulse when Timothy, Aengus, and Ashton burst into the alley.

"What the fuck happened?" Timothy demanded as he dropped to his knees beside her.

Ashton checked for a pulse. "He's alive."

"I kicked his ass, that's what happened," Paislee's voice held no humor though. Truth was, she couldn't blame him for hating her.

"You could have died Paislee, this is not a joke," Ashton scolded her for the first time.

"I know it was dumb, but I needed to know who

he was. Now I do, and now we have him in our custody."

"We need to get out of this alley, can you call a car and have them come get him? He may know something, and we don't want him falling into the hands of the police. At least not yet," Timothy added.

"On it." Ashton pulled out his phone.

Timothy turned his attention back on Paislee, and using his fingers, tilted her head up to see the bruises already forming on her throat. "What happened?" he asked her softly.

She shook her head. "Not here."

Moments later a car pulled into the alley, and after zip-tying his hands, Aengus and Ashton loaded Jake into the backseat.

"I'll go with Ashton in case he needs my help." Aengus climbed into the backseat as well, and the car left the alley.

"Come on." Timothy tugged the ball cap back onto her head and tucked her into his arm. "Don't look up, the last thing we need are nosy people asking why you look like you just had the shit beat out of you."

They walked quickly, and he relaxed slightly once they were back in his building. He guided her out of the elevator and then over to the couch. After pouring them both a drink, he took a seat.

"Tell me what happened?"

"I saw him staring up at the building, so I rushed downstairs to get a closer look."

"You didn't think that perhaps that would be a bad idea?"

She shot him a glare. "Want me to tell you or not?"

He nodded and lifted his glass to his lips.

"I followed him down the street and saw him disappear into an alley, so I continued walking past it and was going to catch up on the other side. As I was turning the corner, I bumped into him." She took a drink and savored the warmth the whiskey offered her. "He dragged me into the alley and told me he just wanted to talk."

"About what?"

Paislee swallowed hard. "About how I was the reason his brother was killed."

"How so?"

"When I was about sixteen, a man came to see Malcolm. He had two sons with him and the older boy, I would guess was about my age, kept staring at me. Malcolm had told them, of course, that I was a witch, he loved to brag to everyone who came to see him. Most didn't give me a second glance, but this boy did.

Whether it was because he was fascinated by the idea of magic, or he felt bad for me, I'm not sure, but I saw an opening, and I used it. I convinced him to open the cage and let me out. It took some coercing, but I promised I would show him some magic if I did, so he opened it." Tears stung in her eyes at the memory.

"I made it as far as the front door before I was

caught and dragged back to that cage. Malcolm reviewed his security tapes, and learned it was the boy who set me free, so in front of me, the boy's father and his younger brother, Malcolm killed him, and made us all watch as punishment."

"Sadistic son of a bitch."

"No question about that, but it worked because I never tried to convince anyone to set me free again. I still remember giving the boy a hug and thanking him. He'd had kind eyes, I don't think he ever would have harmed anyone, and now he's dead because of me. I can't blame Jake."

"He was the younger brother?"

She nodded. "I would hate me too."

"None of that is your fault Paislee, you're a victim in this too."

"I understand that, but the guilt of that boys' death is on me, and nothing you say will ever change that."

CHAPTER 32

"*Y*our man failed, again." Allison scolded.

Malcolm's hand tightened on the receiver.

"He was captured by McGinley and his men after he went for the girl."

"Can you get to him?" he asked, studying the object in his hand.

"Not yet, but I'll keep looking for an opening."

"Good." Malcolm ended the call. *Idiot*! He had been so close to having Paislee back, and because his vengeance was more important, Jake had ruined that chance. He had always known who the boy was, even though he had gone to great lengths to hide his true identity.

The fact that he had sought out Malcolm had pleased him. It was a great feeling to have those you knew hated you under your thumb. Malcolm smiled down. *He had gotten it!* If that jackass had done nothing else for him, he could still call his employment a success. It wouldn't be long now, mere hours before he met his goal, and the world would be his.

CHAPTER 33

"*A*nything?" Timothy asked Ashton into the receiver.

"He's awake, and so far, the only thing he has said is that he wants to talk to Paislee."

"Not happening."

"I don't want her near him either, but if we want to get a handle on Malcolm, he may be our best bet."

Timothy ground his teeth together. This was a bad idea, he knew it was, and yet it was the only one they had. He looked at Paislee who stood staring at the darkening sky, she was tired of being treated like a victim, and if he weren't careful, she'd tire of him as well. He knew that feeling of needing to do *something*. Knew that it could eat at you.

"I'll bring her down." He hung up the phone just as she turned to face him. "Jake wants to talk to you and only you."

She nodded.

"You don't have to do this."

"I do. I have this horrible feeling that we don't have as much time as we think we do."

They made their way downstairs into the basement, Paislee was surprised they were keeping Jake in the same building, but she supposed it made sense. *Keep your enemies close,* and all that.

They stepped into a room behind a hidden panel, and Paislee looked through the one-way glass at Jake whose hands were chained to the table. It reminded her of the interrogation rooms in police stations on TV.

"I don't remember hitting him that hard," Paislee commented at the fresh blood and bruising on Jake's face."

"I questioned him earlier," Ashton said easily. She looked down at his bloody knuckles.

"Learn anything new?"

He shook his head. "He's a tough son of a bitch."

Paislee stepped towards the door. "I'm going in."

Timothy stopped her. "Not alone."

"I don't think he will talk if you're in there with me. You can watch the entire thing from right here." Paislee pointed to the glass. "Or stand right outside the door, and I'll scream if he comes at me. Deal?"

Timothy ground his teeth together. "Deal."

She stepped into the interrogation room, and Jake grinned at her. "I'm surprised to see you."

"Why? You asked to talk to me."

"Didn't think your master would let you off your leash."

"He's not my master."

"Oh, my mistake, your fuck buddy then."

"What do you want Jake?"

"First off, stop calling me Jake. That guy was a loser, a waste of intelligence. Who has that many degrees, studies overseas, and then decide to play fucking video games?"

"Then what should I call you?"

"Mark."

"Fine, Mark, what did you want to talk about?"

"You are running out of time."

She straightened. "What do you mean?"

"I know what Malcolm is planning, and if you want to kill him, you had better move quickly because he already has it."

"Has what? What is he planning?"

"I'm not going to tell you that. I will tell you that he is going to be damn hard to kill at this point."

"Why?"

Mark shrugged. "If you want him, I can give you his address."

"Why would you do that?"

"Because as much as I hate you, and trust me I do, I hate him more." He leaned across the table. "You know it really is a shame you weren't more interested in me. I would have loved to have fucked you just before I killed you."

"Are you trying to get yourself killed?"

Just as she thought he would, Timothy came into the room. "Tell us the address," he insisted, and Jake smiled at him.

"Tell me, McGinley, she as fiery in the sack?"

"You're going to want to stop talking," Paislee warned him.

He looked smugly at her. "Give me a piece of paper and a pen, and I'll write down his address."

"Do you think he's lying?" Aengus asked Timothy when he and Paislee stepped out.

"It's possible, but I doubt it," Paislee responded. "He hates Malcolm, that much is true. And it would serve his purpose if we killed him."

"Don't forget he also wants you dead. It could be a trap," Ashton added.

Timothy, who had been silent, spoke up. "It's more likely that it's not a trap. Paislee is right, if he can't get his own revenge on Malcolm, it is possible he would want to help us get him."

"You don't have long. Only a few hours by my estimation," Mark said from behind the glass. The tone of his voice made Paislee queasy. "Then boom!" He laughed.

"He's insane." Aengus gaped at the glass.

"Yeah, a big bucket of crazy," Paislee commented. "We need to move."

"We need to do some recon."

"We don't have time for that, a few hours remember?"

Timothy ground his teeth together. "Aston, get a team together. We will scout the perimeter and decide if it's worth it to go in."

"On it."

Ashton disappeared, and Timothy turned to Aengus. "You need to not go in with us."

"Don't be ridiculous, I told you I'm here."

"We could all die Aengus, I cannot have your death on my hands. You have a family."

"How many times do I have to tell you that you are a part of my family? You were there for me Timothy, let me be there for you."

"That was different. Caipre was crazy, yes, dangerous, sure, but not like this. This is different."

"I'm not going anywhere." Aengus headed back towards the stairs. "Shall we prepare for war?"

"CAN I ASK YOU WHAT HE WAS LIKE? BEFORE?" Paislee asked Aengus as they waited for Timothy to return. He had gone down to check on Ashton's progress and left them to finish loading weapons.

Aengus laughed. "Stubborn, tough, kind, and loyal as hell."

"Kind? That's a new one," she joked.

"He's a good man Paislee. Again, he can be stubborn, but it's only because he cares for you."

"I know that. I love him." The words spilled out of her before she had even finished processing them.

"Oh?"

She nodded. "I never thought I would survive this. If I'm, honest with myself, I didn't want to. But with Timothy in my life, I find that I'm looking forward to an after."

"I know how you feel. After Aine was killed I went through a very dark period, trauma and grief can do that to a person."

"You guys were friends as kids?"

Aengus smiled. "The best of friends. We were a force to be reckoned with, and one that got into trouble fairly frequently."

She smiled "I can see that. It must have been nice to see him again."

"It was, but I've been kicking myself for not finding him earlier."

"You didn't know he was alive."

"I didn't know he was dead either. It was entirely too painful for Myria and I to look into those we had cared for. She knew Timothy had married, and after that, I think she forced herself to forget."

"Did she love him?"

"Not in the way you're thinking. She had always cared for him and had things worked out differently I suppose it's possible she could have grown to, but she didn't really love anyone until Sheamus."

The jealousy she carried in her heart for what Timothy and Myria could have been loosened, what right did she have to hold onto it anyway? He had never given her any reason to think he still loved Myria.

"Thank you for being here," she said to Aengus.

"I wouldn't be anywhere else."

They went back to loading the weapons in silence. A feeling of dread had settled itself into the pit of her stomach, and no matter how many times Paislee told herself everything would work out, she couldn't get a single thought out of her head, *someone she cared for was going to die tonight.*

"Can I talk to you?" she asked Timothy once he returned.

He nodded, and they walked into the bedroom together. She was nervous, her hands fidgeting with the hem of the black t-shirt she wore.

"What is it?"

"Give me a minute."

Timothy stood quietly while Paislee worked up the courage to say something she never thought she would say to anyone. *Just do it Paislee, like ripping off a Band-Aid. You don't want to regret it later.* "I love you."

She looked at him and repeated. "I love you. I wanted you to know that just in case."

"Just in case what?"

"You know what."

"Is there something you aren't telling me?"

"Can you just take it, please? Even if you don't feel the same, can you give me a thank you? Anything?"

He closed the distance between them and cupped her face with his hand. "I never thought I would feel this way again Paislee. After Cait, I did what I could to close myself off from the world, from feelings. I know what you're doing, you're saying goodbye because you think you aren't going to make it out of there tonight. But I'm telling you that you will because I love you too and I can't lose you." He pressed his lips to hers, and she leaned into him.

When he released her and left the room, tears burned her eyes. The words he had spoken were sweet and should have lifted her spirits, but his accusation had stuck with her. She wasn't saying goodbye because she was worried she was going to die, she was saying it because the pit in her stomach told her it was going to be him.

THEY ARRIVED OUTSIDE OF MALCOLM GENTRY'S estate at just after ten p.m. A black sedan was parked in front of the house, the engine running, and Timothy guessed they had gotten there just in time.

Dressed head to toe in black and carrying assault rifles, the team Ashton had brought together crept towards the car. They managed to drag the driver out and knock him unconscious before locking him into his own trunk, and then they tossed the keys into the bushes and made their way towards the house.

The man in charge gave Ashton a hand signal, so they moved forward. Timothy had his gun at the ready, and Paislee couldn't help but be impressed with the way he handled it.

The black sweatshirt he wore was tight on his body, and she could see the muscles in his back coiled and ready for anything.

"Stay with me," he whispered to her as they

followed the men into the house. Gunshots rang out, and everything moved so quickly that Paislee could hardly keep up. The blood thundered in her ears as adrenaline pulsed through her veins.

A man popped around a corner, his gun aimed at Timothy, and Paislee let loose a blast of magic that sent him flying backward. For the first time in her life, she felt completely in control, with those she loved on the line, she didn't have a choice.

She watched as Aengus took down a man with his hands and had to be impressed by his level of skill. Ashton was hands-on as well, and the man handled himself like a lethal weapon.

She and Timothy made their way up the stairs and towards Malcolm's office. When they stepped inside, Paislee let out a cry. Her old cage sat in the corner of the room, and a woman was curled into a ball on the inside. Her eyes were wide but empty, and fresh tears still stained her cheeks.

"She's dead," Paislee whispered in shock. How had Malcolm found another witch?

"She wasn't nearly as powerful as you," Malcolm said as he stepped from the shadows, Lindsay next to him. "None of them have been."

"You monster!" Paislee screamed.

Lindsay laughed. "You are a naïve child. We have plans, and all plans require sacrifice."

"I'm going to kill you both." She promised.

"Big words from someone who is powerless." Malcolm pulled the necklace out, and Timothy fired on him.

Paislee watched with satisfaction as blood pooled onto the white dress shirt he wore. He looked down at his chest with fascination, and then back up at them. "Good to know this works." He held his wrist up where a cuff glistened in the light.

Paislee glanced at Timothy who looked rattled.

"Do you now know what this is? I thought of everyone you would recognize it. It's the cuff of immortality. While I'm wearing it, I can't die."

"That's not all we have."

Paislee noted the earrings in Lindsay's ears, the garnets impossible to mistake. In front of their eyes, she transformed until she was an exact match for Paislee. Even the earrings disappeared.

"Well, this is disgusting." Paislee tried to steady her voice, but it was anything but.

"You aren't getting out of here Malcolm, I have dozens of men with me, and the authorities are on their way."

"You mean those men?" Malcolm mocked just as Ashton and two other guards came flooding up the stairs. He waved his hand, and the doors slammed shut, locking them inside with two maniacs. "Now, how about we have some fun? Immortal man too well, mortal one?"

"How about her?" Timothy turned his gun on Lindsay. "She immortal?"

Something flashed in Malcolm's eyes, and he flung his hand out, when Timothy didn't budge, his eyes widened.

"You have your tricks, and I have mine." Timothy said with an arrogant grin.

Paislee tried to not look surprised, why didn't the magic work on him? Hope surged through her. Maybe they did stand a chance! If Timothy could get to Malcolm, he could kill him and then it would all be over.

"Yes, I do have my tricks." Malcolm turned on Paislee in an instant, and she was shot back into the mirror above the fireplace. She crumpled to the ground, and Malcolm attacked Timothy. He fired nearly his entire clip into his enemy, but it didn't even faze him.

Timothy dropped the gun and rushed Malcolm. They locked into a hand to hand, and Timothy was winning.

Paislee got up just in time to see herself, or rather Lindsay, stalking towards her.

"You know they say imitation is the best form of flattery," Paislee commented as she got to her feet. "But I find I'm not flattered." She let the magic spark at her fingers and attacked.

She didn't waste time going for anything else, she simply used her magic to knock the other woman to the ground. "Did you honestly think you would stand a chance?" Paislee mocked.

"You aren't immortal." Lindsay grinned and slashed out with a dagger she'd pulled from her waist.

Paislee wasted no time and slammed her hand down onto Lindsay's chest. The woman screamed, and Paislee felt her life force fade away. The dead woman changed back into herself, and Malcolm howled.

"YOU KILLED HER!" he screamed and pulled the necklace out from under his shirt.

Paislee screamed and fell to her knees as the magic was pulled from her blood again. She wasn't sure if it was because the necklace already held so much power, or that she had exerted some herself, but she felt the drain taxing on her more than it ever had before.

"Timothy," she whispered.

Timothy tackled Malcolm to the ground and ripped the cuff off him. They fought for control of it, and Timothy ripped it out of his hands. His focus was on getting the necklace, but if he didn't kill Malcolm, who knew what other items he'd gotten his hands on.

Timothy pulled a knife from his waist and drove it down into Malcolm's heart. The necklace didn't stop though, and Paislee was moments away from death. Knowing it could be dangerous for them both, Timothy carried the necklace over to Malcolm's desk, and set it on the wood. He lifted the orb paperweight off and slammed it down full force into the gemstone.

It shattered into three pieces and magic began to swirl in the air. Paislee screamed again as everything that had been in the necklace surged back towards her.

"Run!" she screamed. "I cannot control it! You'll die! Don't you understand that! Run!" she screamed again, tears pouring down her face. She could feel the magic pulsing through her veins as it continued to fill her. She had nearly killed a man because her power had overflowed before, but then that had only been hers.

Now she could feel the magic from others as well. How many witches had Malcolm killed after she'd escaped?

"Timothy, please," she pleaded. "I cannot hold on it's going to decimate everything, you have to leave."

Timothy walked to her and knelt down. "I'm not going anywhere." He wrapped his arms around her as the world came crashing down on them both.

THE MAGIC SLOWED AROUND HER. SHE COULD SEE everything as it happened, the wood splintering around them as power surged out of her.

Timothy's face was clearer than anything, though. His eyes were closed, his face contorted in pain, still he held onto her. She cried out when blood began to trickle from the corner of his mouth, he was going to die. She was killing him, and she couldn't stop it. The magic simply poured from her body, saturating the air, and destroying everything around them.

No mortal man could survive this blast of power, and Timothy was no longer immortal.

She watched as her life flashed before her eyes. She could see every memory with complete clarity as she knelt on the floor.

Then suddenly, the magic was gone. Timothy slumped to the floor in a lifeless heap and she cried out. Her body was exhausted, aching, and her heart was broken.

"Timothy? Please no," her voice hoarse, she cried and touched his face. "You can't leave me."

His eyes opened slightly, and the tears she had been holding back came out full force. He lifted the blood-soaked sleeve of his shirt, and she saw the silver cuff, now scorched, against his wounded skin. He pulled it down, revealing a burn mark on his arm where the magic had been blocked, and then he smiled. "I told you, I'm not going anywhere."

The door burst open, as Ashton and Aengus pushed inside. Paislee took a quick stock of their injuries. Aengus was bleeding on his arm and cheek, Ashton had a cut on his side, but overall, they looked fine.

"What the hell happened?" Ashton stalked towards them.

"Paislee had a bit of a meltdown." Timothy joked from the floor, his body still charred as if it had been burned.

Paislee choked on a sob. "Are you seriously making a joke right now? You almost died!"

He shrugged. "I didn't."

"Well, this is a bit of a mess." Ashton studied the gaping hole in the room where the exterior wall was.

"Why didn't the rest of the room get leveled?"

"Iron in the walls would be my bet," Ashton responded. "He probably couldn't risk a certain witch getting into the house and bringing it down on top of him."

"Would make sense then I suppose to not line the exterior walls."

Sirens sounded in the distance. "I think Detective Schultz is going to have her hands full with this one."

"I've got Jake, or rather Mark's full confession on tape, so we're safe," Ashton assured them.

"Fuck, I have a headache." Timothy sat up and leaned against Paislee's chest.

"I'm sure you do." She commented as Ashton and Aengus turned to talk about the next steps. Paislee kissed the top of Timothy's head. "I should give you a worse one after that crap you pulled. You should have run."

"I told you, I'm here no matter what. You're stuck with me."

"There are worse things."

"Let's see if you're saying that in ten years."

"Ten years huh?"

"For life, Love." He looked up at her, and she pressed her lips to his.

EPILOGUE

*P*aislee leaned against Timothy in the back of the town car. His body was warm against hers, and she breathed him in. It had been two weeks since she'd thought she had lost him. A week of dealing with the police, including detective Shultz, who was not nearly as grateful as they thought she'd be seeing as how they took down a terrorist who had killed her partner.

She had simply warned them that if they stepped out of line again, she wouldn't hesitate to arrest them. They had turned Mark over to her, and he offered a full confession to nearly everything, minus the magic.

He had promised her with the utmost conviction that he would be coming after her though, which made his death on the way to prison more of a convenience than anything. No one knew who killed him, and while Shultz would have loved to pin it on them, unfortunately for her, they had a solid alibi.

Allison Carver had been captured trying to flee the country and was currently awaiting trial on multiple treason charges. Her entire company was shut down, her assets seized, and it looked as if she wouldn't be getting out anytime soon, if ever.

As for the attacks, the FBI raided Malcolm's residence and had been able to stop what he had planned. Of course, that information was classified, and they couldn't directly share it.

Ashton had done his own research though and determined that Malcolm was headed for Washington and had every intention of using a combination of explosives and magic to put himself in charge. It seemed it wasn't just magic he had been after, but also political power.

The second week had been spent wrapped in each other and barely stepping foot outside of the apartment. She lightly pressed a hand to her stomach and the tiny force of life she could feel blooming there. Three days ago, she'd felt it for the first time and confirmed it with a doctor.

Timothy smiled down at her and laid his hand on the top of hers. A family would come from their time together, a family that they would raise together.

The car pulled up in front of a bright looking house with the words, ADDICTION RECOVERY CENTER in bold across the front. She looked at him, confused, but he just smiled at her and handed her a hand-written note.

She opened it and read the words that had been so carefully written. Paislee touched the letters with the tips of her fingers as tears streamed down her cheeks. She rushed out of the car and towards the building.

Anxious, Paislee followed Timothy through the bright halls, passing medical personnel and patients, before arriving into the common area.

Her eyes searched the crowd and landed on the one person in the world she had never expected to see again. A mixture of disbelief and excitement rushed through her. Even after reading his note, she wasn't prepared to see him standing there.

Zeke stood, a beacon of home for her even after all these years. She could feel the lump in her throat and didn't bother to try and stop the tears as she ran to him. For the first time in over fifteen years, she wrapped her arms around her big brother.

"Paislee," he said into her hair and squeezed.

"I missed you, Zeke."

"I'm so sorry, Paislee. I'm so damn sorry."

"It's okay, it's all okay. It wasn't your fault, I know that."

"It was, I shouldn't have gotten involved with them."

"He would have come for me anyway."

Still hugging, they sunk to the couch and Paislee smiled against his chest. With Timothy by her side, she had found love and her home. Now that she had her brother back, she would be able to leave the past behind her and move on into the bright future she finally felt she deserved.

ACKNOWLEDGMENTS

Oh goodness I'm not even sure where to start! Collateral Damage has been a work in progress for the last year (and an idea long before that!). I am so beyond ecstatic to see Timothy's story finally making it out into the world!

First, I would like to thank God for giving me the inclination and persistence to write. Without Him, none of this would be possible.

I want to thank my wonderful and supportive husband Nathan, for being by my side, listening to all of my crazy book ideas, dealing with the conversations I sometimes have with myself when trying to work through a scene, and for picking up all the parental duties when I have a deadline. I could not imagine my life without you baby, you are my best friend and the love of my life and I am so incredibly blessed that God led me to you.

To my daughters, you two spark my imagination. Keep dreaming baby girls.

To the rest of my family, you guys are truly amazing and I am so glad you're all nuts on my family tree!

For my PA Angela. Oh my gosh girl, I seriously do not know how I did anything before you. Between me changing schedules at the last minute, coming up with new marketing ideas, switching up which book I want to work on, you keep up with it ALL. You have become my friend over the last year and I am so grateful for that! Thank you so much for everything you do and for putting up with all my crazy!

To my wonderful friends who support an encourage me- you guys have no idea how incredibly important you are to me! Without you guys, I would be a hermit, LOL, so thank you for taking the time to make me get out of my office and relax.

#SquadPod, you guys are my rocks and keep me sane when I feel like I might implode. Thank you for your endless support, wonderful advice, and friendship as we navigate this book world together!

To my Wayne-O's, I CANNOT begin to tell you guys how much your support means to me. Every single comment, like, message, e-mail, review, and just general interaction keeps me motivated and focused on the next book. You guys are the absolute best group of readers an author could hope for, and I love to see how our group grows!

To Jackie, Claudette, James, and the rest of the Author's Round Table Society, you guys are absolutely the best. I cannot tell you how nice it is to be part of such an amazing group of people!

To Nora Roberts, Karen Marie Moning, JR Ward, and Amanda Bouchet- you ladies will never know how much your books mean to me. Every single time I open the cover to one of your stories, I know I am going to be transported to a world full of action adventure, and sometimes (most of the time) love. You are all my inspiration and I hope to one day be able to sit down at a table and tell you just that.

To the readers- without you none of this would be possible. Thank you for reading books and helping to spread my stories throughout the world!

I love you all!

Jessica

ALSO BY JESSICA WAYNE

SUSPENSE

THE BASTARDS OF CORRUPTION SERIES

THE CHARITABLE BASTARD

THE RUNNER'S DAUGHTER

THE CAPTAIN'S DILEMMA- COMING SUMMER 2019

FANTASY

THE PROPHECY SERIES

THE PHOENIX

THE FIGHTER

THE SORCERESS

THE PROPHECY- COMING JANUARY 2019

A TETHERED DUET

COLLATERAL DAMAGE

THEIR OWN TIME: A TRIO OF TIME TRAVEL NOVELETTES

ABOUT THE AUTHOR

Jessica Wayne was born and raised in southern California where she and her family trained horses. She grew up traveling to different competitions, as well as showing sheep and rabbits for 4-H and the FFA. After moving to Texas with her family, Jessica joined the Army National Guard where she served for seven years.

From the moment her grandmother introduced her to Nora Roberts' wonderful world of romance, Jessica knew she wanted to create her own stories and share them with the world.

She has been writing full time for the past four years, and is a stay at home mom. She currently resides in Texas with her husband, their two children, and their dog.

You can get in touch with her using any of the links below:
E-mail: authorjessicawayne@gmail.com